Furious, Amuro yelled, "Let me at him!"

Forgetting for the moment the other Zak descending toward him from his left, he made the Gundam charge straight for the enemy. The hilts for the Gundam's twin beam sabers were stored in the Suit's backpack, so he reached back with his right hand to unsheathe one. The instant an electronic lead in the palm of the Gundam's hand connected with that of the saber hilt, a particle beam nearly ten meters long stabbed forth to form the blade. Beam sabers could slice through thirty centimeters of solid titanium in less than a second.

With his eye on the digital readouts from the MS computers, Amuro fired the vernier jets built into the Gundam for 0.3 second. The Zak in front of him turned around and its mono-eye flashed, as if in fear. By the time it raised its rifle up, it was already too late . . .

Screaming in rage, Amuro brought the Gundam's poised beam saber slashing downward in a blur of light. The beam blade entered the Zak's left shoulder and sliced all the way through the right side.

But Amuro had cut too deep. Like the Gundam, the Zak's main engine was located in its waist, and damaging it could be a fatal mistake for the attacking pilot. It was, after all, a nuclear fusion engine . . .

By Yoshiyuki Tomino
Published by Ballantine Books:

GUNDAM MOBILE SUIT:
Volume I: Awakening
Volume II: Escalation*
Volume III: Confrontation*

*Forthcoming

Gundam Mobile Suit Volume I

AWAKENING

Yoshiyuki Tomino
Translated by Frederik L. Schodt

A Del Rey Book
BALLANTINE BOOKS • NEW YORK

A Del Rey Book
Published by Ballantine Books

Translation Copyright © 1990 by Frederik L. Schodt

All rights reserved under International and Pan-American Copyright Conventions. Published in the United States of America by Ballantine Books, a division of Random House, Inc., New York, and simultaneously in Canada by Random House of Canada Limited, Toronto. Originally published in Japanese by Kadokawa Shoten in 1988. Copyright © 1988 by Sunrise, Sotsu Agency.

Library of Congress Catalog Card Number: 90-91838

ISBN 0-345-35738-8

Manufactured in the United States of America

First Edition: September 1990

English-language map by Shelly Shapiro

CONTENTS

CHAPTER 1	Side 7	1
CHAPTER 2	Escape from Side 7	34
CHAPTER 3	The *California* Crush	59
CHAPTER 4	New Types	91
CHAPTER 5	Zeon	112
CHAPTER 6	The *Texas* Zone	133
CHAPTER 7	Lala Sun	165
CHAPTER 8	The Beginning	188

SPACE MAP UC0079

A WORD FROM THE TRANSLATOR

The Gundam Mobile Suit is no ordinary three-volume science fiction series. It is but one part of a fantasy universe and a social phenomenon of gargantuan proportions, Made-in-Japan.

GUNDAM began in 1979 as an animated television series, titled "Kidō Senshi Gundam," or "The Gundam Mobile Suit," but it had its roots in a long Japanese tradition of giant warrior robot animated TV shows for children (mostly boys). These stories were usually about struggles between good and evil forces, and adhered to formula plots—after an invasion by alien monsters or crazed robots, a young hero typically climbed into a "drivable" giant robot (a state-of-the-art model designed by his scientist father or uncle, who had been killed by the attackers), and then proceeded to save the world. As directors often lamented, because the shows were essentially commercials for toys based on the robot characters, they had to show robots in absurdly dramatic poses in as many action scenes as possible. The result was an endless series of hyped battles between thirty-stories-tall, sword-wielding, transforming warrior robots stomping through smashed cities.

Yoshiyuki Tomino, a veteran animation director, had long chafed at the constraints of the genre, and was determined to demonstrate that it had a greater potential. With GUNDAM, in 1979, he created a far more realistic storyline, and lavishly detailed both its characters and *mecha*, or high tech hardware. Influenced partly by Robert Heinlein's 1959 novel, *Starship Troopers*, he abandoned traditional Japanese robot concepts and made the "Mobile Suit," a type of armored suit or piloted exoskeleton, the centerpiece of his story. He paid attention to the laws of physics and limits of believability, and he introduced characters with complex personalities that were difficult to pigeonhole as simply good or evil.

The first television series did not begin with high ratings, but it ended as a sensation, and marked the start of a GUNDAM decade in Japan. It also gained a near fanatical following among a much older audience group than would have normally been expected—many viewers were junior and senior high school, even college, students. The success of the first TV series thus led to a second in 1985, titled "Z Gundam" (Zeta Gundam), and then a third in 1986, titled "Gundam ZZ" (Gundam Double Zeta). The first TV series was reedited for theatrical release as three features, and in 1988 an original theatrical release, titled *Gundam Mobile Suit: Char's Counterattack* followed. Yet another feature is planned for 1991. In conjunction with TV broadcasts and theatrical features, a series of original animation videos, "The Gundam Mobile Suit 0080" has also been on sale since 1989.

Films are only one part of the GUNDAM universe. Toys are traditionally merchandised in conjunction with animation in Japan, and GUNDAM has been no exception. But instead of gaudily painted, sturdy robot toys for little boys, GUNDAM is famous for its beautiful scale models of the show's *mecha*, detailed with an unprecendented aura of "realism." These, too, have been a sensation. On one Sunday morning in 1982 nineteen young Japanese were injured in a near riot that broke out at a department store where crowds were vying to purchase the models. Nearly one thousand different types of GUNDAM plastic models have subsequently been produced, and over one hundred million have been sold—nearly one for every man, woman, and child in Japan.

Books are another component of GUNDAM. The original edition of the first three volume series of GUNDAM novels was published in 1979 by Asahi Sonorama, and followed in 1987, by another, re-worked edition published by Kadokawa. Authored by Yoshiyuki Tomino, the creator and director of the animation shows, the novels have allowed him to develop the GUNDAM universe with even more detail and sophistication than possible in the animation. Appealing to an even older age group, the books have also been wildly successful. The original three-volume GUNDAM series (this one) has sold well over one million copies, as has a subsequent five-volume Z GUNDAM series. In addition, over one hundred different illustrated and special interest GUNDAM books have been marketed.

An entire generation of Japanese has been raised on GUNDAM stories and images, but the ultimate testimony to the concept's success is that there has even been a parody animation series created, called "SD (Super Deformation) Gundam." It, of course, has also been accompanied by heavy merchandising—miniaturized, comical versions of the original GUNDAM scale models have been the rage among young children since 1988.

This Del Rey edition of the Gundam Mobile Suit is an English translation of the 1987 Kadokawa edition of the first series of three novels. I have tried to be as faithful as possible to the original Japanese in my translation, while striving for an English structure that is as natural as possible. This may seem an easy task, but with a language as different as Japanese, it is not always so. Luckily, Yoshiyuki Tomino's epic is set in outer space, and most cultural and historical differences have been neutralized as a result, making the job of translator far easier, and giving the novels a truly international atmosphere. Careful readers, however, will occasionally note Japanese names and a uniquely Japanese flavor.

To hardcore U.S. GUNDAM fans a caution is due. In much of the English language promotional material that has emerged from Japan over the last decade, character names have not been transliterated into English in a unified fashion. I have therefore given priority to the original Japanese text, and some of the spellings I employ therefore differ from those popular in English language promotional materials and fanzines. For example, the name of Amuro Rey's arch rival is often written as "Char," whereas I have chosen "Sha," which is closer to the original.

GUNDAM has inspired countless imitators in Japan and set a standard for science fiction that few have equaled. And despite the fact that neither animation nor books have been officially introduced in the United States, GUNDAM has already had a major, albeit indirect, influence on the American SF-fantasy world, in terms of both character and *mecha* design. With the Del Rey English language edition of the GUNDAM MOBILE SUIT, American sf fans can now finally read the original novels of the story they have heard so much about. But the GUNDAM universe is vast and still expanding and these novels are but a small peek into it. Hopefully they will soon be followed by many others.

Frederik L. Schodt

CHAPTER 1

SIDE 7

"The instrument panel's decoration—to let you know if you're facing front or back. The only thing you can really rely on is your eyes! And they're useless unless you use your brains! Understand? God help you idiots when you become pilots!"

With spittle flying, Lieutenant (jg) Ralv thundered at the five young pilot cadets standing at attention in front of him, but they were having a hard time concentrating; their empty stomachs were making too much noise.

When the *Pegasus* entered inertial flight, they were required to stand in the command center and observe the warship's seven regular pilots practice takeoff and landing in their Core Fighters. And they had to do more than just watch. When a Core Fighter was about to land, they had to yell out the correct landing procedure—before the pilot actually executed it. And if anyone failed to respond with the proper spirit, Ralv's left hand would let him know right away. Despite its realistic fuzz, the thing was artificial, and if it ever really connected in the weightless environment, it could slam a cadet into a fixture in the command center and lay him out for three days; unlike most warships, when last in port the *Pegasus* had not been fitted with protective padding.

The *Pegasus* was finally on a real mission, to proceed to Side 7 and pick up the new Mobile Suits. It was time for Ralv to teach the newcomers about the ship, about the Core Fighters. It was time for young men to learn to submerge their wills to that of the ship. On the *Pegasus*, the best of the White Base class, that was the way things were done.

The ship's seven regular pilots were lucky; they had already experienced real combat two or three times on the space carrier *Trafalgar* and as a result needed only three trial runs to learn the ropes to takeoff and landing on the new ship. For the five cadets, hell was just about to begin. First, they performed a textbook preflight check on five Core Fighters. Then they each climbed into one. It was their first time in a real Core Fighter. And it was their first time attempting a takeoff.

"Follow me!" Ralv yelled.

The lieutenant was irritated, and he had a right to be; he was one of the regulars. If the ship picked up six Mobile Suits as scheduled, and the higher-ups ordered them into action on a round-the-clock basis, even twelve pilots would not be enough. The cadets were young and fresh out of training. The only way the regulars would be able to lighten their own load would be to make sure the boys could take up the slack.

Ralv's Core Fighter catapulted out of the ship's port hatch, and the cadets followed: Ryu Jose and Kai Shiden from port and Amuro Rey, Sean Crane, and Hayato Kobayashi from starboard.

Ahead and to the left Amuro Rey could see the revolving red light on Ralv's machine. Using it as a guide, he gingerly twisted his Core Fighter's joystick to the left—like turning

AWAKENING

an egg in an egg cup. It was a good analogy, he thought while marveling at the stars blazing silently all around. His sun visor had a reflective coating on the outside, but from his perspective it was colorless and transparent, and through both it and the fighter canopy he could sense the indescribable stillness of space. But inside his helmet his ears were filled with noise. Amid the static caused by Minovski particle interference, he could hear the sounds of transmissions between Lieutenant Ralv and the *Pegasus* and the calls of the other four cadets, echoing over and over again.

"To be a pilot, you gotta learn to sort the important crap from the noise," Lieutenant Ralv had often said. He belonged to the amoeba-brain school and was not into sophisticated logic. "Don't worry about your eardrums rupturing," he was also fond of saying. "Your headphones've got an automatic volume control."

The six Core Fighters were now strung out in a curve like a strained fishing pole as the lieutenant's machine led them back around to the mother ship. On the right, the sun; on the left, Amuro saw the *Pegasus* floating in its rays. The ship was one of the White Base class, and its body was a beautiful, pure white. The bridge was in the center. On the right and left sides heat-dissipating panels with built-in solar batteries stretched out like wings. The prow was divided into two separate units for catapult decks, and the stern was similarly split into two units for the main engines. Viewed from this angle, Amuro thought the ship's profile resembled a rather skinny sphinx or even a dog lying prone with front and back legs extended. Sometimes it even looked like a wooden horse . . . In fact, Amuro decided that a name like *Pegasus* was really too limiting for a ship like that.

"Amuro!" Lieutenant Ralv barked.

Amuro's Core Fighter had strayed two degrees off course.

"Sorry, sir!" he yelled back with force, imagining how nice it would be if he ruptured the lieutenant's eardrums.

In front of him Ryu Jose's fighter plowed into the arresting cables strung under the *Pegasus*'s portside front hatch. Amuro, next in line, raised the landing hook behind his Core Fighter cockpit and sailed into the cables under the starboard hatch.

Ralv always said pilots should be able to spot the ship's arresting cables with the naked eye, but it was not that simple. In the vacuum of space the resolution was too extreme, and even with the cables painted bright red it was still hard to judge the distance to them relative to the rest of the ship. Landing manually, instead of on auto with the computer reading information from laser search beams, was an art that would take over ten years to learn and then still be hard. On Earth all one had to do was hook the cables, and gravity would bring one down. Here in space one had to worry about the relative distance and speed of both ship and Core Fighter and hit the wires at just the right speed so they would not snap, or else in an instant one would shoot by the ship or smash into its walls. And even if the *Pegasus*'s arresting cables snared the fighter's landing hook properly, there was still a risk. If they slowed one too fast, a fighter—worth its weight in gold—might flip and smash into the side of the ship.

The lieutenant always said the safest thing was to bring the fighters in by the book, following the digital readouts on the instrument panel. "But remember," he would add, "if the power fails, your instruments are about as useful as sunglasses in a cave at midnight." The analogy was a little oblique, but it got the point across.

Amuro felt the cables stop him with about the same force as slamming on the brakes in a car on Earth, and when his

AWAKENING

fighter came to rest, he felt rather proud of himself. Above him was a docking hatch that connected with the ship's catapult deck. The hatch opened, and a crane arm with a giant hook emerged and hoisted the entire Core Fighter up to the deck, where it was reset on the catapult mechanism, ready to go again. The entire process took only twenty-five seconds.

"Core Fighter Number 4! Chief Petty Officer Amuro Rey, prepare for launch. You are cleared for takeoff!" The confident voice came through loud and clear from an officer in the command center. Inside the *Pegasus*, all communications were hard-wired to avoid interference from Minovski particles, and even subtle nuances could be read in a man's voice.

"Ready for launch!" Amuro yelled back with vigor, trying to sound like a proper pilot should. If a cadet used the wrong language or tone, it would be reflected in his grades. Then his Core Fighter soared once more into space.

The Core Fighters piloted by Amuro and the other cadets were an integral part of a larger mission to pick up two new Mobile Suits developed by the Federation, models called Gundam and Gun Cannon. Mobile Suits, MS, were giant humanoid, heavy armor machines, a new type of weapon designed for close-quarter combat in outer space and introduced for the first time in the current war. Externally they resembled a robot, but they were operated by human pilots in a cockpit in the core module. Unfortunately, Federation MS development had begun only six months earlier. The Zeon forces had already finalized their models the year before.

Core Fighters, as the name suggested, could be incorporated into the central core of a Mobile Suit, where they functioned as its cockpit and, in emergencies, as a specially designed escape pod. They had heat-dissipating wings with built-in vernier rockets that could fold up into the fuselage and fairly powerful nuclear engines. They could perform a combat function independent of the Mobile Suit, but to call them fighters would have been stretching it a little.

Back at the ship, Lieutenant Ralv continued doling out advice to his pupils. "The Gundam and the Gun Cannon Mobile Suits are even trickier to pilot than Core Fighters. Gotta handle 'em like a good woman in bed, with care. But what would you boys know about that? This war's wiped out so many people, you'll never know unless we beat Zeon and you get to sow a few oats with their women! Don't ever forget that!"

Amuro, standing at attention, stared at the lieutenant. He had an awful habit of waving his artificial left arm when he talked, probably to compensate for a complex about it.

He's probably right, Amuro thought. He could not help thinking of Fra Bow, who lived on Side 7 colony. He had lived there himself until enlisting in the Federation Forces, and for the first three months or so thereafter he had received video letters from her on a regular basis. But then they had stopped. Now, on the *Pegasus*, he was headed back to his old colony.

"Switch to the nuclear fusion engine the instant your Core Fighters connect with the Gundam or Gun Cannon," the lieutenant intoned. "That'll give you some *real* power."

But then Ralv suddenly punctuated his monologue with a "Damn you!" and his metal fist sliced through the air, barely missing Amuro's left temple. Amuro did not mean to duck but did so out of reflex when he felt the hand crease his hair. The lieutenant, for that matter, left the floor from the inertia of his own swing.

AWAKENING

If that thing had connected, Amuro thought, *I'd be a goner* . . . But he had no time to feel relieved. The lieutenant quickly spun on his feet and with his own weight and momentum regained his balance. Then he turned to Amuro.

"Not a bad dodge for an idiot with his head in the clouds. But not good enough! You two on either side of Mister Amuro! Restrain him!"

As ordered, Chief Petty Officers Ryu and Kai reluctantly held Amuro's arms. Ralv then grabbed him by the collar with his right hand and slapped him across the face four times in a row with his left.

"Enough for now! It's chow time," he yelled. "You're all dismissed for an hour. We meet later in the briefing room. Hop to it!"

None of the cadets needed to be told to hurry. They were gone in an instant. Twenty feet above the Core Fighter launch pad was a catwalk, and from there it was a short hop by lift-grip to the mess hall. Lift-grips were special moving handholds that ran on rails built into both sides of the ship's passageways, and the crew used them to move through weightless areas. When the cadets grabbed on to one, they could zip along at speeds between six and twenty feet per second.

"Hey, Amuro!" Ryu Jose said, laughing at his friend's red cheeks. "Try a little harder to stay out of trouble next time!"

On the Zeon cruiser *Musai*, Lieutenant Commander Sha Aznable flexed the tip of his toes and floated up to the bridge. *Musai*-class ships were so quiet that when he landed, one could hear only the Velcro on the soles of his boots mesh with that of the floor. But Dren, a junior grade lieutenant, had sharp ears. Turning, he said, "We'll reach Side 7 in fifteen minutes, sir."

Sha grunted in acknowledgment and stared out the bridge window at the panorama that unfolded before them. It was something he always enjoyed. There, down to the left, was Earth, an illuminated crescent floating in space. And next to it was the reddish rock of Luna II, reflecting like a rusty little hand sickle.

Luna II was the nickname for Juno, an asteroid between Mars and Jupiter that had long ago been moved near Earth. Shuttled around in the same orbit as the moon, it had been used to supply important minerals and landfill to over two hundred colonies, and after years of mining it was now a lemon-shaped clump of rock less than eighty kilometers in diameter, with little of its original shape. Twelve years earlier it had finally been parked polar opposite the moon, in an area referred to as the Shoal Zone, which Earth Federation space forces had heavily fortified since the beginning of the war. Zeon cruiser-class warships rarely attempted to enter, but that did not prevent regular skirmishes between patrols sent out by both sides.

"Laser scope!"

At Sha's command, the monitor on the port side of the bridge displayed an image from the laser system; it showed the warship Sha sought, floating in space between two asteroids on the other side of the Shoal Zone. But the image was not a true depiction of reality. The system detected what information it could; the computer analyzed it and then, using inference and extrapolation techniques, finally output a detailed computer graphics image. Since the computer data base did not yet contain specific information on such a new design of ship, however, the system could only display a silhouette of what looked like a resting 180-meter-long wooden horse.

"Looks like a horse," Sha had remarked when he had first seen the silhouette, coining the code name for the en-

AWAKENING

emy ship on the *Musai*. Unlike most other Federation warships he had seen before, the shape of this one also reminded him of an old navy landing/transport craft.

"Something about that ship worries me," Sha muttered. Then he called out: "How far are we from Side 7?"

In response, an enlisted man stationed in front of the monitor typed in a command on a keyboard. Something about the torn seam on the man's left shoulder distracted Sha, but the data he wanted nonetheless soon appeared on the lower right corner of the display, and he pored over it through his antiglare face shield. All the crew members wore similar face shields on combat duty, but Sha was unique. Beneath his, he had another mask that he wore constantly. It was technically allowed because of a horribly disfiguring facial scar, but in reality he had another reason for wearing it; he did not want the higher-ups in the ruling Zavi family to learn his true identity.

"How long has the Federation been developing Side 7?" Sha asked Dren.

"About two and a half years, Lieutenant Commander Aznable, sir," came the response. Dren, a junior grade lieutenant, was ten years Sha's senior. His reply was overly formal; rank was important, but last names were rarely used anymore. "Only a third of Side 7's first colony had been completed when the war began," he continued, "so it's probably still a little primitive."

"Hmmm . . . And it's in the area controlled by Luna II, isn't it . . ." As Sha said that, something suddenly dawned on him. Ahead of them lay both the odd wooden horse-shaped ship and Side 7. It had to be more than a coincidence. "The V-strategy!" he exclaimed. "Dammit! I'll bet the Feds have developed their own MS!"

"Mobile Suit? The Federation?" Dren said skeptically.

Dren's stupidity irritated Sha. But the man had begun his

career as a civil servant. What could he expect? "Any troops occupying the Side?" he asked.

"Yes, sir!" called out the young crewman by the monitor. "A small unit under the Ministry of Colony Administration. According to information received two months ago, it's Company Number 8 from the Third Sector Patrol Forces."

"Two months ago?" Sha thought out loud. "My God, that's already ancient information. Our intelligence forces must really be shorthanded."

"Furthermore, sir," the crewman continued, "according to intelligence received seven months ago, there are 13,800 civilians."

"Understood."

The *Musai* had just completed a guerrilla-style raid on the Federation Forces and was headed home. It had almost no missiles left. Two of its four mega-particle beam cannons had been out of whack since the start of the operation, a single blast having fried the magnetic coating in their barrels and rendered them useless. The ship's three Mobile Suits—the Zaks—were usable, but there were only two cartons of ammunition left for their 120-mm rifles. There was only one way to find out if the Federation Forces were testing their Mobile Suits on Side 7, and that was by sending in Zak scouts.

It was 0079 U.C., seventy-nine years since the start of the Universal Century. By the Year Zero of the new calendar system, mankind had already begun to move in force into outer space.

At the end of the twentieth century—under the old system—Earth had plunged into crisis. Horrendous overpopulation had wreaked havoc on a civilization dependent on the burning of fossil fuels. It had brought out the worst evils of capitalism, aggravating a struggle for finite resources and exacerbating the greenhouse effect. And when an attempt was made to switch to giant orbiting photovoltaic cells, the transmission of power to Earth nearly destroyed the ozone layer, making radiation damage a serious danger. There was only one way to avoid destruction of the planet's entire ecosystem, and that was through collective action on the part of mankind to manage its own population growth.

With the planet's very future at stake, a bold massive program to colonize space was proposed and quickly adopted. In what seemed like a science fiction dream at the time, groups of floating colonies called Sides were constructed at the Lagrange points, specific locations around Earth and moon where the gravitational fields of the sun, Earth, and moon all neutralized each other. In the early days the individual colonies were giant floating cylinders three kilometers in diameter and thirty-eight kilometers long, but later they doubled in size. Emigration was made compulsory and was enforced by state mandate on a global basis, with no cultural or regional exceptions permitted.

The first group of forty colonies—Side 1—was constructed at the Fifth Lagrange point. It was followed by the construction of another group called Side 4. Sides 2 and 6 were built at the Fourth Lagrange point. Side 5 was built at the First Lagrange point. And then Side 3 was built at the Second Lagrange point in an area colloquially known as "the back of the moon."

By 0045 U.C. Luna II had already been created, and immigration to Sides 1 and 2 had been completed. When construction on Side 3 began, the colonists on the first two Sides had already begun to think of themselves as somehow different from Earth. Construction of the remaining Sides thereafter proceeded at an increasingly fast pace. By the time emigration to Side 6 had concluded and construction had begun on Side 7, a nearly centurylong colonization and emigration project had almost ended, and nearly eighty percent of mankind lived in space.

But on Earth more and more people began to rebel against the idea of emigration, and they petitioned the Earth Federation for permission to continue inhabiting the planet, to "preserve the native human stock," as they put it. As Earth residents, however, they still insisted on retaining the right to rule over all the space colonies. Inevitably, perhaps, a schism occurred between the Earth residents and the Colonists, or Spacenoids, as they were sometimes called.

The most dramatic example occurred on Side 3. In 0054 U.C. a young revolutionary named Zeon Zum Daikun declared the colonies of Side 3 to be an independent republic. But four years later he suddenly died, and he was succeeded by Degin Zavi, who resurrected an ancient concept of a sovereign state, established the Zeon Archduchy, and declared himself archduke.

The men and women on Earth, needless to say, were in no mood to relinquish control to an upstart archduke and were determined to continue ruling the colonies from the home planet. But adherence to this idea ignored both the difficulties of remote rule on such a vast scale and the realities of a changing time.

Degin Zavi decided that he would no longer be at the mercy of unilateral decisions made by a distant Earth Federation. Rallying the Colonists of the Zeon Archduchy around him, he organized an independent military and decided to resist by force. And thus mankind slid into its first war in space.

Two things made Degin's audacious military stance possible. The first was the use of Minovski particles, named after their discoverer. When several types of the infinitesimally small, charged particles were scattered in space, they

AWAKENING

fused with plasma and created an unstable ion state that absorbed rather than reflected radio and radar signals. Minovski particles were short-lived and were limited by the fact that they had to be scattered in space continually, but they nonetheless fundamentally altered the rules of combat. For all intents and purposes they rendered radar-based weaponry unusable.

Then two grown children of Degin Zavi, Gren and Krishia, developed a new weapon that cleverly exploited the new situation. Called the Zak, it was a Mobile Suit. Like warships of the time, it was powered by a nuclear fusion engine and could therefore engage in long-term sustained combat. But because it could use a variety of firearms interchangeably, it was also highly effective in close-quarter combat, even in the presence of Minovski particles. This, combined with its maneuverability, hit-and-run attacks, and tactic of jumping directly into the middle of a battle, meant that one Zak could single-handedly destroy an Earth Federation's Magellan-class ship. Zaks, more than anything else, enabled the Side 3 Zeon Archduchy to embark on its War of Independence and helped the opening rounds of the One Week Battle to go more or less as Gren and Krishia Zavi had expected.

Zaks were not without their flaws. When they were armored with a compound triple honeycomb construction, a sixteen-meter-tall Suit was said to be the maximum that a man could operate. And the pilots complained about the cockpits. The entry hatch was right in front of the instrument panel and was difficult to get in and out of. Weightlessness usually made this no problem, but pilots griped that the instruments were always dirty.

The Zak's 120-millimeter rifle, however, was exceptional. Only called a rifle because the Mobile Suit actually held it like one, in reality it was a cannon. When used in close-in fighting, it enabled pilots like Lt. Commander Sha Aznable to accomplish the previously unthinkable. Piloting a single Zak, Sha had destroyed three of the enemy's Magellan-class ships and seven Salamis-class cruisers. This feat had earned him a special promotion to lieutenant commander and the fear and respect of the Earth Federation Forces, who knew him and his red-colored Zak as the Red Comet.

As ordered by Sha, Lieutenant (jg) Denim launched his Zak fifty meters behind that of Ensign Jeen. First he detoured around the Side 7 colony and positioned himself with the sun to his rear. The cylindrical colony looked as bright as a full moon. Then, shielding himself with fragments of Luna II that drifted in the Shoal Zone, he led the way to the colony core.

It was hard to keep a cool head when closing in on an object three kilometers in diameter. The colony glared bright white in the sun, and the vacuum of space skewed Denim's perspective. Squinting, he could even make out the details of the looming walls, but soon his main monitor showed nothing but wall, making it even harder to keep a sense of relative distance. He stopped looking at the monitor and fixed his eyes on the range finder beside it. Since the Zak carried a 120-mm rifle in its right hand, he also made sure the gun sights were aligned with the Mobile Suit's mono-eye so that he could fire at a moment's notice.

There was no response from the colony. Monitors on the left and right sides of Denim's cockpit displayed the colony's periphery and revealed its relative scale; a protruding framework of several hundred meters was still under construction.

Denim swore under his breath. "Jeen's a lucky bastard. All *he* has to do is follow me. If I cream into something, I bet he'll turn tail and run."

AWAKENING

Eventually Denim was so close to the colony wall that even the range finder was of little use. He had to use the main orthoscopic monitor whether he wanted to or not. Just when it looked like he might smash into the wall, the details of a giant hatch used for entry and exit came into focus, as did what looked like human graffiti. He could make out *Toilet to the right, I wanna do it with Hanes,* and worse.

He snorted, "Uh oh . . ." But he was not responding to the graffiti. He had spotted the cargo hatch in the colony's center module, and it was open. It might be a trap.

"It's a gamble," he muttered. "The moment I touch the wall, an alarm might go off. But what can a few Federation clowns do right away against a Zak?"

Denim maneuvered his Suit to touch the wall. Nothing happened. With Jeen following, he entered through the first door on the cargo hatch and tried the inner lock hatch. Incredibly, the manual door was open.

This proves Zeon doesn't have a monopoly on idiots, he thought.

One by one, he opened the four layers of shuttered doors on the inner hatch. The last one was welded shut, but the laser burner built into the Zak's hand took care of that. And then he and Jeen emerged onto a deck that overlooked the inside of the colony. They were on the central axis of the cylinder, and had it not been for the clouds that obscured their view, they would have seen a 360-degree panorama of "land" surrounding them.

From the inside, the colony cylinder wall, or "floor," was divided into six equal sections, which alternated between glass-walled areas that let in sunlight and "land" areas where people actually lived. The artificial land below their feet was their "earth"; the transparent walls of the colony three kilometers directly above them formed their "sky." Natural sunlight was evenly distributed throughout the colony by an enormous array of mirrors built outside the colony next to the glass sections, and by adjusting the angle of the mirrors to Universal Mean Time, it was possible to create an illusion of day and night and even to generate a sense of seasons and regional differences.

Ensign Jeen made his Zak's left hand reach out and touch the shoulder of Denim's machine, initiating what was called skin talk—a form of communication utilizing the voice vibrations that could travel through the Zak's armor. Skin talk also could be used when one was wearing the helmets that were part of Normal Suits—the term used for regular space suits ever since Mobile Suits had come into vogue.

"Look, sir . . . a spiderweb," Jeen said.

Normally Denim would have chewed out his subordinate for such an asinine comment, but instead he actually looked in the direction Jeen pointed. In the corner of the deck above them there *was* a beautiful spiderweb. In the Zeon colonies insects were strictly regulated, and outside of the entomological room in a museum no one ever saw them.

"I'd love to climb out of this Suit and see what that stuff really feels like," Jeen opined.

"Win the war, Jeen," Denim replied, "and you can play with as many spiderwebs as you want."

With that, Denim made his Zak jump off the deck they were standing on, into the mist. The pair had to drop 1,500 meters from the core to the ground, or inner walls of the cylinder. But construction on the first Side 7 colony had stopped with only a third of it complete, and compared to the Zeon colonies, the clouds were still quite wispy.

So far, so good, but if the enemy spots us, we're goners, Denim thought. Noting that there seemed to be a fairly high concentration of Minovski particles diffused throughout the colony, he realized Sha's hunch had been right. *Something's going on here*, he concluded. Minovski particles meant that

AWAKENING

he and Jeen did not have to worry about being detected by radar, but someone might still spot them visually. He would just have to rely on the fact that it was early morning on the colony—4:30 A.M., to be exact.

As Denim dropped closer and closer to the ground below, he was surprised. He had imagined that a colony still under development might look a little like this, but compared with Zeon's ergonomically designed, calculated environments, the area below seemed awfully primitive. Nonetheless, he soon could see an open undeveloped zone with what looked like a military facility. While keeping the trajectory of his Zak aimed at it, he noticed something flash in the corner of the site.

I wonder if it's their MS, he thought.

Ten seconds later the two Zaks touched down in a pile of earth. Since they were still around three kilometers away from the military facility, Denim switched his main monitor to telescope mode. In the distance, almost eleven kilometers away, he could see the colony's "mountain." It was an artificial construct on the central axis of the colony, on both ends of the cylinder. The mountain peaks contained the colony's port facilities and industrial sectors, and from there the "ground" sloped into the colony's flatlands. As Denim watched, a giant elevator platform built into the side of the mountain began to rise slowly. There was no mistaking the exposed red-colored machinery it carried: It was a humanoid Mobile Suit.

I wonder if they've actually completed the thing, he thought. The Suit on the elevator platform was still divided into a humanoid upper and lower torso. Even more interesting, it had what appeared to be missile or cannon barrels built into the shoulder sections. It was a rather crude design, but it made a lot of sense to Denim. *A design like that would free up the MS's hands. With a rifle the thing'd be deadly!*

Then Jeen initiated skin talk. "Sir," he said, "look at that trailer down there on the left. That white thing on it might be another MS."

Sure enough, a self-propelled flatbed trailer was pulling another Mobile Suit, half-covered with a tarp, out of a gigantic building. But it was clearly a different model from that on the elevator. Its "eyes" were in exactly the same place as a human's.

"Jeez, it looks uncannily human," Denim grumbled. "But makin' a weapon lifelike doesn't always make it better."

Denim had now confirmed the existence of two enemy Mobile Suits, but it occurred to him that if, as it seemed, the Federation Forces were doing final operational tests on them, there ought to be two or three more around.

"Well, Denim," he said to himself, "it's time to make your move."

The best plan would be to capture the two Federation Mobile Suits right in front of them. But it might also be the right time to show Lt. Comdr. Sha Aznable—that young upstart so favored by the Zavi family—what a *real* combat veteran could do.

"Now, how many Suits have we really got here?" he thought out loud.

The *Pegasus* entered the Side 7 colony port, and the instant the docking lock mechanism was activated, the crew opened the hatches on the front "legs" of the warship. The conversion system for the new model Mobile Suits was ready and waiting.

"Prepare to receive three Gun Cannons and three Gundams in three minutes! All crew to stations!"

With the announcement, Amuro and the other four cadets assumed their assigned stations on the left and right decks.

AWAKENING

At the same time four of the regular pilots left the *Pegasus* and headed on lift-grips toward the port hatch that led to the inner colony. Being higher in rank, they would get to see the new Mobile Suits first.

"On the double, men! As soon as we finish loading the Suits, we blast off from this Side. That *Musai*'ll be on our tail!"

On the *Pegasus*'s bridge, Captain Paolo Cassius was worried. Twenty minutes earlier in the Shoal Zone he had spotted a Zeon ship but then had lost sight of it. And he was bothered by the high concentration of Minovski particles around the colony. Maybe it made sense for the Mobile Suit development team to scatter them in the area to confound enemy transmissions, but there was always a negative side to it. "If only they'd do things in moderation," he grumbled.

From the bridge Paolo could see the module that formed the Side 7 colony's port. The central command section was built into a wall only a hundred meters away, and in the reddish glow of its lights Paolo could make out the forms of a few workers. Just as he was noting how terribly understaffed the facility seemed, he heard an alarm sound. And at almost the same instant one of his communications men turned around and suddenly yelled. "Captain! There's an attack *inside* the colony!"

"An attack?" *It must be a joke,* Paolo thought.

Zeon scout Lieutenant (jg) Denim had, after all, decided to demonstrate what sort of stuff he was made of. The two Federation Mobile Suits first sighted were temporarily hidden in mist, but four other flatbed trailers with loads emerged from the shadow of an enormous building nearby. After waiting a couple of seconds to make sure there were no more, Denim ignited the jump verniers on his Zak. With the thrusters he could make his giant suit jump eight hundred meters in a normal-gravity environment. Ensign Jeen followed in his Zak.

When his field of vision was free, Denim trained his gun sights on the Mobile Suit on the mountainside elevator and fired in midair. Two shots hit their mark. The elevator platform crumpled and slid down the slope of the mountain, carrying the red Mobile Suit with it. Jeen fired a volley at the base of the mountain, and one of the flatbed trailers burst into flames. Watching the column of black smoke that bellowed from the site, Denim wondered if the Federation Forces were still using old-fashioned gasoline.

When the Zaks touched down, their legs skidded in the soft earth of the colony floor, and they were met by a wire-guided missile zooming toward them from off to the left. (Inside a small colony, guided missiles had to be wired to avoid Minovski interference.) Denim tilted his Zak's upper torso a tad to let the missile zip by harmlessly and slashed the guide wire with his left arm. He had not expected any resistance, yet to his astonishment the Federation Forces seemed to have at least considered the possibility of an attack from inside the colony. Several enemy ele-cars carrying missile launchers appeared, but the Zaks picked them off like sitting ducks with their rifles. The Federation crowd did not seem to have any idea how to properly use the slow, electrically powered vehicles in combat.

Five hundred meters in front of the *Pegasus*, over in the port area, a hatch leading to the inside of the colony opened, and Amuro suddenly heard a roar from behind him. To his amazement, two Core Fighters launched from the ship and entered the colony. Core Fighters were not really designed as fighter planes, and it was sheer madness to take them into combat in the narrow confines of the colony. The Side 7 colony, after all, was only around twenty-five kilometers

AWAKENING

long and three kilometers wide. It would take all a pilot's skill just to avoid smashing into the walls that alternated between terrain and the transparent sections bringing in sunlight; intercepting the enemy would be almost impossible.

Inside the colony, Zeon Lieutenant (jg) Denim was shocked by the sight of the two tiny craft bearing down on him out of a crack in the clouds. Since no one had warned him of fighters stationed inside the colony, he could only deduce that they were from that odd-looking wooden horse warship spotted earlier in the Shoal Zone. But did the Federation crowd really believe they could destroy his Zak with a simple strafing? If so, they were grossly underestimating his ability. He quickly had them in his sights, and then he fired. The 120-mm rifle was not equipped with diffusion shells, but he managed to pick them off anyway. The Core Fighters disintegrated in midair, fragments of them raining noisily down on the Zak's armor.

In the port area Amuro and the four other cadets quickly donned their Normal Suits, grabbed some recoilless rifles, and headed on lift-grips for the inner colony.

"I heard two companies of combat troops have infiltrated the colony!" Kai Shiden yelled. He had a way of stating the outrageous, and no one could ever figure out where he got his information.

"We don't have any seasoned combat troops on the *Pegasus*," Hayato Kobayashi said softly. "I wonder if we'll be all right inside."

Luckily, Amuro, standing next to Hayato, was the only one who overheard his friend's doubting voice.

"One thing's for sure," Ryu Jose said, taking his hand off the lift-grip handle and sailing through the air. "The enemy's not gonna run out and shake our hands." Ryu was big, and his body had a lot of inertia, but by grabbing on to the lift-grip on the other wall and using it as a brake, he was able to get to the C deck—the deck that led down to the section of the colony where the attack was taking place.

Explosions taking place on the floor of the colony below reverberated through the air. And then two more Core Fighters took off from the central port entrance and promptly disappeared into the clouds in the cylinder's atmosphere.

"Not bad," Sean Crane said. "It must be their small size that lets them turn on a dime."

With Ryu in the lead, the cadets approached one of the colony's giant elevator platforms and on their way got their first glimpse of a Gun Cannon Mobile Suit. The upper half of the machine, on a trailer, was over eight meters tall, but it nonetheless looked smaller than it had seemed in slides and videos. It was the twin 28-centimeter cannon built into each shoulder that really gave it a strange sense of power and enormousness. Despite a month of field tests, its shiny bright red body looked brand new.

"Why don't they take the offensive with this thing?"

"It's got no legs yet."

While listening to his companions' comments, Amuro noted the Gun Cannon's heavy armor and decided that if he had any choice in the matter, he would have preferred to pilot an MS with that kind of protection.

While they were riding on an elevator platform that led down to the colony floor, the power failed. The cadets therefore found an unused ele-car, piled into it, and began half sliding, half driving down the rest of the colony's central mountain slope. As they gradually entered the world of gravity, they could again feel the flesh settle around their hips and the blood pulse toward their extremities. Try as they might, they could not suppress the knots growing in their stomachs. It was their first exposure to real combat,

AWAKENING

and the closer they got to ground level, the louder the explosions sounded. Blasts from guns. Roars from missile launches. Even with helmets, the noise in their ears was so deafening that they ducked despite themselves. Seventy or eighty meters away, the elevator platform they had just been riding on received a direct hit.

Their ele-car veered sharply from the shock waves, and then, with a *whomp*, its metal frame buckled and white-hot flames shot in all directions. An explosion must have occurred slightly above them; it tossed the cadets into the air and then, aided by a gravity half that of Earth, flung them against the foot of the mountain.

Amuro hit the ground just as he remembered that he should have lowered his sun visor fully, but it still caught enough of the shock to protect his face. The visor was made of incredibly tough bulletproof plastic, and any impact strong enough to smash it would probably have decapitated him.

"Everybody all right?"

At the sound of Ryu Jose's words, the cadets all momentarily took off their helmets and checked themselves. Luckily, no one was injured. They picked up their rifles again and resumed scrambling down the mountainside on foot. Once they were below a layer of clouds, a flat expanse of ground—the battlefield—came into view. And in the midst of the growing "morning" light, they heard the approaching roar of a Core Fighter, its engine sputtering. It soared up over Amuro's head, creased the foot of the mountain with its fuselage, and exploded in flames.

Immediately, Amuro heard a scream. The automatic volume control on his headphones cut the top end off the decibels, but it nonetheless assaulted his ears. And he knew who it was.

"Sean!" he yelled. He spun to his right just in time to

see Sean Crane's lemon-yellow combat Normal Suit fly into the air in an arc. The suit looked limp, almost empty, and fresh blood spewed from a huge hole in the side. It smashed into a big rock on the mountainside and lay arched at an odd angle. What seemed to be a long cloth belt streamed out of the suit, apparently dyed bright red by blood. A piece of the exploding Core Fighter must have hit his friend, Amuro surmised, only later realizing that the cloth belt was his friend's intestines, unraveling before him.

But there was no time to dwell on such thoughts. Still shaking from the Core Fighter explosion, the cadets resumed running. Behind them they could hear the battle cries of a combat company of thirty-some men from the *Pegasus*, charging forth.

I wonder if Fra's all right, Amuro thought. Four years ago he had lived next door to her on Side 7. She was a year younger than he, and because he had lived alone with his father, her mother had been sort of a surrogate for him. Like her mother, Fra had been kind and gentle. At the time he had not really been aware of it—and he still was not sure— but perhaps she had been his first real girlfriend. While pondering this, he realized that he and his friends were headed for Block C in the colony, where he and Fra had lived. *Wouldn't you know,* he thought. *Of all places, the military has to requisition my old home as a weapons test site!*

Then Amuro felt the shock of another type of explosion, and he hit the ground out of reflex. The others did the same, only slower. Something gigantic was skirting the base of the mountain, climbing toward them. When it neared, Amuro saw a huge machine with a 70- or 80-centimeter mono-eye in the center of a round "head," glowing as it scanned nearly 180 degrees to the left and right. The ma-

AWAKENING

chine kept coming, and it was walking. It was a white Zak, one of the Zeon forces' Mobile Suits.

The *Pegasus* troops near Amuro began firing at the Zak, but when their bullets merely bounced off its armor, their bold cries turned to groans of fear. Amuro felt a round from the Zak zip through the air by his ear, and he shuddered. He began to run and headed straight for the metal monster's huge legs. He had no way of knowing exactly in what direction they would move, but on a hunch that he could make it, he ran right between them and kept running without pausing for breath.

To his rear a Zak shell aimed at the soldiers exploded on the ground, and the blast from it sent fragments flying through the air. A boulder landed only a few meters below him, and a stone hit him in the back. He tripped but got up and kept running. Before firing a single round from his own rifle, it seemed, he had experienced more than he had ever wanted to know about combat.

With a *whommp!* another earth-shaking roar occurred, and Amuro saw the mountainside elevator platform collapsing in flames. To no one in particular he yelled, "This isn't fair!"

In a few minutes Amuro arrived in front of the military evacuation capsule, where he was joined shortly by Ryu, Kai, and Hayato. The capsule was designed to be ejected with the aid of the colony's rotational force in times of emergency, but the cadets were not there to escape. As one of the most conspicuous objects on the mountain slope, it was simply a natural place for them to regroup.

"I hear there's only two Zaks," Ryu reported with assurance, "but they already got three of our Core Fighters."

"Nope," Kai replied. "Four."

The cadets looked out over the colony floor. A ball of flame was falling toward a river.

Amuro turned to Ryu. "I wonder if the colony itself can hold up under this much fighting inside. If there are two Zaks here, that means other Zeon forces must be nearby, right? Shouldn't we be even more worried about that *Musai*-class ship we saw?"

One of the Zaks had by then stationed itself at the base of the mountain; the other was occupying the middle of the Federation's Mobile Suit test site. Together they had more or less succeeded in quelling the opposition.

At the first lull in the firing, a crowd of forty or fifty civilians rushed out from the right of the cadets toward an elevator platform. Almost all of them were old people and women and children. Other groups were trying to escape to another section of the colony by crossing over one of the transparent parts of the colony floor. Yet others headed for an elevator built inside the central mountain, which they knew was one of the more sheltered spots in the whole colony and would take them to the port area for possible escape.

Amuro scanned the fleeing crowds, hoping to see Fra Bow, but with no luck. Over a kilometer away to his right, he saw a company of Federation troops rolling out five elecars equipped with antitank missiles, which launched with a roar. At almost the same instant other soldiers on the mountain slope began directing their fire at the Zak on the flat.

Seeing the fairly organized resistance, Amuro and the others became acutely aware of how little they were contributing to the fight despite the uniforms they wore. Hoping to locate more weapons, they dashed into a nearby military facility built into the mountainside, only to find that the guards had taken everything with them. But scrambling about, searching for something somehow made them feel

AWAKENING

better. At least they were involved in the action, if only indirectly.

An incoming round missed the building they were in but shattered its windows. On the other side of a grove of trees they could see the legs of a giant Zak bearing down on them. It suddenly occurred to Amuro that it might be the same MS they had seen higher up on the mountain slope earlier. Perhaps, he thought, it had somehow jumped down to where they were.

"We'd better get out of here." The instant Amuro uttered the words, the cadets all dashed out of the building, and just in time, for an enormous boulder came crashing through the roof. Outside, to their dismay, they found themselves directly exposed to a barrage of friendly fire aimed at the Zak.

Hayato screamed in frustration. "Don't shoot! We're on your side!" But Amuro knew that even if the Federation defenders could have heard his friend, they had only one thing in mind, and that was to eliminate the Zak, regardless of who was in the way. Sure enough, a volley of fire rained in the midst of some civilians who had taken refuge among the trees, scattering them. It was impossible to tell for sure where the fire was from, but it appeared that the Zak had jumped into their midst, trying to use them as a shield.

The cadets found an overturned ele-car, righted it, climbed in, and managed to start its engine, but just then a Zak, now only ten meters to their left, fired a burst. First the shock waves from the explosion reached the cadets; then empty cartridges the size of oil drums rained around them in a clatter. Ryu, in the driver's seat, tried to steer clear. "Damn!" he yelled as a cartridge scored a direct hit on the front of the ele-car and tossed the cadets from the vehicle.

Amuro, luckily, landed in a bomb hole, where his fall was cushioned by newly overturned earth. But when he picked himself up, he shuddered at what he saw at the bottom of the crater. In the old days colony floors had been built with a soil layer of only around three meters. Nowadays the average was more like six. Nonetheless, the blast had exposed the basic structural elements of the colony cylinder's framework. "A few more explosions like this," he noted with a low whistle, "and the whole colony'll be destroyed."

Superstitious soldiers said that a new bomb crater was the safest place to be during an attack, so Amuro hesitated to leave. But when a fresh round hit directly in the middle of the road fifty meters ahead, he changed his mind fast. First he saw a plume of smoke, and then he saw a bloody human hand flying through the air. It was small, and its middle finger was still wiggling, and later he realized it must have belonged to a child.

Perhaps such a shocking sight triggered something in Amuro. Whatever it was, he dashed from the shelter of the crater with an idea. He knew there was one Federation MS still undamaged on a flatbed trailer at the test site. He was not sure why he knew, but he just did. He ran over three hundred meters, jumping over the charred bodies of several colonists, but then lost his footing when he stepped on what seemed to be a blackened log. On closer inspection, the blackened bark of the "log" had been stripped away, revealing salmon-pink mixed with the bright red of human capillaries. Much to his horror, he realized that the soles of his Normal Suit boots had literally skinned the flesh off a charred corpse. For a second he wondered how such a beautiful color could exist under a carbonized exterior, but then the sight made him nauseous. Steeling himself, he resumed running.

When he reached the site, sure enough, there was a Gundam model Mobile Suit on a trailer. Not only had the Zaks

AWAKENING

not yet captured it, but it was intact and even seemed to be outfitted with a Core Fighter. He hurriedly climbed up the ladder affixed to the trailer and found the hatch used to enter the cockpit in the Gundam's midriff. Tearing away the canvas that covered it, he exulted in the fact that his hunch had been right: Incredibly, the Gundam's engine was even idling.

Before entering the cockpit, Amuro scanned the surrounding landscape for the Zaks. One of them was still busy warding off Federation troops in antitank ele-cars, but there was no doubt about who was going to win. The other one had just downed its fifth Core Fighter and was in the process of scrambling down the mountainside in Amuro's direction.

For the past three months Amuro had trained daily on a simulator for the Gundam model MS, so he immediately knew what to do, or at least thought he did. When he actually slid into the cockpit and looked around inside, he realized he was in a machine with quite a few quirks. The instrument panel, for one thing, was covered with notes made during field tests, with corrections listed for numerical readouts.

First he checked to see if the control system had been switched from the Core Fighter to the Gundam MS, and then he stepped on the left and right pedals. The Gundam was powered by an ultracompact magnetic confinement fusion engine and was known to overheat easily. At first it responded to the increase of power with a contented purr, but within seconds indicators slammed into the red zone and hot gas spewed from the twin exhaust nozzles on the left size of the Gundam's chest area, filling the cockpit. Amuro quickly turned on the ventilator, but this was already more than he had ever experienced in simulation.

When he closed the Gundam's triple-layered armored front hatch, a central orthoscopic video monitor on the inside began displaying an image. Since it was linked to other screens on the right and left sides of the hatch, it could automatically convert the Gundam's eye-level view to a human pilot's perspective and provide a sense of distance almost identical to what the pilot would have actually seen with his naked eye. Moreover, if the image happened to be a target registered in the Mobile Suit's data base, the computer system could accurately augment it with computer graphics or provide a warning to the pilot if it was unidentifiable. Surrounding the Gundam's main screen, there were also eight smaller monitors that provided a true 360-degree panorama; if needed, the image on any one of them could easily be switched to the main screen. In addition, although they often suffered from poor reception, there were two monitors for communicating with friendly forces close by.

Amuro quickly noted that there were eighty rounds left in the Vulcan cannon in the Gundam's head—good enough for at least two series of blasts. He slowly pulled on the left and right operating levers to start the Gundam. Sensors in its legs took readings on the environment and activated the system. The exhaust nozzles belched forth pent-up gas.

I wonder where the beam rifle is. While watching the monitors in the cockpit, he made the Gundam's cameras scan the trailer and its environs but could see no sign of the weapon he wanted. But then, on one of the left-side monitors, he caught a glimpse of a Zak at the base of the mountain. It seemed to hesitate, and he wondered if he had been spotted.

When the Zak took aim with his rifle, there was no room for doubt. Amuro fired the Vulcan cannon on the Gundam's head. But the Vulcan had been developed for close-quarter fighting, and its barrels were too short to be very accurate; the shells exploded harmlessly around the Zak. To top it off, Amuro realized he had forgotten to use the hinged sighting

AWAKENING

scope on the right side of his headrest. He quickly swung it around, positioning it in front of him, but while he was doing so the other Zak—the one that had been attacking through the trees earlier—turned toward him.

In haste, Amuro pushed the right lever away from him and twisted it into the third zone on the left. It took speed, a strong handgrip, and considerable pressure on the right steering pedal, but the Gundam's huge body did spin to the right. At the same time the rifle aimed by the Zak at the foot of the mountain flashed, and Amuro felt his entire cockpit reverberate from the explosion of a near miss. His left upper monitor flashed pink and indicated the shock, but there was no time to look.

"Damn!" he cursed. "This thing's slower than the simulator!" He was stunned at first by the fact that the Gundam's entire control system differed from the one used in training, but he was not about to let it get the better of him. His initial terror of combat gradually subsided and a newfound confidence welled up inside him and helped transcend the very craziness of what he was attempting.

Leaning the Gundam's upper torso forward slightly, Amuro headed straight for the Zak at the base of the mountain while dodging the attack of the other one farther up. In the woods, the tallest conifers helped hide his machine. His main monitor began to display the Zak. There were no civilian evacuees in sight.

"Hah hah! Now we're rolling!" He exulted in the thrill of the moment. He could tell by the way the Zak on the other side of the woods was moving that its comrade on the slope above had not yet spotted him. But then he saw its legs crush the body of an earlier victim of the fighting. Blood spattered out onto a concrete surface.

Furious, Amuro yelled, "Let me at him!"

Forgetting for the moment the other Zak descending toward him from his left, he made the Gundam charge straight for the enemy. The hilts for the Gundam's twin beam sabers were stored in the Suit's backpack, so he simultaneously flicked a switch under the instrument panel to free up enough energy for them and reached back with his right hand to unsheathe one. The instant an electronic lead in the palm of the Gundam's hand connected with that of the saber hilt, a particle beam nearly ten meters long stabbed forth to form the blade. Like the beam rifle, beam sabers required an enormous amount of energy and could be used only for a short time, but their blades could slice through thirty centimeters of solid titanium in less than a second.

With his eye on the digital readouts from the MS computers, Amuro fired the vernier jets built into the Gundam's backpack, waist, knees, and ankles for 0.3 second. The g force that resulted was mild, but it was enough for the Gundam to jump over the coniferous forest. The Zak in front of him turned around, and its mono-eye flashed as if in fear. By the time it raised its rifle up, it was already too late.

Screaming in rage, Amuro brought the Gundam's poised beam saber slashing downward in a blur of light. The beam blade entered the Zak's left shoulder and flickered for a second, but it had more power than in the animation sequences Amuro had seen in training and sliced all the way through to the right side. The Zak looked like a monster severed in half and spurting blood; sparks flew from its severed circuitry, and oil spurted out of its hydraulics.

But Amuro had cut too deep. Like the Gundam, the Zak's main engine was located in its waist, and as the training manuals noted, damaging it could be a fatal mistake for the attacking pilot. It was, after all, a nuclear fusion engine.

Damn! he thought, realizing his mistake. He turned the Gundam's chest verniers on full and jumped backward. The Zak descending the mountain slope tried to pick him off but

AWAKENING

missed. Amuro cursed its pilot for even trying; he must have known his colleague had been mortally wounded, and they both had to get out of the way of the nuclear blast that would ensue. It would not go off like an atomic bomb, but it was far more powerful than normal explosives and could cause contamination.

When the Zak piloted by Zeon Ensign Jeen finally blew, it carved a hole in the base of the mountain and blew a hole in the nearest wall in the colony. The blast of air that resulted even shook the *Pegasus*, docked way over in the colony port. Amuro, tossed backward in his Gundam, was able to slow his own speed by firing his vernier jets in reverse, but he was still thrown over four kilometers into the colony's Zone B residential area, where he finally came to rest on top of six smashed civilian houses. Lieutenant (jg) Denim's Zak was blown in the opposite direction, into the area normally called a river—a glass wall that let light into the colony—where he smashed over two hundred 50-centimeter panels of glass.

"Jeez, what've I done?" Denim sobbed. In the space of a few seconds a Zak had been lost. It was far more serious than losing an ordinary human soldier. Even though a Zak might not have as much firepower, his superiors had always told him that one Zak was worth an entire space cruiser.

Denim cursed his bad luck. *But the Federation Forces weren't supposed to have an operational Mobile Suit yet!* And then he remembered the warning the normally daring Lieutenant Commander Sha had given him when he left. "Remember, Denim," he had said, *"it's a scouting mission."*

Gnashing his teeth in frustration, Denim resolved to leave, alone.

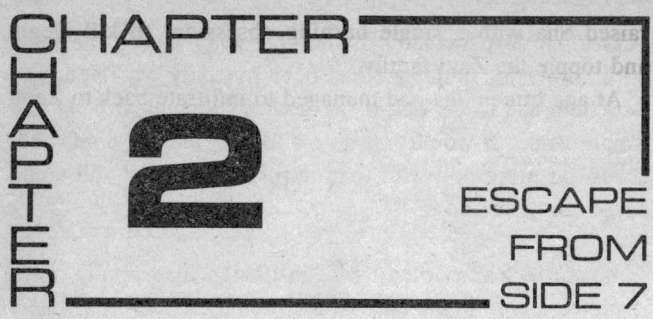

CHAPTER 2

ESCAPE FROM SIDE 7

The Zavi family doesn't trust me, Lt. Comdr. Sha Aznable thought, as light flashed from the Side 7 colony. Something had clearly gone wrong, and he knew he had only two real choices—to send in another strike team or retreat—and given his reputation and character, the latter was hardly appealing. It was he, after all, who had uncovered the information about the new Federation Mobile Suits in the first place, and he was not about to let anyone forget it. And a promotion, which it might lead to, was the only way he would be able to get closer to the Zavi family.

Sha's father, Zeon Daikun, had founded the original Zeon Republic with the help of Degin Zavi, the current ruler. But fourteen years earlier, after Zeon Daikun's death, Degin had repudiated the republican system of government and changed the country to an archduchy, purging it of all loyal republican elements. Sha was too young at the time to understand the difference between the two forms of government, but his foster father, Zinba Ral, believed—was, in fact, convinced—that Zeon Daikun had not died a natural death but had actually been assassinated. Zinba Ral had therefore

AWAKENING

raised Sha with a single burning obsession: to kill Degin and topple the Zavi family.

At age fifteen Sha had managed to infiltrate back to Zeon alone and, with the help of a few loyal friends of his father, obtain papers identifying himself as Sha Aznable. He attended a Zeon high school and upon graduation entered the Officer's Academy. It was there that he became friends with Degin's youngest son, Garma Zavi.

And then the war had erupted. Not surprisingly, Sha saw it as an opportunity. It seemed mere training for his eventual mission, especially when what was supposed to have been a short, neat little victory for Zeon turned into a protracted conflict. Zeon had quickly fallen into the grip of Zavi totalitarianism, but a long, drawn-out war, Sha reasoned, would eventually rock the foundations of the system. In the interim he could try to rally some of the old Daikun loyalists and work to topple the Zavi family from within. It had to be done carefully. As much as Sha despised the Zavis, he had no intention of letting Zeon fall back under the influence of the "absolute democracy" enforced by the bureaucratic Federation on Earth.

The Fates are on my side, Sha thought with unshakable conviction.

Just then the crewman manning the laser search beams yelled, "Lieutenant Denim's Zak is returning, sir!"

Sha ordered, "Put out some covering fire!" and almost immediately, several missiles streaked out of the *Musai* toward Side 7.

"Take her forward," he next directed. "We're going to do some scouting around Side 7."

The *Musai*'s captain, Haman Tramm, frowned. "But Commander . . . er . . . don't you think that's a little risky?"

Sha ignored him. The capillaries in the man's nose indicated someone too fond of the bottle, and Sha despised anyone afraid to take a chance simply out of fear of being demoted if he damaged his ship. Besides, the fact that Side 7 had not struck back indicated to him that even if Denim had gone on the attack without permission, he had at least accomplished something.

Five minutes later, when Denim docked in the *Musai*, Sha could have called him on the carpet, but he did not. Denim had, after all, brought back valuable information on the Federation Mobile Suits, including photographs and videos. Scenes of Ensign Jeen's Zak being blown up could provide rare, concrete information on the new enemy weapon's performance.

"We still need to do more reconnaissance," Sha announced out loud on the bridge. "And if Side 7's as shaken up as it seems, now's the time to get the information we need. We'll infiltrate in Normal Suits rather than Zaks this time."

Shortly thereafter Sha took off from the *Musai* with seven handpicked crew members. "Sorry to make you shuttle back and forth like this, Denim," he said, touching his Normal Suit helmet to Denim's for skin talk while in transit, "but I've got to punish you somehow for disobeying my orders . . ." The reflecting sun visor on Denim's helmet hid the man's face, but Sha could sense his shame.

As the walls of the Side 7 colony gradually filled the men's frame of view, the *Musai* initiated a diversionary attack on the port side of the giant cylinder and finally met some counterfire. With that as a cover, Sha and his men landed one by one safely on the wall of the giant cylinder.

* * *

AWAKENING 37

Inside the Side 7 colony, Amuro Rey had not had time to climb out of his Gundam Mobile Suit since the initial Zeon attack. There was so much to do—help transport an undamaged Gun Cannon Mobile Suit to the waiting *Pegasus*, aid civilian evacuees, and carry heavy construction materials for the Side 7 repair crews. There were an infinite number of ways to put a sixteen-meter-tall giant to work.

To his surprise, Amuro found himself receiving orders transmitted from Warrant Officer Mirai Yashima and Ensign Brite Noa. They appeared alternately on the two-way communications display above the Gundam's main monitor and told him what to do. Sometimes Chief Petty Officer Mark Kran appeared. It seemed that there were no senior officers left, at least not in the command center of the colony's port.

"What in the world happened up there?" Amuro asked Mark. They were on good terms and often spoke to each other.

"There was a direct hit on the *Pegasus*, Amuro, and it took out the main bridge and almost everyone on it. Captain Paolo's been badly wounded, so Brite's taken command of the ship from the subbridge. Not a single man from the surface combat units that went down into the colony has come back up. But more than anything right now, we need you to help get whatever's left of the Gundams and Gun Cannons up here."

"What about the other pilots? Can't some of them help, too? Sean got hit down there, but Ryu or even Kai oughta be around!"

"Ryu's up on the main deck checking the Gun Cannon we already recovered."

"Chief Petty Officer Amuro Rey!" Mirai Yashima's image suddenly appeared on the screen, reading from a file in front of her and telling him what he already knew. "According to this report from the colony, there should be three

Gundam models and three Gun Cannon models. We've got to get those other Mobile Suits up here!''

"There's only one other usable MS on this Side," Amuro answered her, "and that's the Gun Cannon being transported up to you right now." But he knew that there still might be some usable Mobile Suit parts and maintenance equipment left in the colony and that he should haul them up to the ship as soon as possible. He wished his father, who knew something about those things, were around to help him decide what was important and what was not.

At the foot of the colony's mountain core Amuro hoisted the other Gun Cannon's upper torso onto an elevator platform to send it up to the port area. As he did so, a van-style ele-car skidded toward him from Zone B, and a chorus of voices emerged from inside: "You've got to help us . . ."

There were around twenty civilians in the van—worried old people and women—who looked imploringly up at the Gundam. They, too, wanted to ride up on the elevator platform, and Amuro did not have the heart to say no. With the Gundam's left hand he signaled them to climb on board. Up to three humans could have actually fit in the palm of a Gundam's hand, but he did not want to risk their falling out, so he was not about to try that. He was more worried about the Gundam's beam rifle, which he still could not find.

When the elevator platform finally began its ascent up the side of the colony's mountain core, it carried not only Amuro in his Gundam MS but also the Gun Cannon and over twenty people. It rose through the colony's cloud layer, and then another two hundred meters above that it reached the port section, with its nearly weightless conditions. There, Amuro made certain that each of the civilian evacuees with him had a firm hold on the lift-grips that would transport them through the port area to the *Pegasus*.

In another group of civilian evacuees in the port area he caught sight of Fra Bow. She looked tiny as she drifted toward him on a lift-grip, staring up at his Mobile Suit with a worried look.

"*Hey, Fra!*" Amuro called out, switching the Gundam's voice channel to its external mode. "*You all right? Where's your mom? Why isn't she with you? What happened?*"

At the sound of Amuro's amplified voice, the crowd of people moving on lift-grips toward the *Pegasus* all stared up at his Mobile Suit in shock. The Gundam had no mouth, but the bulletproof, heat-resistant yellow glass panels covering its optical sensors resembled eyes and gave its face an uncannily human look. There was also something decidedly weird about a giant machine emitting such ordinary, familiar language.

"*Er . . . excuse me, ladies and gentlemen . . . ,*" Amuro quickly announced, trying to explain. "*This is a Gundam model Mobile Suit, and I am its pilot, Chief Petty Officer Amuro Rey.*"

Then he opened the hatch in front of the Gundam's cockpit and found himself looking down at the civilians nearly nine meters below him. True, he was now in an almost weightless environment where falling had little meaning, but even with his seat belt fastened, the ground seemed far enough down to make him feel giddy.

"Amuro! Oh, Amuro . . . ," a stunned Fra called up to him, "Mom and Gramps are dead . . ."

As if Fra's words were a signal, the lift-grips transporting Amuro's group of civilians began to move through the port area. The grips were rubberized rings two meters in diameter that slid along rails built into the walls and transported people through weightless areas. But if anyone let go of a ring while moving, the inertia alone could easily send him flying over a dozen meters. Because old people and little children lacked the physical wherewithal to control their own momentum, they had to cling desperately to the rings until they came to a halt.

"Go with the other evacuees to the *Pegasus*, Fra," Amuro called out, trying to sound in control. "I'll see you there later."

He made sure she got on the third lift-grip that came along and then turned and hoisted the Gun Cannon's upper torso off the elevator platform. In the weightless environment that took a special technique; to counter the inertia created, he simultaneously had to exert a counterforce in the opposite direction with the Gundam's other hand. Then he activated the electromagnets on the soles of the Gundam's feet and began walking through the port area toward the *Pegasus*.

Arriving at the ship's No. 1 hatch, Amuro found Ryu and several mechamen already working on the other Gun Cannon. As he lowered the upper torso of the Gun Cannon he was carrying, the communications monitor in his cockpit flickered to life, and Ensign Brite's face appeared.

"Mister Amuro! We've got beta test reports on the Gundam from the Side 7 Mobile Suit test site! I want you to go over these and memorize 'em. Understand? Better yet, copy 'em on your computer scanner."

Brite's eyebrows were arched, and his voice was high-pitched. He was doing his best under the circumstances, but Amuro had never liked the man's overzealousness. Nonetheless, when Brite sent the documents to the Gundam's upper right monitor, Amuro scanned and copied them into the Gundam's main memory bank and then began displaying them in enlarged format on the main monitor.

"I'm blowing up the specs now, sir," Amuro said. "Could you explain them to me?" Then, thinking of his father, he asked, "By the way, how'd you get these?" But Brite was not listening and continued his orders.

"The Gundam's spare armor plating's still at the main test site, and so are the magnetic control coils for the beam rifle. And finally, we've got to destroy whatever's left of the Mobile Suits that were hit inside the colony. We can't afford to leave anything behind."

"Can't you let the other Gun Cannon help me, sir? It'll take too long with just me in this Gundam . . ."

"Don't worry, kid. I'm not an idiot," Brite replied. "I'm gonna send Chief Petty Officer Ryu Jose out with you."

Saila Mas had just turned twenty. Two years earlier she had immigrated to the Side 7 colony voluntarily, a rather unusual act since hardly anyone volunteered anymore. Most immigrants nowadays had left Earth against their will; the only people who could remain on the planet were those whose political views were appropriately orthodox or who had some sort of special connection to the Federation government. Saila nonetheless had her own reasons for coming to Side 7. She was the daughter of Zeon Daikun; her real name was Artesia Som Daikun. Her brother was Caspar Lem Daikun, otherwise known in Zeon as Sha Aznable.

When Saila had been three years old, her father, Zeon, had died. One of his right-hand men, Zinba Ral, together with his wife, took in the two Daikun children and fled the collapsing republic with them to live in safety on Earth. To ensure success, the Rals took an enormous amount of money, with which they purchased the respected family name of Mas in southern Europe. This enabled them not only to pass as full members of Earth's elite society but also to safely raise both children under the names of Edward and Saila Mas.

Over the years the Rals repeatedly told the two Daikun

children that their father had been assassinated in one of Degin Zavi's plots. When Sha reached high school age, it was this more than anything else that fostered his unshakable desire to return to Zeon and destroy the ruling Zavi family.

But Saila was different. She had grave doubts about her brother's obsession and about the course of action he had chosen. He was her only brother, and he had always been good to her. She did not want to lose him. When she found out that he had secretly returned to Zeon, she wept for three days and nights. She began to loathe her foster parents' fixation with revenge and began to hate them instead. She thought about running away from home, but upon hearing that construction was due to begin on the new Side 7 colony, she hit upon the idea of emigrating. It took a year to persuade her aging foster father, Zinba Ral, to let her go.

"If a father truly loves his daughter," she had lamented one day, "why should he derive pleasure from her misery?"

"Artesia, dearest," Zinba had finally replied, giving up, "if you insist, you may go."

At first Saila had hoped to become a doctor, but after deciding to join the Side 7 project, she enrolled in a school that trained midlevel technicians in the maintenance of the Side. And when construction began on the Side's first colony, she emigrated. She wanted nothing to do with the Zeon Republic or the Zavi family.

Unfortunately for Saila, when war erupted between the Federation and the Zeon Archduchy, it became impossible not to be involved. Along with other civilians on the Side 7 colony, she was pressed into working for the military, and when she qualified as a communications expert in six months, they wanted her to formally enlist. The military was always looking for more qualified people, and nearly a quarter of all personnel in both Federation and Zeon forces

AWAKENING

were now women, or Waves, as they were called. In some fields, such as supply, communications, and the armaments, the ratio of women was even higher. Still, no matter how alien and despicable Zeon's social system, Saila had no interest in going to war with it—especially when it bore her father's name. But then an event occurred that shook her beliefs.

As one of the communications personnel on the Side 7 colony, Saila was assigned to work at the Gundam Mobile Suit test site and, in case of an emergency, given strict orders to destroy any and all documents to prevent them from falling into enemy hands. After the first Zak rocket attack she therefore hurriedly collected and destroyed all the important-looking documents she could find, even if they were only simple code lists for internal use or work schedules.

When the attacking Zaks grew closer and closer, Saila and the other communications technicians left the test site and moved over to the Air Defense Capsule—an emergency escape system connected to the outside world that could, in time of disaster, use the spinning colony's centrifugal force to shoot out of the Side. But when the Federation Gundam destroyed one of the Zak intruders, the resulting explosion warped the escape system rails and rendered it unusable. The sergeant in Saila's unit therefore issued the order "Move to the *Pegasus*," and the group began to head toward the colony's port area.

Along the way Saila spotted files that someone else had discarded, so she stopped to pour acid on them and burn them. Technically it was someone else's responsibility, but she did not want to take any chances. If any of the documents survived and the test site supervisor found out, Saila's entire unit could be slapped around, and she did not want that. She was not about to invite the military, with its love of corporal punishment like slapping and spanking, to apply its hobby to civilians like herself.

As a result of her diligence, Saila lagged behind the rest of the group and had to dash alone across the area where the Zak had been destroyed. She had been taught not to worry about residual radiation after the explosion of a Mobile Suit or even a warship's nuclear fusion engine, but she knew there were limits to this assurance. After all, if an explosion were big enough to blow a hole in the colony's outer wall, even the *whoosh* of escaping air could kill a person. Luckily for Saila, the hole from the Zak's blast seemed to have been blocked already, probably by objects sucked into it, and the fierce wind had died down.

But as she ran toward the elevator platform at the base of the colony mountain, she spotted someone in a red-colored Normal Suit dash into the ruins of a building. How odd, she first thought, that a Federation unit would use red for its suits. There was also something odd about the way the man carried himself. She stopped in her tracks, picked up a revolver from the body of a fallen Federation soldier, and snuck back toward the ruins. Much to her amazement, she saw the man in the red Normal Suit pointing a camera at the wreckage of a Gun Cannon destroyed earlier by a Zak, taking pictures. And then she remembered. She had recently seen a Federation report describing the uniforms used by the Zeon military. The man before her fit the description.

Being a civilian, Saila was under no obligation to engage a Zeon soldier in combat, but in times of stress theory did not always fit reality. Something about the bearing of the red-suited man made her heart pound; implausibly perhaps, she almost felt attracted to him. *I've got to capture him . . . ,* she thought as her legs propelled her out from the cover of a shattered wall in the ruins.

AWAKENING

"Take your helmet off and put your hands over your head!" she yelled as threateningly as she could.

The man in the red Normal Suit—Sha—was mystified. Why had he not sensed the approach of such an obviously rank amateur? True, he had been preoccupied with collecting materials on the Federation's new Mobile Suits. But that was no excuse. Normally his entire nervous system would have been scanning 360 degrees for anything unusual; it was this ability more than anything else that made him and his Zak feared far and wide as the Red Comet. Perhaps, he considered, the Fates wanted him to meet this person and had deliberately created a blind spot in his consciousness. He stood stunned as a young blond woman in double-handed firing posture pointed a revolver straight at him.

Before completely recovering his senses, he noticed that the woman's gun was shaking and realized that she would never be able to hit him even if she fired. He jumped at her. He heard the gun discharge, but he ignored it. The toe of his Normal Suited foot connected with the gun and sent it flying into the air. The woman staggered back, amazed. The instant he looked into her blue eyes, he knew. It was Artesia, his sister. She flinched and then glared back at him. In her expression he read terror and a defiant refusal to give in.

"Artesia!" Sha cried.

She looked at him, at first puzzled. Then she straightened and looked again.

But just then Sha felt the reverberations of giant footsteps, which he knew belonged to one of the new Federation Mobile Suits scrambling down the foot of the colony mountain toward him. That meant he had to get out of the area immediately. By the time Saila recognized him and rushed forward calling "Caspar!" he had already spun around, ignited the small vernier rocket strapped to his back, and soared into the air. As he maneuvered through the air to get out of the Gundam's field of vision, he heard his sister behind him exclaim "Caspar!" once more as she tripped and fell.

Moments later Saila was still staring in the direction in which the man in the red Normal Suit had disappeared, thinking he might have taken refuge in some other distant ruin. To her surprise, behind her she heard the voice of a very young man say, *"Climb up on the Gundam's palm. I'm gonna raze this whole area."* When she turned and looked up, she saw a giant Mobile Suit kneeling next to her, extending its left hand.

"Hop on board, but keep your head down . . . ," the voice said.

Immediately below the Mobile Suit's chest, in the area equivalent to a human solar plexus, Saila saw a hatch open and a young pilot peer down at her from it. As directed, she climbed onto the Mobile Suit's hand, whereupon its fingers slowly but gently closed around her, as if forming a shield. It was not a pleasant sensation. She kept her head down and tensed and then felt a floating sensation as the Gundam stood up and began transporting her. Pushing as hard as she could with her arms against the sides of the steel hand, she tried hard not to fall out; the hand was not designed to carry people. Moving ten meters above the ground, she closed her eyes to avoid a sense of vertigo.

By now Amuro had found the beam rifle, and when the Gundam reached and boarded the elevator platform at the colony's mountain core, he turned and fired at the MS test site, scoring a direct hit on a stockpile of napalm shells. *That fries the documents, all right,* thought an astonished Saila, *but it'll contaminate the remaining colony air.*

When the elevator platform reached the colony port level,

AWAKENING

a giant hatch opened to receive the Gundam, and Saila saw the same red-suited man of her earlier encounter zip by in the air in front of them. He had his vernier jets on full and roared through the hatch into the weightless environment of the port area. Saila could feel the Gundam's hand holding her twitch. Its other hand rose up and pointed the beam rifle toward the port but did not fire. Using a beam rifle on a single man would be overkill and might even hit the *Pegasus*, which was moored two kilometers straight ahead. But just when the red Normal Suit disappeared from view, Saila heard gunfire coming from the direction of the ship. "Caspar . . . ," she murmured.

As the Gundam strode quickly toward the *Pegasus*, each footstep created a loud echo. The sound of gunfire ended, but Saila heard a small explosion from the direction of the port exit hatch.

When the Gundam reached the *Pegasus* in the docking bay, one of the crewmen running around on the warship's deck yelled, "A Zeon infiltrator has blasted a hole in the outer air lock and escaped!" No one paid any attention to Saila as the Gundam gently lowered her to the ground.

Behind her, Saila heard a nearly hysterical voice call out, "Over here! Please. You've got to help me treat some of these wounded!" Turning around, she saw that it belonged to a young Colonist woman she knew, Fra Bow, on a gangway two levels above her. She kicked off the floor and floated up toward her.

On the subbridge of the *Pegasus*, Ensign Brite ordered, "Have the Gundam MS precede us supported by the two Gun Cannons. And give me full combat speed as soon as we clear the colony's port!" Then, turning to the ship operators strategically seated above him atop a cranelike arm that gave them a maximum monitoring capability, he called out, "Keep me posted on every move that *Musai* makes!"

The operators, Chief Petty Officer Mark Kran and Petty Officer First Class Oscar Dublin, were awfully young, but they were among the most dependable survivors on the bridge and had actually had formal training. Mirai Yashima, the young warrant officer standing in as helmsman, was part of the same student group mobilized into military service as Brite. It was all she could do to cling to the ship's wheel.

Almost everyone on the *Pegasus* was inexperienced. The ship's normal chain of command had been wiped out earlier when the *Musai* had fired one of its four large Tam missiles at Side 7's core, piercing four layers of armor and nearly destroying the *Pegasus*'s primary bridge. With Captain Paolo and other officers gravely wounded, except for the men who had been in the ship's engine room, the rest of the surviving crew, including those now manning the warship's guns and the missile launchers, were almost all new recruits. The only Mobile Suit pilots left alive were all cadets; Amuro Rey would have to handle the Gundam with Hayato Kobayashi as a backup and Ryu Jose and Kai Shiden at the two Gun Cannons.

The giant four-layered air lock doors of the Side 7 colony opened, and the *Pegasus* sailed forth from the port. Mirai, manning the helm, bit her lip and looked deathly pale.

"You can relax a little, Mirai," Brite said, tapping her on the shoulder. "The laser sensors'll help lead us out of here . . ." He was so scared himself that unless he did or said something, he would not have been able to stand the tension.

As the *Pegasus* advanced into the vastness of space, the shining orb of Earth came into view, fully illuminated by the sun. Sometimes it was possible to see little Luna II shining above it, but now the asteroid was overwhelmed by the brilliance of the mother planet.

Brite called out to the operators, louder than need be: "Mark! Oscar! Where's the *Musai*?"

"It must be in the colony's shadow, sir. We can't get a reading on it!"

"Mirai! How far out are we from the colony?"

"Th—three kilometers, sir . . ."

As soon as Brite heard Mirai's nervous reply, he asked no one in particular, "Can the Mobile Suits keep up with us?"

There was no answer, because no one on the bridge knew. But just then the rear door to the bridge opened, and the ship's medic, Samaro, wheeled Captain Paolo into the room on a gurney.

Beads of sweat oozed from Paolo's brow as his eyes hurriedly scanned the instrument readouts. "Don't . . . don't worry about the performance of the Mobile Suits, Brite," he whispered between stabs of pain "First get the *Musai* off our tail!"

"Maximum combat speed! Ready stern missile launchers!" Brite yelled, switching the captain's phone to shipwide. "All crew double-check the air in each section of the ship!"

It was not easy to move through space using a Normal Suit's vernier jets. Sha and his men could not see their destination, the *Musai*, so they navigated using Luna II and the Side 7 colony as reference points. Checking them every once in a while to keep their bearings—the sun being a primary reference point—and taking into account their own speed, they calculated how many seconds to fire their verniers and in what direction. But they had to be careful to avoid the worst enemy of all free space walkers—panic. The physical sensation of floating in a weightless environment could psychologically resemble that of falling, and unless one was constantly reminded that one was positioned "above" Earth or "above" a colony, it was all too easy to become totally disoriented.

"*Musai*, do you read me?" Sha spoke into his radio receiver while double-checking to see that his squad of seven men was still following him. The Minovski interference was intense, but at close range radio communication was often possible.

"Yes . . . We . . . read you," came the faint reply from the ship.

"Get my Zak ready, and Denim's, too," Sha added. "The enemy's headed our way."

Sha was determined to engage and fight the new Federation Mobile Suit he had just seen. From what he could tell, it was probably a high-performance model, but he had no way of knowing how well it performed in the vacuum of outer space. After losing a Zak to the machine inside the colony, he felt that the least he could do would be to find out specifically how it operated. After all, he was not called the Red Comet for nothing.

The far right corner of the main monitor in Chief Petty Officer Amuro Rey's Gundam indicated two enemy objects approaching. Laser sensors could be accurate on their own terms even with Minovski interference, but as Lieutenant Ralv had often said, until one confirmed something visually, it was not confirmed. That aside, the monitor indicated something approaching at high speed.

On the bridge of the *Pegasus*, Operator Mark read the same signals and yelled down from his perch at Brite.

AWAKENING

"Judging by the size, sir, it looks like Zaks, but one of them's closing in on us faster than I've ever heard of!"

"The other's speed matches a Zak profile exactly, sir," chimed in Oscar, the other operator. "I'm sure they're both Zaks!"

"Ready antiaircraft guns!" Brite screamed, at the same time glancing behind him at Medic Samaro and Captain Paolo.

Thinking he had heard the skipper say something, he went over to the wounded man strapped in his gurney. He bent over and listened and heard a whisper. "If . . . if it's a fast red Zak . . . it's . . . it's Sha Aznable. He's taken . . . over ten Federation warships . . . with his machine. They call him the Red Comet . . . You've got to get the ship . . . out of here!"

Paolo's face looked contorted, not from the pain of his wounds but from fear. And he said it again: "Get out . . . of . . . here . . ."

Out in space in the Gundam Suit, Amuro saw a reddish point of light weave through the stars toward him at high speed, and he felt a chill run down his spine. For a second he thought he was looking at a real red comet, but then his main monitor showed a close-up of a Red Zak. In its head, behind a panel that looked like the windshield of an ele-car, a pink-colored mono-eye flashed. It was sighting down the barrel of a hand-held rifle.

Amuro gently twisted the left and right joystick levers in front of him toward each other and felt the sudden *g* force as the entire Gundam spun sharply to the right. The Zak fired, and a tracer streaked brightly through the darkness. But Amuro knew that a single tracer meant his opponent had actually fired a burst of five rounds.

With a horrible sinking feeling he remembered the lieutenant's lectures: *"You gotta watch out for the guys who fire long bursts with rifles or machine guns, 'cause one of the rounds might hit you. But as long as you can still see the barrel of the gun, you're okay, 'cause it means you're still alive. It's the guys who never waste a shot you really should be scared of. They'll really make you stay on your toes. What's that? You wanna know how to spot them? Lemme tell ya. In real combat, you'll just know. And when you know, you'll probably be dead. The first thing to do when you sight an enemy is to pray he's an uncoordinated idiot. That's your only hope."*

Amuro felt lucky. He had managed to dodge the Red Comet's blast. The left and right monitors in his cockpit began displaying data, but he did not have time to look. It was all he could do to track the enemy Zak streaking across his main monitor. When the red machine seemed to hesitate, he pulled the trigger for his beam rifle.

A multipolar superelectromagnetic coil pulled energy from the engine in the Gundam's midriff, oscillated and accelerated heavy metal particles inside the beam rifle, and then blasted them out of the barrel. Because each shot was accompanied by an enormous burst of light that revealed one's position to the enemy, the rifle was best used only when one was in constant motion. But the magnitude of destruction a blast could cause more than offset the risk. Zaks were so well armored that they could withstand a direct missile hit; the Gundam's beam rifle and beam saber were the only weapons that could take them out. And Zaks did not have them.

The blast from the Gundam's rifle sliced through the darkness of space, leaving a trail of white light, but the Red Comet was already bearing down from another direction. If Amuro had kept his eye on the light, he would have completely overlooked the Zak. But the moment he pulled the trigger, he knew he had missed, so he deliberately broadened his focus. Like a real red comet, the Zak bore down on him, and its mono-eye again flashed. Amuro fired the Vulcan cannon built into the Gundam's forehead, knowing it could not destroy the Zak but hoping to at least knock one of its camera eyes out of action.

The Red Zak swooped left, executing an almost perfect ninety-degree turn. Amuro maneuvered the Gundam to square off against it and saw the small monitor on the left side of his instrument panel flash a warning. He jammed the joysticks to put the Gundam into an evasive maneuver and saw two bands of tracers. The Zak had fired twice as many shells as the last time. It was trying for a death blow, but Amuro had managed to dodge it again. Amuro's reflexes were better than average, and the Gundam was responding to them instantly.

Against Amuro in his Gundam, any other Zak would have seemed leaden in reaction. Sha's Zak had undergone finetuning, it was true, but he had really earned the name Red Comet for his unnerving ability to coax his machine into giving 110 percent of its potential performance and to engage the enemy at breathtaking speed.

Nonetheless, Sha was amazed. As soon as he had obtained information about the new enemy Suits being developed, he had conducted mock battles once or twice using other Zaks as stand-ins. But that had been like child's play compared to this. The real white Federation MS turned on a dime above and to the left of him, and beams of light zapped toward him from its rifle. They seemed so powerful, at first he thought they must have come from the big guns on the Side 7 colony itself, and his hair practically stood on end. Then he realized that making a beam gun compact enough to carry as an MS rifle was a diabolical act of genius. Whatever was sacrificed in destructive power was more than compensated for by the MS's innate agility. And it would take only one blast to wipe out a Zak.

The very thought of it made Sha's blood boil. There had to be a way he could put the white MS out of action. The Federation pilot was no doubt good, but although he could not really put his finger on it, there was something about the slightly awkward movements of the suit that convinced him the man inside was still a novice. This encouraged him, and he was seized by the same rush of adrenalin he had felt in the past when he had moved in on one of the Federation's Magellan-class warships. The only difference this time was in the size of the target. But Sha was too smart to judge an enemy by size. He had an uncanny ability to evaluate total strengths and weaknesses.

Turning his Zak hard toward where he sensed the enemy would be in a few seconds, Sha exulted "Got him!" when he spotted the white Suit. His main monitor displayed the cross hairs of his rifle scope. He lined them up with the gun sight and cranked the MS up to maximum combat speed. It was not a rash act but a tried and true tactic used to overwhelm the enemy. Then he fired . . .

But something unexpected happened. Unlike the Federation Forces Sha had met in the past, the white Suit had somehow dodged his attack. What was going on?

It was then that Sha thought the unthinkable: Could the Federation pilot possibly be a New Type?

No one in the Federation, he was certain, was yet truly aware of the New Type concept. After all, he himself had first heard about it only a few months earlier when he had contacted the Flanagan Agency. It was a theory regarding the emergence of a new type of human. The last thing in the world he wanted to believe was that he was really confronting one now. He wanted desperately to believe that the

AWAKENING

Federation Forces were just using some uncannily skilled pilots. But as implausible as it seemed, although the enemy pilot had first moved like an amateur, he was now appearing more and more like an expert. There seemed far more to the incredible leap in skill level than first met the eye.

Biting his lower lip, Sha fired a burst from his rifle. The tracers from it left a trail of light that disappeared between the stars. And then, in the midst of the battle, he heard a brash voice cut through the static in his headphones: *"This is Lieutenant Denim. Do you read me?"*

"Watch out, Denim!" Sha yelled back. "The white Suit's a tough customer!"

The fool, he thought, noticing a light on the top right of his instrument panel flash. Denim's Zak was emitting its FOF—Friend or Foe—laser ID signals, and in the presence of an alert enemy that could be tantamount to suicide. Denim obviously thought he should identify his position to his superior to avoid a case of mistaken identity or to avoid getting in the way, but this was underestimating Sha's ability. It was being unnecessarily cautious.

Sha barked over the intercom. "Denim! Turn off your damn ID signal!" But it was too late.

Enemy fire streaked out of the area in space where the Federation warship—the Horse—was and converged on Denim's Zak. But Denim was a seasoned warrior, a veteran of the Battle of Ruum, and he was not about to let anyone turn him into space dust *that* easily. He skillfully evaded it and went in hot pursuit of the white MS.

And then it happened. A direct blast from a beam rifle pierced Denim's Zak at its midriff. And it came not from a Federation warship but from the white MS. First the Zak slowly scattered beams of light into space, and then it emitted an enormous flash. In an instant it evaporated.

"D . . . Denim!" Sha screamed, hardly believing his eyes.

It was true. The white Mobile Suit's beam rifle did have as much power as a cruiser's main cannon.

Amuro had just dodged a blast from the Red Comet above and to the right of him when he first detected an odd signal to his FOF ID monitor. The signal source was around four degrees above the Red Comet, and it was another Zak, apparently moving at about half the speed of the Red Comet. *Just give me three seconds,* Amuro prayed as he drew a bead and fired two shots from his beam rifle so close together that they almost formed a single band of light. When the beams scored a direct hit in the Zak's waist, his main monitor reacted to the enormous burst of light that followed by instantly activating an automatic filter. Nonetheless, the screen showed a huge white saucer-shaped orb of light gradually fading into the blackness of space.

One down, Amuro exulted to himself. But the next instant he spotted the Red Comet bearing down on him straight out of the residual light of the blast. And when his monitor returned to normal, he saw—almost heard—the red Zak's mono-eye flash. Instinctively, he pulled the trigger for his rifle. Another beam shot forth and crossed in space with one of the tracers fired by the Zak. On Earth, the sound of a 120-millimeter cannon merging with the supersonic roar of a beam rifle would have been unbearable. But this was outer space. The two Mobile Suits silently crossed paths in the vacuum. And with a shock, Amuro suddenly realized his Suit was running low on energy.

At the same time Sha began to curse himself: He had run out of ammo. In theory, Zaks were supposed to conserve enough ammunition to last until they returned to the mother

AWAKENING

ship, but the irksome sight of such a humanoid face on the white enemy MS had made him squander his shells. Now, to have the enemy where he could polish him off and to be out of ammo . . . Glancing back at his opponent, he gritted his teeth in frustration, convinced that he could have scored a direct hit.

"How could I be so stupid?" he swore as he pulled away from the combat zone at high speed.

Amuro had no way of knowing the fight was over. He had six spare shells built into the Gundam's head, but once the beam rifle's energy was depleted, it took thirty minutes to recharge. There was little he could actually do, but he was too psyched up to quit. He scanned the heavens 360 degrees several times and wandered through the combat zone until the *Pegasus* finally issued an order to return to ship.

When he at last neared the *Pegasus* again, he opted for the safest docking procedure of all and had the ship reduce power on its main engines as much as possible so he could enter through the rear hatch. Guide sensors all around him went into action, and all he had to do was to line up with them and leave the rest to the computer.

"Good work, Mister Amuro," said Brite, ensconced in the captain's seat in the middle of the subbridge. "Now that the *Musai*'s lost two Zaks, they won't come after us for a while. And judging by the way the Red Comet pulled out of the fray, I'd say he ran out of ammunition. In the meantime, I want you to work on getting the Gundam and the Gun Cannons ready again. Some of the mechamen on board were involved in testing on Side 7, and they can help."

Amuro formally saluted and intoned: "Yessir! Chief Petty Officer Amuro Rey, descending to the second flight deck!" He noticed a young woman to his left on the bridge with her back turned. It was Mirai Yashima, the warrant officer. She had a friendly, gentle face, and he wished she would turn around and look at him. But she did not.

On the *Musai*, Sha finally returned and ascended to the bridge, where he was greeted by an overfriendly Lieutenant (jg) Dren. "That white Mobile Suit's absolutely terrifying, isn't it, sir! Why, those Feds—"

Sha held up his hand to stop the prattle. He stared out the window of the *Musai* bridge at the area into which the Federation Horse had disappeared. Luna II had moved out of the glare of Earth and was visible on its own as a shining half circle.

There had been nothing wrong with his basic strategy, but Zeon's intelligence-gathering efforts clearly left something to be desired. And never in his wildest dreams had he expected to run into his younger sister, Artesia, on the Side 7 colony, of all places.

For a moment he started to feel a little sentimental, but he quickly restrained himself. Forcing himself to reflect on the day's action, he muttered to himself, "I hate to admit it, but maybe I made a mistake. I'll just have to write it off to youthful inexperience . . ."

CHAPTER 3

THE CALIFORNIA CRUSH

The *Pegasus* was headed for Luna II, the former asteroid Juno. Now a Federation base, it had had a traumatic but pivotal history. The plan to move it to a lunar orbit had been announced in 0035 U.C. but had taken ten years to complete. It first had been mined and hacked at for resources, and the Federation Forces had already begun fortifying it by 0067 U.C., when construction on Side 7 began. And then, in one week of January 0079 U.C., when the Zeon Archduchy simultaneously struck Sides 1, 2, 4, and 5, annihilating several hundred Federation colonies, Luna II was heavily bombarded with missiles, and any and all surface construction was shattered beyond recognition. Largely because of this attack, Federation Forces were deprived of one-third of their entire fleet of ships before they could effectively resist.

There was one exception. General Revil's fleet was on Side 5 at the time and managed to put up a fight. And because Zeon was unable to destroy them in its initial strikes, it was forced to throw much of its remaining forces into yet another attack. And this time the Federation Forces rallied in a counterattack. The result was the first major fleet battle in outer space. The Battle of Ruum, as it came to be known, ended tragically in the nearly total devastation of Side 5 and the destruction of most of the warships in both the Zeon and the Federation fleets.

For over eight months afterward the Federation Forces frantically rebuilt Luna II and refurbished and expanded their fleet. Zeon similarly attempted to consolidate its position by constructing its *Granada* fortress on the moon and its *Solomon* space fortress in the area where Side 1 had formerly existed. Several smaller, strategic skirmishes continued throughout space as both forces attempted to expand the territory under their control.

One of Zeon's strongholds was a giant, ultraadvanced satellite called *California*, which orbited on a thirty-degree slant to the plane of the ecliptic. It served as base for a Zeon reconnaissance unit and was primarily charged with scouting enemy movements on Earth and monitoring Federation activity on Luna II. To avoid direct enemy attacks from Luna II, it moved constantly in a random orbit and sowed as many Minovski particles as possible in the vicinity.

On *California*, a sallow-faced young captain, Garma Zavi, read an electronic message from Lieutenant Commander Sha.

HAVE INFORMATION ON FEDERATION FORCES' V-STRATEGY. WILL DRIVE WHITE BASE-CLASS SHIP CARRYING NEW MOBILE SUITS INTO YOUR AREA. CAPTURE AND DESTROY THEM. WILL CONTACT AGAIN.

"Not bad for the class valedictorian," Garma said, smiling and indulging in his habit of curling a lock of his bangs around his right index finger. "Sounds like Sha's going to bring me a little present."

* * *

Garma, the youngest son of Degin Zavi, had been eight years old when his father had crowned himself sovereign of the Zeon Archduchy. Whether from upbringing or from genetics, he grew up to be extremely indulgent of other people. If tolerance was his good quality, it also made him an ineffectual leader. Worse yet, he was far too immature for the level of responsibility he possessed as a result of his family connections. On *California*, instead of waiting until contacted again, as Sha had recommended at the end of his message, he excitedly ordered Rear Admiral Zom, the nominal base commanding officer, to take off with three Gow attack carriers and intercept the *Pegasus*.

Traveling at full speed, the *Pegasus* would normally take over ten hours to reach Luna II from Side 7, so to divert the Federation ship from its course, the *Musai* periodically fired blasts at it from its twin mega-particle guns. In reality, the *Musai* had only two of its large Tam missiles left, but Ensign Brite was no match for Sha's experience, so the *Musai*'s feints worked, with the result that both ships proceeded on a zigzag course just as Sha had planned.

"If *California* wasn't in its southerly orbit now, we'd never be able to pull this off," Sha said, laughing, to Dren on the bridge of the *Musai*.

"You really think it'll work, sir?" Dren asked, unable to conceal his nervousness about the plan. "They say the Federation ship has an awful lot of firepower."

"Well, it's working right now, isn't it?" Sha retorted. Then, turning to the beet-nosed skipper of the *Musai* for a change, he added, "Isn't it, Haman?" As long as there was no threat to his own life, the captain had no problem with diversionary attacks.

"Haman?"

At the sound of his name, the captain blew his nose and laughed. But at Sha's next words he fell silent, and the color drained from his face.

Sha commented, "We'll probably lose a *Musai* in the process of testing the Feds' new military capability, but it can't be helped. I want the crew's combat rations increased. We're going to try to catch the Horse at *California*."

The *Pegasus* was in an unusual situation; in addition to its crew, it was carrying nearly five hundred evacuees from Side 7. Normally this would not have been permitted. Two or three holes blasted in a colony such as Side 7 usually did not entail the loss of the cylinder's atmosphere or even require the total evacuation of its residents. Basic functions would continue. Total malfunction was almost inconceivable. Solar-powered colonies such as the one at Side 7 were almost perpetual motion machines; once activated, their ecosystems went through their natural cycles, and basic materials were largely recycled. Being man-made, they would not last forever, but as long as the sun continued to shine, they were exceedingly stable environments, especially compared to the permanent energy crisis on Earth. Their future was also guaranteed by the Treaty of the Antarctic, which both the Zeon and Federation governments had signed after the carnage of the One Week Battle. The depopulation caused by the war had terrified both parties so much, they had agreed not to completely destroy each other's colonies.

Fra Bow moved to the gravity sector of the *Pegasus* and busied herself treating the injured. She was becoming inured to it now, and open wounds and exposed organs were no longer a shock.

"Get me some type A and type AB blood for transfusions," said Samaro, the nervous, bespectacled medic, to Fra. "There's got to be some left."

Jumping over the bodies of several wounded soldiers, Fra ran to the ship's blood bank as asked. Along the way, she could not help thinking what a horrible situation the ship seemed to be in. It was supposed to be a warship, but she saw so few military men in the sector, she wondered how in the world the Federation could ever win the war. And she was irritated by the fact that she had absolutely no idea where they were headed.

I wonder where Amuro is, she thought. It occurred to her that he might have been killed. She had known him, after all, not as a particularly strong boy but as one who always needed someone to keep an eye on him. But she swept the thought out of her mind, remembering how he had looked when he had opened the Gundam hatch to greet her back at Side 7. Amuro was now a full-fledged military man.

At the half-empty blood bank she picked up two bottles of the blood type requested and started to return to the room where the medic was. Along the way, she was startled. In among a crowd of civilians milling about, she heard children crying and saw a young boy—certainly under ten—trying to calm two even younger children while sniffling himself.

"What happened?" Fra asked.

"My mom . . ." The oldest boy started to say something but then began weeping uncontrollably. It was almost as though the gentle sound of Fra's voice had broken the dam of his pent-up tears.

"Now, you just wait here," Fra soothed. "I'll go look for all of your parents later."

She took them into what seemed like an officer's vacant quarters, had them sit down, and, after comforting them again, started running back to the medic with the blood.

They bawled mightily when she left, but that somehow reassured her. With that much energy in their lungs, she knew they would be all right. Besides, despite their own tears, the two older boys had tried to comfort the little girl. Somewhere, she thought, she had seen the girl before.

On the subbridge of the *Pegasus*, Ensign Brite remarked to Saila Mas, "You're just what we need. We're incredibly shorthanded. All you'll have to do is relay any messages that come in from Luna II or Side 7. I'll take care of most of the calls inside the ship, but I could sure use your help when things really get hectic around here." Brite should have been strapped in the captain's chair, but he felt better talking while standing.

Saila answered, "Understood, sir."

Then she floated over to the communications panel on the right side of the bridge. An enlisted man drifted by her, his head covered with blood from a wound. For a second she thought he was smiling at her, but then she realized the expression was frozen; he was dead.

The communications panel had five monitors on it, and Saila had no way of knowing which section of the *Pegasus* each showed. Nor, if there was any voice contact, did she know how to prioritize it. The main laser communications channel appeared to be open but was silent. Then she saw a close-up of a cadet's face on one of the right-hand monitors, and he seemed to be yelling. She pressed the button activating his voice channel.

"I finished readying the Gun Cannon," yelled an awfully impatient young man of mixed ethnic background. "Now what?"

"The . . . er . . . Gun . . . Cannon, you say?" Saila answered tentatively.

AWAKENING

"Yeah. This is Ryu Jose! Right, I'm talking about my Gun Cannon!"

Saila turned and called over to Brite, standing under the operator crane behind her. "Sir! A Mister Ryu Jose says his, er, Gun Cannon is ready."

"What?"

Brite picked up the captain's phone and curtly ordered Ryu to stand by.

"I don't mind standing by," Ryu snapped at Saila from the little monitor, "but I wanna know what the hell's going on. How're we doing?"

"He wants to know how the battle's going," Saila relayed.

"Tell him we're sending the information to the control room and for him to look at it there!" Brite screamed, forsaking any politeness toward his new-found crew member. Turning to one of the operators perched on the bridge crane, he added, "I want you to compile information on our status and send it to each combat sector. On the double!"

"Yessir!" Petty Officer Oscar Dublin called out with a gesture that looked almost like a salute. Watching the exchange between the two men, Saila sensed that things were not going very well.

Ryu Jose laughed bitterly in the monitor in front of Saila and said, "Well, I guess I just learned what I wanted to know by overhearing Brite's scream. By the way, I'm Chief Petty Officer Ryu Jose. I'd love to take you out on a date sometime."

Rather than being put off by such forwardness over official communications channels, Saila found herself staring at the image in the monitor in front of her. Was he half black and half Caucasian? Or was he part Arab? She could not really tell, but when he smiled, his white teeth flashed beautifully against the dark tone of his skin. "Well," she replied flirtatiously. "Maybe, if I have the time. By the way, my name's Saila Mas."

Why did she say that? She was shocked by her own friendliness to a total stranger.

Ryu's image said: "We know you're a newcomer, Saila, but hang in there!" Then his monitor went blank, and almost on cue, a close-up of a different enlisted man appeared on a monitor on the far left of the panel. It was Petty Officer Mark Kran, the operator, calling out to Brite.

"*Musai* approaching at seven o'clock, below us at an angle twenty-five degrees! It's coming at us at maximum combat speed, sir!"

When she heard Mark's voice, Saila looked up. Both the main bridge and subbridge ceilings had display screens built into them that showed a three-hundred-degree panorama of the heavens. The balance—sixty degrees—could be seen on another monitor to her rear.

"You absolutely sure, Mark?" Brite questioned.

Images generated from laser sensor readings were useful even when there was a heavy Minovski concentration, but they were only a simulation, a computer graphics model created by extrapolating from prior data corrected for Minovski-induced errors. They were far less precise than the three-dimensional displays used in the days of uninterrupted radar, but they nonetheless gave an idea of what was going on. Without those models, a skipper like Brite—a rank amateur—would have been completely helpless.

"Launch Mobile Suits!" Brite yelled into the bridge phone. "Antiaircraft units stand by! No, wait. Prepare for a direct ship attack."

"Looks like they've launched one of their Mobile Suits, sir," Mark said. Then, interpreting his own reading, "It's . . . a Zak . . . the Red Comet!"

"You absolutely sure?" Brite said, again feeling a tinge

of embarrassment because he kept asking the same question. He scanned a multiscreen display in front of him that monitored the inside of the ship. In the left corner screen he could see the two Gun Cannons being loaded into the catapult mechanism. The Gundam was already poised for ejection. Brite grabbed the bridge phone and barked.

"Amuro! Sha's on his way! Get ready to—"

Before Brite could finish his sentence, he heard a "Yessir!" and saw the Gundam blast across the screen of his launch deck observation monitor. The mere sight of the MS, fully equipped with its beam rifle and shield, made him feel better. The others were next.

"Chief Petty Officer Ryu Jose launching, sir!"

"Chief Petty Officer Kai Shiden taking off!"

As the two red-colored Gun Cannons soared out of *Pegasus*'s portside hatch, Brite felt a lump form in his throat. Here he was, using trainees—still teenagers—as Mobile Suit pilots, sticking them in cockpits the mechamen called coffins, entrusting the defense of the *Pegasus* to them.

Through the static, he could hear a fragment of a message from Amuro: "Gundam intercepting Sha! *Musai* heading straight under me. You'd better ready your stern missiles."

The *Musai* was on a course that would take it beneath the *Pegasus*. Sha, approaching ahead and slightly above the *Musai* in his Zak, apparently intended to take on all three Federation Mobile Suits.

Brite yelled out a command: "Elevation minus 2.5 degrees. Launch missiles in a fan pattern! Two barrages!"

Mirai, gripping the ship's helm, glanced over and commented, "I hope our boys are a match for the Red Comet."

Brite stared at her and said nothing. *Why*, he wondered, *do women say things best left unsaid?*

Then Oscar's yell assaulted Brite's ears from above: "Our

stern missiles missed, sir!" Eight precious missiles had vanished into space.

"What about scattering some mines?" Brite asked Oscar. "Think it's possible?"

"We're outside the Shoal Zone, so it's a little hard to hide them. But if we use Model 2s, they might not spot 'em."

"Model 2s, eh? Those won't work against the *Musai*."

Model 2s were contact mines with a diameter of ten centimeters; when dispersed in space, they were almost undetectable, but they would not even put a dent in a cruiser-class ship.

Then Oscar let out what sounded like a wounded cry. "A heat-emitting object's headed straight for us!"

"Missiles?" Brite instinctively clutched the armrest of his captain's chair and looked up at the ceiling display screen.

This time Mark answered with a strained voice. "It looks like a Tam, sir!"

"Just one?" Brite demanded, immediately learning the answer. One of the multiscreens to his left clearly showed a computer-generated image of a single large Tam headed toward them, along with its estimated course and time of arrival.

"Mirai!" he barked out. "Initiate evasive maneuvers! Angle the ship up nineteen degrees. Hard starboard!"

The *Pegasus*'s emergency alarm sounded, and the crew first felt the *g* force with their legs. For humans used to weightlessness, it was not a pleasant sensation. The blood drained from their heads, and those with low blood pressure felt dizzy. The instrument monitor went into countdown mode, ticking off each hundredth of a second. When the readout reached 1.5 seconds, Brite looked out the window of the bridge and saw, with the naked eye, a bright white light bearing down on them. The sensors built into the bridge

AWAKENING

window detected the light and automatically activated a protective filter shutting out much of it, but it was still too bright to look at directly.

The next moment the entire *Pegasus* was suddenly tossed violently upward, and its metal frame screamed as it twisted. The crew members on the bridge wearing seat belts hung on for dear life and prayed their bodies would not be severed at the waist. Mirai, standing at the helm when the blast hit, ricocheted back and forth between the ceiling and the floor three times and, had she not been wearing her Normal Suit, would have broken several bones. As it was, the shock was enough to kill some of the wounded soldiers on the ship. They had had no protection at all.

Before the ship stopped shaking, Brite grabbed the phone built into the armrest of the captain's chair and yelled, "Main engines! Give me every ounce of speed you have! Maximum acceleration!"

Mirai, wincing from a blow to her chest, carefully monitored the gauge for the ship's main engines. It read ninety percent of the way to redline but could conceivably go thirty-five percent higher. She realized what Brite was trying to do: use the force of the blast to help accelerate the ship and escape from the combat area.

"I wonder how our Mobile Suits are doing out there?" Brite said, half to himself. To his surprise, a voice behind him rasped in an almost scolding tone, "Don't . . . don't worry about them . . ."

It was Captain Paolo. Fortunately, his gurney had been secured to the bottom of the bridge crane when the blast had occurred, but the restraining straps had ripped open his wounds, and the blankets covering him were soaked in blood.

Turning to the ship's medic, Samaro, Brite yelled, "See

to the captain!" Then, speaking over the phone, he bellowed an order to the entire crew of the ship to inspect all stations for damage. A computer-generated image on a screen to his left displayed potential problem areas. The ship's external skin looked all right; besides, wall film—a viscous plastic film that could seal off most holes—would automatically go into action. But only humans could restore the equipment inside the ship, and any that had a direct affect on the ship's combat status would have to be fixed right away.

Brite asked Mark, "How many Tam missiles does a *Musai* normally carry?" and felt a chill run up his spine when he instantly received the answer: "Four, sir."

Out in space, Lieutenant Commander Sha had one weak spot in the way he attacked; the instant he fired his rifle, he would make his Zak run in a straight line for two seconds. But Amuro, Kai, and Ryu were too inexperienced and too busy fighting for their lives to take advantage of the opportunity presented to them.

Amuro would spot the cometlike streak of Sha's Zak in his center monitor, fix him in the sights of his rifle scope, and then . . . fire! But the instant the beam left the gun barrel, his foe was nowhere to be seen. Instead, Sha kept firing at him. Like the Gun Cannons, the Gundam wielded a shield for protection, but it was not armored heavily enough to withstand direct hits from a Zak's 120-mm rifle forever. It had already absorbed several rounds, and one more direct hit would render it useless. And Amuro's brain was reaching a state of overload. At one point Sha's Zak came so close that its red mono-eye seemed to fill Amuro's entire scope, and he reflexively screamed in terror. But then a miraculous thing happened—the Gundam moved with the agility of a trained fighter.

Amuro kicked the Gundam's left leg forward and felt the impact as it connected with something. If he had had time to look he could even have seen a readout on the instrument panel giving the force of the blow.

Sha was elated because he had caught the white MS suit within a one-kilometer range. If he could just destroy its head, he could knock out its main TV camera. He confidently fired again, but the catlike MS somehow managed to evade the burst. He cursed under his breath.

At almost the same instant he felt the impact above the ceiling of his cockpit. His center monitor went blank for a second, and the *g* force threw him back into his seat. The white MS incredibly had kicked his Zak and smashed its head camera. The Zak spun backward.

"And they call me the Red Comet?"

Sha felt humiliated. Mobile Suits had not been in use for very long, and his Zak was certainly the first ever to be physically kicked by the enemy. Smoldering anger erupted into fury. "You won't get away with this!" he screamed.

His center monitor automatically switched over to an auxiliary camera and came to life again. Fifteen kilometers ahead, he could see the white MS. Its beam rifle flashed again but as usual missed.

"Even a cruiser's beam cannon won't do you any good if you don't know how to aim," he yelled.

But then a barrage of fire swept between the two dueling Mobile Suits. Kai and Ryu in the Gun Cannons had started firing in support of Amuro's Gundam. Outclassed in firepower, Sha initiated a zigzag evasive maneuver. He knew he had to close in on the white MS fast, but he also knew that his opponent was no sitting duck. With his ammunition running low, he started to feel impatient.

* * *

"Incoming Tam!" yelled Mark, the operator on the *Pegasus*.

"Launch AMMs!" Brite ordered, suddenly remembering the ship's Anti-Missile-Missiles. They might not hit the target, but they were better than nothing.

Elsewhere in the *Pegasus*, Fra Bow's back throbbed in pain as she headed back to the officer's quarters where she had earlier deposited the three young children. When the Zeon missile explosion had rocked the ship earlier, she had been tending the injured with Samaro. One of the wounded had not had a restraining strap on him and had bounced back and forth several times between floor and ceiling, splattering the room with blood from his wounds. She had grabbed him and tried to restrain him and was now covered with his blood. Her blouse still soaked and her hands still slippery, she drifted along on the ship's lift-grip. Her own pain paled in the memory of it all.

"Well, you've been fine, haven't you?" she said to the children when she reached them.

"Yeah . . . um . . . but . . ."

The oldest boy started to say something through his sniffles, when the ship's alarm sounded again.

"Hurry! Put your seat belts on!" Fra said, seating the three children on the sofa in the officer's cabin and strapping them in.

Then the *Pegasus* shuddered again. This time the explosion seemed even closer than before. The covers on the bunk in the room, normally fastened with Velcro, flew off, and the three children screamed in terror and pain. Seat belts, even if made like restraining harnesses with two or three straps, dug deep into flesh. The younger boy's body slipped, and the strap around his chest pressed hard against his lungs;

AWAKENING

he began hacking. Then, as Fra and the children exclaimed in surprise, the emergency combat room lights went out.

The little girl wiggled out of her seat belt, crawled into Fra's lap, and clung to her in fear. She still had the softness of an infant, but Fra hugged her as hard as she could. In the semidarkness of the room she made a mental note of the emergency oxygen source, the video monitor that connected them to the bridge, and the shipwide phone.

"Everyone stay still now." Fra took off her seat belt and tried to stand up, but the little girl would not let go. Feeling indulgent, Fra carried the child as she felt her way along the wall to the officer's desk. With a little light leaking in from the hallway, she could barely make out objects in the room; she needed a flashlight. She searched the desk, wondering who normally used it; there were only two ring binder notebooks in one drawer. Another contained the flashlight she sought and a gun.

Maybe I'd better take it with me, she thought for a second, looking at the gun and then realizing she would never have an opportunity to use it. She picked up and switched on the flashlight, turned, and spoke to the boys on the sofa.

"You know what?" she said. "I forgot to ask your names."

"My name's . . . my name's Kats. Kats Hoween," said one.

"I'm . . . um . . . Rets Ko Huan," said the younger boy. Then, squinting in the glare of the flashlight, he asked in a worried tone, "Did you find my folks?"

Fra, at a loss for an answer, felt herself panic. Ignoring him for the moment, she turned to the little girl. "And what's your name, honey?" she said.

"Kika. Kika Kikamoto," she stated. Then she blurted: "You said you'd look for my mom."

"I'm sorry," Fra apologized, trying to be as gentle as

possible. "I haven't searched the whole ship, but when the fighting's over I can look some more." She wondered if there wasn't some easy way she could disengage from the kids. She had already looked through several of the ship's civilian areas but had not run into any parents searching for these children.

"They've made quite a nice course correction," Lieutenant (jg) Dren said, watching the Federation ship through binoculars from the bridge of the *Musai*. One more blast from a Tam missile would make things perfect, but there were no more left.

"I guess we'll just have to threaten them with our megaparticle cannon," Dren said.

"You're entitled to your opinion," the red-nosed Captain Haman Tramm replied in a mocking tone. "But Captain Garma is part of Rear Admiral Krishia's Space Attack Force. If we drive the Horse toward *California*, we'll have an argument on our hands with Vice Admiral Dozzle later."

"That's Lieutenant Commander Sha's problem, not ours," Dren retorted.

"No, it's a problem for me. I'm captain of this ship," Haman said.

"Well," Dren said, "then why did you agree to go along with this plan?"

Dren knew that correct protocol required that they obtain some sort of permission from Dozzle Zavi's Mobile Assault Forces before Sha contacted *California*. But they were in the Shoal Zone, and Dozzle was on the space fortress *Solomon*, which was blocked by Earth. Laser transmission was impossible.

"It all depends on how much one of those new Federation Suits is worth," Haman added. "If it's really so important

AWAKENING

to snare one, then arguments over turf will be irrelevant. If not . . ."

Then Dren replied. "I guess we'll just have pray its performance knocks our socks off."

Against this, Haman was at a loss for words. He turned his gaze to a computer display beside him, in a huff.

How about that, Dren thought. *He hates Sha even more than I do.* In war there were always brave young men who distinguished themselves and soared in the ranks, and it was not easy to serve under them, especially when they were like Sha Aznable—a young lieutenant commander, overly talented and overly deferential to his superiors. Social class had little meaning in the young Zeon hierarchy, but Sha's attempt to reach *California* and deliver a "present" to Garma Zavi, his classmate from the Officer's Academy, was nonetheless the act of an overly ambitious ingrate. Someday Sha would probably slip and show his true colors. Someday, Dren thought, Sha's luck would surely run out.

In his Gun Cannon, it was all Kai Shiden could do to keep his balance. The suit's left leg had taken a direct hit and thrown off his sense of equilibrium. Then, through the static, he heard the faint voice of Ryu Jose in the other Gun Cannon, saying, "That's enough . . . withdraw . . ."

"Withdraw? Where the hell to?" Kai screamed to himself in his cockpit in frustration. He had no idea where the *Pegasus* was. All laser search beams had been turned off because they were in an area where Sha could attack at any moment. And Kai could not very well wander leisurely around in open space looking for the mother ship.

Ryu, for his part, tried to support Amuro by training his sights on Sha's Zak for the third time. He knew it was risky since the Red Comet tended to move in close to Amuro's Gundam, but he fired anyway. Three times the 28-centimeter twin cannon on his suit's shoulder's flared. Nothing happened, but at least he did not hit the Gundam. Then he took his eyes off his gun sight, and to his surprise Sha had disappeared. He activated his 360-degree monitoring camera and sent out laser sensors that traced the heavens. Thirty seconds passed, and nothing happened, but then something emitting an FOF ID signal approached. It was the Gundam. Amuro's static-filled image and voice appeared in Ryu's cockpit.

". . . to . . . the *Pegasus* . . ." it said.

Ryu tried to query him: "What happened to the Red Comet? Did he turn tail?"

He knew it was a dumb question. Three state-of-the-art Federation Mobile Suits, after all, had gone after one Zak and had not even scored a single near miss.

Amuro made the Gundam hold up its shield so Ryu could see.

Ryu whistled low in appreciation. "He did that to you?" One-quarter of the shield was gone, revealing a cross section of its honeycomb construction.

Ryu was impressed not only by the accuracy of Sha's attacks but by the fact that Amuro had been able to ward them off with the shield. To himself he muttered words he had heard recently: "Maybe the guy's a New Type."

"Sha only retreated because he ran out of ammunition." Mirai's statement was delivered with such conviction that Brite felt compelled to ask how she knew.

"Sure, Sha lives up to his reputation of being a fearless pilot," she explained, "but I think he's a lot more than that. He's also a brilliant tactician. Look how he made those mincing little attacks on the Gundam. Seems to me he wasn't even trying to destroy it. I think he's just trying to gather information on it."

AWAKENING

As Mirai spoke, it also dawned on her that even if Sha had run out of ammo, his decision to about-face had been too sudden.

"You mean he seemed *too* in control?" Brite pushed.

"Well, yes," Mirai said, hedging. "Seems odd, doesn't it?"

Returning her gaze, Brite was impressed by how intelligent and perceptive she suddenly seemed.

Then Mark, perched above on the operator crane, announced something that gave Brite a chill. "Sir," he said, "if we continue on our current course, we won't be able to descend toward Luna II."

Since loading the Mobile Suits on Side 7, Brite and the others had had no way of knowing the *Pegasus*'s true assignment, as most of the ship's key officers had been killed in the initial attack. And now Captain Paolo was fading in and out of consciousness from losing too much blood, and unless he came to and told them they would never know. Given his condition, returning to Luna II seemed the only logical choice, but every time the *Pegasus* tried to head toward the base, the *Musai* unleashed another beam attack; unless they were prepared to confront the Zeon warship head-on, they would never make it.

"Well, Miss Saila," Brite called out across the bridge. "Any communication with Luna II?" For the first time he noticed how pretty she looked. When the light was from behind her, her medium-length blond hair almost seemed to glow.

"Something's creating interference," she ventured. "I think it's an enemy ship . . . maybe the *Musai*. There's a horrible distortion in the laser oscillation."

"Hmm . . ." Brite said, pondering a minute. "I think we've been led into a trap by Sha."

Then a voice came from near the entrance to the sub-bridge: "What's happening, Mister Brite?" It was Amuro Rey, but he was not alone in wondering. More than fifty other crewmen were assembled in the room, all looking at Brite with the same worried expression on their faces.

"For the last three hours," Brite explained, "we've been traveling at full speed, but we haven't been able to shake the Zeon ship. If, as it seems, they're trying to prevent us from landing on Luna II, I had planned to take the *Pegasus* into a broad loop around it, turn our prow 180 degrees, and approach from the opposite direction. But I just recalled one thing—Zeon's base, *California*, is in the way."

Hayato shouted out the next question. "You mean they might send some Gow attack carriers after us?"

California was not a particularly large base, but to the inexperienced crew of the *Pegasus*, if it could dispatch two or three Gows after them, it was terrifying.

Then a crewman mentioned, "I heard Captain Garma Zavi's in charge of *California*." A commotion ensued among the rest of those assembled. If they had been forced in range of Zeon's *California* base and Degin Zavi's youngest son was there, it had to have been part of a master plan by Sha.

Brite spoke bluntly. "We're all in this together, crew, and I need your opinion. Should we turn around and attack the *Musai* head-on, or try to scrape by *California*, use the Earth's gravity to boost our speed, and make it back to Luna II?"

The first answer came from Mirai. "Let's turn around and face the *Musai*," she said. "If *California* hadn't been in Sha's plans from the beginning, he wouldn't have attacked like he did earlier. And if the *Musai* had had enough fire-

AWAKENING

power on board, it would have come at us a lot more aggressively."

"I agree with Mirai," Ryu Jose said. "The *Musai*'s probably out of ammo, and probably outgunned by us, in which case we should attack it. And who knows how many Gows they have on *California*?"

No one seemed to take issue with Ryu's assessment, so it appeared a consensus had been reached. After a pause, Brite turned and announced, "All crew don Normal Suits again. We'll reverse course and destroy the *Musai* ship. Then we'll head straight for Luna II." The crowd assembled on the subbridge scattered.

Next, Brite broadcast an appeal throughout the entire ship. "Some civilians on board have had prior military training or are former military personnel. All of those to whom this applies, whether male or female, are hereby ordered to help in the defense of the ship. Infants, children, their adult guardians, and any wounded troops must immediately move to Ward E in the gravity sector. We will engage the *Musai* in fifteen minutes!"

The subbridge fell silent. Taking advantage of the moment, Saila Mas turned and looked up at Brite. "Excuse me, sir, but isn't there a map of the layout of the *Pegasus* somewhere? I'm having a little trouble understanding what's going on."

"We can display one for you on one of the top screens," Brite said, "but maybe Mark knows where there's a printed version."

"There should be one in the right-hand drawer over there," Mark replied. "Take a look."

Following his directions, Saila finally found a document that graphically showed both the ship's layout and its internal communication channels.

"Anyone want some coffee?" Brite asked.

At the sound of the word, Saila realized how parched her throat was, but it was Oscar who replied.

"Good idea," he said. "Let's send Recruit Tamura down to the galley to bring us some."

As if that were a signal, the crew members on the bridge fell silent and returned to their assignments. Before Saila had time to digest the new information she had been given, the communications monitors in front of her all suddenly sparked to life with questions, requests, and protests from people stationed throughout the ship. There were not enough Normal Suits to go around. What station to proceed to? Where was an assigned gun turret? The questions were all new to Saila and were more than she could possibly have handled. All she could do was relay them to Brite.

"The rule of thumb on this ship," he explained, "is that the officers stationed on each deck make those decisions. Tell them not to bother us with stuff like that."

In the end, the only job Saila could perform with confidence was to check the monitors, oversee the movement of civilians and wounded troops throughout the ship, and then relay the information to Samaro, the medic.

"Five people in Sector 24 being moved to Ward E," she announced. "No wounded among them."

Immediately afterward, a young civilian woman appeared on a screen, saying, "Hi, I'm Fra Bow. I've got three kids with me. How do I get to Ward E?"

"Where are you currently located?" Saila asked, thinking the woman looked awfully young to be their mother.

"I'm in an officer's cabin," Fra reported. "Number 16, I think."

* * *

AWAKENING

In the midst of all this confusion, a gray-haired old man suddenly rushed into the subbridge area, yelling. "Where's the captain? What the hell's going on?"

"What do you want?" Brite asked.

"Hmph. I asked to see the captain, not an ensign," the intruder sniffed.

"Captain Paolo's in a coma right now, sir," Brite replied. "I'm standing in for him."

"You're taking over for Paolo Cassius as skipper?" The man was incredulous.

"Yes, I am," Brite said, feeling irritated. "And what can I do for you?"

"Listen," the man huffed, "I hope you're not serious about that earlier announcement—about taking on an enemy warship! In the condition we're in, it'd be madness!"

"We've no other choice, sir," Brite retorted. "If you've nothing further to say, I'd appreciate it if you'd leave the bridge."

"I'm Jarma Amov, son," the man said, drawing himself up. "I may not know much about this ship, but I once commanded the heavy cruiser *Buchanan*. I'm here to help you."

The old graybeard did look like he might have been a military man in his day, but he also looked like he could cause trouble. Brite decided he was probably a by-the-book ex-officer who had left the *Buchanan* after ten years of service, unable to advance in the ranks beyond commander.

"Times are different now," he said to the man. "The combat tactics we use these days are more like those of the preradar age. It's a whole new ball game."

"I know that," Amov protested.

"Well," Brite sighed, "I don't have the time to explain the *Pegasus* to you, but we've got twenty-four missile launchers up in the fore of the ship. Why don't you take charge of those for us."

"Where's the command post for them?"

"On the deck below us. Petty Officer Dublin should be down there. Take over from him and tell him to move forward to the launch tubes."

"Er . . . understood, skipper." Reluctantly, the former commander turned around and started to leave.

"There's a radar display in the command post," Brite called out after him, "but it's useless."

The old man said nothing. He was wearing a Normal Suit and tottered as he reached out to grab the lift-grip. For a moment it looked like he would not make it.

Brite got Dublin on the ship's phone immediately. "Dublin. A former ship commander named Jarma's on his way to your area. I want you to pretend to let him take over. But you'll actually be in charge of all the missile launch tubes from one to twenty-four."

"But skipper," Dublin asked, confused, "what should I tell him?"

"Just say the communication channels are out or something. He's one of those radar-age military men, you know. Let him think he's still in command."

Brite put down the receiver and congratulated himself on having handled a sticky situation well.

"Now, who's in charge of the stern missiles?" he asked.

"Seaman Torkum, sir," Mark replied. "And he's a veteran, so he's no problem." As operator for the ship's internal operations, Mark sometimes had an uncanny ability to remember every last detail, all the way down to the number of shells left.

"Understood," Brite said. Then, turning to Mirai, he added, "Okay, let's turn this ship around."

He switched his communications link to shipwide and wondered why the coffee was taking so long to arrive.

* * *

AWAKENING

On the *Musai*, Lieutenant (jg) Dren announced, "Captain Garma's leading three Gow attack carriers, sir, and he'll be in firing range of the Federation ship ten minutes from now."

"Sounds like Garma," Sha answered. "The guy'll never grow up."

"I think he wants to distinguish himself in battle, sir. You know how he always says he doesn't want to be a desk-jockey type of leader."

There was something about Dren's know-it-all look, Sha thought, that rubbed him the wrong way. He blurted out to the other man, "And that's why Zeon'll never win this war against the Federation. Understand, Lieutenant?"

The instant he uttered the last two words he knew he had gone too far. Dren turned his back on him, as if saying in silent accusation, "You're just as young and inexperienced as Garma, Lieutenant Commander."

The younger a man, the more sensitive he is to perceived slights. If Sha differed at all from other people, it was in his normally superb self-control. Despite the fact that he was exceedingly young for his rank and responsibility, he possessed a type of maturity that gave him a powerful advantage in dealing with others and was especially useful in the Zeon forces. Garma Zavi, on the other hand, had the typical psyche of someone his age, and it showed in his actions.

"If Garma's leading three Gows," Sha continued smoothly, totally ignoring the overtones of the conversation with Dren, "it means he has eighteen Dopp fighters. Here's hoping he can pull it off."

Dren suddenly turned toward Sha again, smiled, and said, "So if Captain Garma spots the Horse first, he ought to be able to capture it, right?"

"Sure," Sha answered, deliberately being affable. "He's got a hyperbazooka with him, doesn't he?"

Dren punched a couple keys on a terminal in front of them and displayed an answer. "Yessir. But he only has three shells available. And all three are refurbished duds from the battle the day before yesterday."

"That tells me enough," Sha announced. "I'm going out to help him."

When he estimated that Garma's Gow attack carrier had launched its Dopp fighters, Sha took off in his Zak.

A Gow was fifty meters long by sixty meters wide and actually looked more like a fat rounded aircraft than what used to be called a carrier on Earth. The main fuselage carried five Mobile Suits; the front part of each wing section had bays that contained four Dopp space fighter-bombers. The aft part of the wing section flared into giant nozzles, which, when the twin nuclear fusion engines were on full power, could propel the ship at twice the speed of a normal cruiser. The ship was also equipped with two mega-particle cannons.

The Dopp fighter carried by the Gows was one of the first fighters developed by Zeon, and had first been put into operation when Minovski particles were still largely a rumor. It bore a resemblance to the twentieth-century craft of the same name. The cockpit was stacked on top of the engines, giving the fighter a rather quaint silhouette but providing the pilot with a superb field of vision in dogfights, where it was generally believed Dopps easily outclassed the Federation Flying Manta fighters. But in terms of modern firepower, the Dopp was pathetically underequipped; it had only Vulcan guns and small missiles.

Dren had tried to stop Sha when he had first announced he was going to help Garma. If there was a heavy concentration of Minovski particles in the area, he feared friendly machines might misinterpret Sha's Zak's FOF ID signals.

AWAKENING

There was a real danger, in other words, that he might be blasted out of the picture by his own forces.

But Sha had sniffed at the idea, saying, "How can I possibly play the coward now, Dren, when Garma's always been my friend? I want to help him out by ramming as many bazooka rockets as I can into the Horse. I want to make the guy look good."

Realizing that the crew of the *Pegasus* had resolved to turn about, take on the *Musai*, and break through to Luna II, Sha found himself sympathizing with the captain of the enemy ship. *He's too late,* he thought. *Thirty minutes earlier and he would've only faced the* Musai *with its single MS, and he might have had a chance.*

The eighteen Dopp fighter-bombers from the Gows, each equipped with four Lim antiship missiles—two classes under a Tam—could turn on a dime. With them dodging fire from the *Pegasus*'s gun turrets while boring down on the ship, and with blasts from the twin mega-particle cannons on each Gow carrier, it should have been easy to deliver a fatal blow. But ten minutes later the error in Garma's carefully laid plans was revealed. Six particle beams from the three Gows streaked toward the *Pegasus*, but somehow, with stunning agility, she managed to evade them.

Even Mirai, manning the *Pegasus* helm, could not explain it. She had not relied on directions from the ship operators, Mark and Oscar. To her surprise, she had merely noticed a strange feeling piercing her body, and she had piloted the ship as if to avoid it. But even Brite, watching the enemy's particle beams zip by on either side of the ship, marveled at the speed with which she reacted. It occurred to him then that if she could just keep it up, they might even be able to trick the enemy into blasting each other out of the sky.

The three Mobile Suits launched from the *Pegasus*—the Gundam and two Gun Cannons—squared off against the Dopps attacking from the *Pegasus*'s port side. If used right, the explosive shells fired from the Gun Cannon's shoulders could take out more than one Dopp, and sure enough, when Ryu fired, he turned three of them into star dust.

"Hooray!" Ryu yelled, having scored the first kill.

Hayato Kobayashi was standing in for Kai Shiden as pilot of the other Gun Cannon. Like Ryu, rather than use its handheld beam rifle, he chose to fire the cannons built into the MS's shoulders and immediately knocked out two more Dopps. The Gundam, for its part, destroyed another two.

Fortunately for Sha, his Zak managed to approach the *Pegasus* without being hit by friendly fire. Weaving through the blasts from the Federation ship, he executed his famed multiple S-shaped maneuver and then headed straight toward the ship's blind spot—its underbelly.

He held his fire. The bottoms of Federation ships were built with reinforced armor that no Zak bazooka or rifle had ever managed to pierce. He therefore moved around from the ship's belly, almost creasing the side of the ship, trying to head first for the bridge, then for the main engine's magnetic core. Both sections were practically devoid of armor, and two blasts from his bazooka could put the ship out of action.

As soon as he was in position, Sha sighted on the bridge.

Then something impossible happened. At almost the same instant Sha had the bridge in his rifle scope, a white Federation MS slipped into view like a dog following a scent. Stunned, he felt a moment of real fear, but he was not called a Zeon ace for nothing. Fear became anger. He yelled out loud from inside his cockpit: "What the hell do you think you're doing here?"

It was not supposed to have happened. He had closed in

AWAKENING

on the ship's blind side and maneuvered his red Zak into striking distance so fast that no one should have noticed. By the time they did see him, they should have been pulverized. But there was his nemesis, the white MS, again.

It caught the first shell he fired with its shield and appeared to shake violently, but that was all. Then it lifted up the beam rifle it had in its right hand and moved as if to draw a bead on his Zak. Sha gritted his teeth and fired his bazooka again. The white MS's beam rifle also flared.

It must have been sheer luck, but the beam from the enemy rifle vaporized the rocket Sha fired and merely creased the top of his Zak. A few particles diffusing on the edge of the beam burned part of the shield on his Zak's left shoulder. It still looked fine, but he knew it was useless; millions of tiny holes invisible to the naked eye had been blasted in it.

Only one more shell left! Sha thought to himself. He felt the same fear he had felt the first time he had gone into combat, when he had narrowly missed a Federation Flying Manta fighter-bomber.

The sixteen-meter giant white MS came at Sha at high speed, and he could almost sense the war cry of a seasoned pilot radiate from inside it. Had he known that the pilot of the MS—the Gundam—was a youth named Amuro Rey who had logged a grand total of two hours of flying time, he would have again suspected a true New Type. But he had no way of knowing.

The white MS unleashed one more blast from its beam rifle. Sha managed to evade it but then saw the enemy MS's left arm, which carried a half-destroyed shield, reach behind its back. Something flashed, and for a second he thought he saw an explosion. But he was wrong. The flare of light from a beam saber swept toward him, aiming for a point right between his eyes. Under his face mask, he felt as though cold ice had been shoved against his brow. The main orthoscopic monitor in front of him automatically filtered out the overexposure, and there, on the darkened display, the white MS's eyes appeared to glare at him in mockery.

Zaks did not have beam sabers, although a month earlier Sha had observed a test of a new Zeon MS model—a Rik Dom—that did. When its hand had connected with the saber hilt, a direct link was formed to the main engine, and the hilt then emitted particle beams, which, when focused, formed a beam of mega particles over a dozen meters long— the "blade" of the saber. But in the demonstration Sha had seen, the Rik Dom's saber had lacked a filter of sufficient precision to contain the particle diffusion. The final beam blade was too broad. It still needed more work to be practical.

The sixteen-meter-tall white MS now in front of him was far beyond the experimental stage and looked like a human fencer with a saber in its hand. The beam blade had a sharply defined edge, and it was coming right at him.

Sha started to unsheathe the heat ax built into his Zak's waist, knowing full well that although it, too, was made for close-quarter combat, it was like a toy compared to the destructive power of beam sabers.

Then he put his Zak into reverse, and not just because he was outclassed by the enemy's weaponry. Despite the heavy Minovski interference, he heard Garma's voice issuing orders, saying *"Dopp fighters, pull back. Gows, start countdown for the mega-particle cannons!"* Sha was not dumb enough to let himself be blasted to smithereens by a barrage of friendly fire. Following a few of the surviving Dopps, he quickly steered his Zak out of the area.

AWAKENING

And then the impossible happened. Two of the Gow carriers were destroyed. With its mega-particle cannon, the Federation ship scored a direct hit on the main engine of one, and the ensuing nuclear fusion explosion incinerated the entire ship, creating an enormous fireball that temporarily enveloped Garma's command ship. When Garma's Gow emerged from the inferno, it looked like a giant fire-spewing bird-monster, with the jets on both wings on full thrust for maximum speed. Nose first, it plunged forward toward the Federation Horse, looking for a moment as if planning to ram it.

Sha, watching from far off, felt helpless. He knew Garma was personally manning the helm. Only Garma, the brash young Zavi kid, would do such a crazy thing. His mind screamed, *Garma!! Stop!*

But at the same instant another, utterly different thought flashed through his mind. Garma was, after all, one of the Zavi family. So what if he died? The Federation ship was merely aiding his own quest for revenge. He should feel lucky.

He looked over toward the *Musai*. He could not make out his own ship's shape in the darkness between the stars, but he knew Dren was doing his job. One after another, blasts from its mega-particle cannon streaked toward the Federation Horse. Still, to his amazement, the Horse never received a single direct hit despite being in the line of fire of both the *Musai* and the Garma's Gow. Perhaps, he thought for an instant, the Horse was possessed by demonic forces.

Yet another, even more chilling notion then occurred to him: Perhaps the entire crew were . . . a specially formed unit of New Types. No, he reminded himself again, that would be impossible. The only people in the world who knew about New Types were himself and Rear Admiral Krishia, and Dr. Rolm Flanagan of the Flanagan Agency.

Suddenly a beam of light pierced the prow of the Horse.

Even Sha could see the ship shake violently. And as if on cue, the white MS that had been dogging him reversed course. Sha knew it was a useless gesture, but he fired his last bazooka rocket at it anyway, and the enemy pilot dodged it with ease.

Although the area was heavily saturated with Minovski particles, Sha miraculously heard a transmission. It was intermittent and hard to make out amid the static, but it sounded like the voice of young Garma Zavi shouting "Glory to the Zeon Archduchy!"

"Glory to the Zeon Archduchy"? That's Garma, all right, Sha thought, now convinced that his former classmate was at the helm. Twenty kilometers out from the Horse, Garma's Gow carrier caught three blasts from the enemy's megaparticle cannon and turned into a ball of light. The image of a young man teasing a lock of his bangs with the fingers of his right hand flashed through Sha's mind. Now, he realized with a twinge of sadness, Garma Zavi would carry that trait to his grave. In war, it occurred to him, the reward for Garma's type of overzealousness was death.

Sha signaled the order to retreat with his laser oscillator and began heading back to the *Musai*. Six Dopp fighters fell into line behind him, but he wondered if any of them would be able to make it to the *Solomon* base. It was odd how little he felt about Garma. He never would have made lieutenant commander without Garma's string pulling, but that was Garma's problem. At the academy where Sha had always been head of his class, Garma had often said, *"I want you to be my staff officer in the future. I need you to stay alive till then, so don't do anything rash."*

With a growing sense of unease, he thought: *Vice Admiral Dozzle Zavi won't be happy about this.*

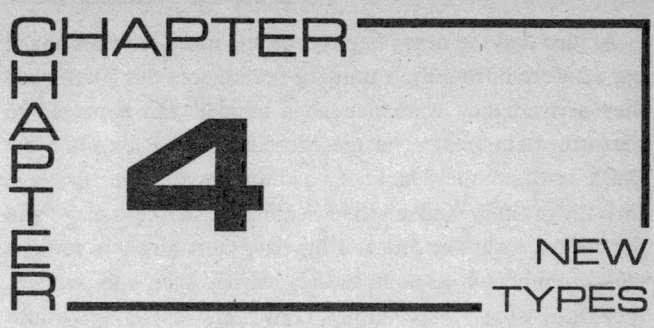

CHAPTER 4
NEW TYPES

"I'm amazed you all made it to Luna II alive."

The lips that formed the words smiled. They were a little full but well shaped. Lt. (jg) Matilda Ajan, their owner, was about the same height as Amuro, and tall for her sex. If she had any flaw, it was the way she wore her reddish hair cut short. Nothing in Federation regulations specifically said officers had to wear their hair short, but among military people who spent a lot of time in a weightless environment it had become a de facto rule, and their hair was often kept in place with a stiff gel. Matilda Ajan's hairstyle was one thing. Her almost transparent blue eyes, her lips, reddish hair, and low, lustrous voice were another. For Amuro it was love at first sight.

Amuro had never met a real officer of the Supply Corps, especially one like Matilda Ajan. She was the skipper of the *Medea*, a Luna II–based transport belonging to the 28th Division, and was normally out supplying the front lines. Since she was currently on Luna II preparing for the next offensive, she had been ordered to supply the *Pegasus*.

* * *

Amuro and the other *Pegasus* cadets had been on Luna II once before during their training period, but this time when they arrived they were handed a manual and expected to perform maintenance on the Mobile Suits. Ever since the Battle of Ruum there had been a chronic manpower shortage in both military and civilian sectors of the economy, and double duty was the order of the day. Only absolute rookies were exempt, but as soon as they learned their way around, they, too, were put in charge of any and everything. Amuro was now a combat veteran.

A flurry of activity swirled around the *Pegasus*. First, Lt. (jg) Matilda Ajan's unit deposited repair parts anywhere they could on the *Pegasus* and left for more. Then men from Lieutenant Woody's Engineer Corps arrived on the ship, and the *Pegasus*'s hangars echoed over and over with arguments between his men and the ship's own mechamen over correct procedures. Because it was the first time most of the mechamen had worked on a completed Mobile Suit, far more than were actually needed milled around the machines.

Inside the crew's Normal Suit helmets, all was bedlam. In theory, of course, one could tune out the racket and enjoy some silence by simply switching off the mike, but that was only theory. In reality, if a mike was not set to a specific frequency for a specific job, it was impossible to know what was going on, and one might be accidentally clobbered by an object being moved about the site. The trick, as usual, was to be able to isolate the voices needed from among all the others echoing inside the helmet. Except for emergencies, within the teams most people found that rather than using mikes it was easier to use skin talk, and send voice reverberations directly through touching helmets.

Recruit Maximillian put his Normal Suit helmet against Amuro's and laughed scornfully. "Hah! At least our team's

AWAKENING

had three chances to practice before with the MS blueprints. Can you believe they call this a combat-ready deployment?"

Following proper procedure, Amuro quickly checked the places the Gundam had been hit and busied himself reloading the Vulcan guns with ammunition. Compared to Amuro, Hayato Kobayashi seemed to perform a better overall inspection. He scurried back and forth among the two Gun Cannons and the Gundam, helping the mechamen at each stage of their work.

"Amuro," Hayato advised his friend, "it looks to me like you depend on the Gundam's armor too much. Look at the effects of all those near misses on its skin. Don't forget the Gundam's designed for movement, and it's not as well protected as the Gun Cannons."

Amuro threw in a bit of flattery to reward Hayato for his consideration. "Hey, you're my buddy out there in space, aren't you? I know you'll keep me out of trouble."

"Don't hold your breath, pal," Hayato replied as he drifted over to the Gun Cannons. "Our future assignments haven't been finalized yet, and they won't be till Brite comes back from the General Staff Office."

Watching his friend in action, Amuro marveled at what a skilled, dedicated worker he was. Then, noticing that everyone around him had moved on to other chores, he floated over to the floor next to the hangar and called up to the ship's bridge on the internal video system.

The blond communications operator, Saila Mas, appeared on the display and answered with a "Yes?"

"Er . . . ah . . . I was wondering if you could tell me where the civilian evacuees are located."

"They're still in the ship's gravity module."

Amuro could not help thinking her voice had a rather unfriendly tone, as if she wanted to ask why he wanted to know. And there was something else about her, something he sensed she was holding back.

"Could you switch me over there? I can't contact that module from this monitor."

"Wait a second . . . I think so." She tried to lighten up and with feigned laughter said, "Did you know in the old days there actually used to be a job like this called 'telephone operator'? Hang on. Here we go. Sorry, but I can only reach Ward E in Sector Number 28."

Before Amuro could finish telling her that was fine, Medic Samaro's face appeared on the screen, demanding, "Whaddyou want?"

"I'm calling from the Number 2 deck, sir. If there's someone named Fra Bow there among the evacuees, could you get her on the monitor for me?"

"This some kind of emergency, or what?"

Samaro looked angry, but he did not wait for an answer. His face disappeared, and in its place Fra Bow drifted into view. Since docking in the Luna II port, the *Pegasus*'s gravity gondola had been deactivated, and Fra almost could not stop in time. But she righted herself and peered into the camera.

Remembering that he still had his helmet visor filter on, Amuro quickly deactivated it and put his face close to the monitor-camera, saying, "Fra, it's me, Amuro."

"Amuro? Where are you calling from?"

"The Mobile Suit hangar. You all right?"

"I'm . . . I'm fine, but . . ." She looked pained, and tears began welling in her eyes, but she continued. "When the Zaks attacked Side 7, Mom and Gramps were . . ." That was as much as she could get out. With her face in full display, Amuro watched her break down and cry.

"Fra! Fra! You'll be all right! I know you will!"

* * *

AWAKENING

Amuro had been extremely close to Fra's mother, Fam. Separated from his own mother, Kamaria, at age six, when his father, Tem, moved to Side 7, he had been down to Earth only two or three times after that to see her. She had always spoiled him with kindness but had never agreed to go to Side 7, and Amuro's father never demanded it. In reality, his mother's refusal to leave Earth was a convenient pretext for his parents to separate. His father used his fame as an architect/builder to make a deal with the local officials and obtained a special dispensation for her, so she was spared the forced emigration to the Sides. His own philosophy was simply expressed as "I want Amuro to see the construction of the new Side. The experience will make him grow up to be strong, the kind of man we'll need in the new century."

After arriving at Side 7, Fra Bow's mother had shown enormous sympathy for the single-parent family next door and had become in effect Amuro's surrogate mother. She was just being kind, of course, but her affection helped assuage his longing for his own mother.

"Fra," Amuro continued, "you've got to get hold of yourself . . . think of all the other people."

"Amuro . . . I need to see you so bad. Where are you, Amuro?"

Right on top of Fra's words, a general summons was suddenly announced for Amuro and the other cadets: *"All pilots named report immediately to the subbridge!"*

"Fra, Fra!" Amuro pleaded. "I've got to go—they've called me! Listen, if you move or transfer stations, make sure you leave a message for me! Understand? I know you'll be all right . . . you're stronger than you think." He wished he could wipe the tears from his eyes, but in order to do so he would have had to enter an air lock and take off his helmet.

* * *

Captain Watkins, in command of the Federation base on Luna II, had his office in the centrifugal gravity core. The only decoration on the walls was a copy of an abstract painting by Jube Blanc. Ensign Brite, Warrant Officer Mirai, ship's engineer Ensign Sem Dowai, and Petty Officers Amuro, Ryu, Kai, and Hayato, all told to wait by the soldier on duty, stared at the painting as if trying to find some clue to the captain's personality.

They heard the gentle laughter of General Revil approach from the hallway outside and then Watkins opened the door and ushered his superior in, still chuckling.

"Sorry to keep you waiting, troops."

Watkins said it in a rather curt, almost cold way, but Amuro had read a review of his poetry in the local newsletter, *Luna II News*, and he knew he must be something of a sensitive man. As for General Revil, he had never met him in person before, but he had seen many TV broadcasts of his famous *Zeon Is Exhausted* speech, delivered after his escape from captivity in Zeon, during negotiations on the Treaty of the Antarctic.

The still-smiling general returned the salutes of Amuro and the others and performed a cursory review. When his expression turned more stern, Amuro recognized in it the same power he had felt at the time of the TV broadcast, and felt a chill.

Then the general turned straight to Amuro, grinned, and said, "And are you Petty Officer Amuro Rey?"

Warfare between the Zeon Archduchy and the Earth Federation had first erupted in January 0079 U.C., when—three seconds after issuing a formal declaration of war—Zeon threw its entire military might into an attack on Sides 1, 2, 4, and 5. Each Side was composed of up to forty groups of colonies which collectively held up to a billion people. In one audacious move the Zeon fleets had nearly accomplished the unthinkable, slaughtering four billion people, annihilating the entire Federation Forces, and forcing the Earth government to capitulate. Survivors later sarcastically referred to having received a "three-second warning."

The strategy for destroying the colonies was horrifyingly simple. The colony cylinders had a sealed atmosphere, so the Zeon military simply injected GG gas into them. The gas was poisonous, colorless, and odorless; it took only fifteen minutes to inject ten tons of it, and in five hours nearly twenty-five million people were dead. Had Zeon managed to continue at that rate for twenty hours and then immediately demanded the unconditional surrender of the Earth Federation Forces, they probably would have triumphed. But two factors worked against them.

First, General Revil put up a courageous struggle around Side 5, known as Ruum, and successfully held off the Zeon forces there. Second, immediately after the first gas attacks the Federation Government on Earth began to put up a fierce resistance of its own. It was not solely because nearly four billion of its fellow citizens in outer space had been killed. Human psychology reacted to more directly perceived danger.

It was because Zeon also implemented its diabolical colony crash strategy, which consisted of maneuvering the "dead" colony cylinders into Earth orbit, and then decelerating them until they plummeted toward targets on the ground. When the first colony fell on New York, the horrified people of Earth were driven to action. Taking advantage of the fact that the Zeon forces required considerable time and energy and large numbers of Zaks to prepare for such a massive undertaking, the Earth Federation Forces regrouped and counterattacked. Unfortunately for Zeon, large numbers of Zaks were destroyed.

For once both Gren Zavi and his sister Krishia were in

fundamental agreement on the correctness of the colony crash strategy. They believed that victory could not be achieved only by slaughtering innocent millions with gas attacks; rather, because they saw war as primarily a psychological process, their plan was to crash colonies into Earth's major cities until the arrogant ruling Federation elites trembled in fear. And to a certain extent they achieved their initial objective.

A month after the One Week Battle, as this first stage of the conflict came to be known, Zeon launched another attack. But General Revil had mobilized the surviving Federation ships and was again able to resist effectively. As the opposing fleets clashed in a fierce struggle between the Earth and the moon around Side 5, the Zeon forces were at first outnumbered in ships, but they put their new Mobile Suits—the Zaks—to superb use and succeeded in annihilating most of the Federation ships. Revil's flagship was destroyed by a special team of Zaks called the Black Tri-Stars, and Revil himself was taken prisoner. It was in this same Battle of Ruum that Lieutenant Commander Sha Aznable first distinguished himself as a Zak pilot.

Zeon's Supreme Commander, Gren Zavi, then issued an ultimatum to the Earth Federation government, threatening to crash Luna II into their headquarters at Jaburo unless they surrendered unconditionally. Jaburo was the central command post of the Earth Forces, located deep underground in South America, and had it been destroyed, the planet clearly would have had no choice but to capitulate. Shuddering in fear, high-level Federation officials began negotiating with Zeon representatives, including Supreme Commander Gren and Rear Admiral Krishia, at a site in Antarctica. While most felt unconditional surrender was unavoidable, they asked Gren for ten days to debate the issue among themselves.

AWAKENING

Without waiting for their decision, Gren returned to Zeon, entrusting the rest of the negotiations to Krishia with the advice: *"The Earth Federation leaders are spineless. Be sure to take advantage of that."*

Three days later, the day before the surrender treaty was to be formally signed, General Revil managed to escape and return alive to Earth. And from Jaburo, he broadcast his speech, *Zeon Is Exhausted.*

Fellow Earth Federation citizens. Fellow survivors. I appeal to you all. Zeon is exhausted! It is low on troops! Low on ships, weapons, and even ammunition! Why, then, I ask you, should we surrender to them? Dear fellow citizens, our true enemy is not Zeon now but our own weak-kneed civilian leaders. Hiding behind some notion of "absolute democracy," they are reduced to absolute indecision. Why should we, the survivors of this horrible war, entrust them with the power to make decisions for us?

How can we forget the arrogance of Degin Sod Zavi when he usurped power in Zeon? He claimed that the people of Zeon are a "chosen people." That we of the Earth Federation are hidebound by archaic ways of thinking and incapable of realizing the new potential for expanded consciousness of the human race in outer space. That there is no need for the people of Zeon to obey an "Earth Federation" run by outmoded human relics! Well, fellow citizens, even though I am a member of our armed forces, I have to admit that if Degin was referring to our corrupt Earth Federation bureaucrats, he was correct.

But, fellow citizens, we must not be deceived by Degin Zavi simply because part of what he says is true. Zeon may be the Side farthest away from Earth, but that is no reason to believe its leader's prattle about communing with the universe!

Degin Zavi must not be allowed to justify his Zeon Archduchy simply because of corruption in one part of our Federation. His words are dogma, the dogma of a man plotting a dynasty of Zavi dictators on Zeon. Even if we do the unthinkable and recognize the existence of the Zeon dictatorship, that in no sense means we must also sink to our knees before them! The Earth Federation is a government founded on the premise of sovereign individual rights. Mankind, furthermore, was able to advance into outer space as a result of the Federation government, which is itself a crystallization of all mankind's accumulated knowledge and experience.

Now Degin's son, Gren Zavi, says it is the weak and inept Earth Federation itself that must be destroyed! Well, let him go ahead and try. Strike at the heart of our weakness! But what right does he—who slaughtered four billion innocent people—have to strike such a righteous pose?

Gren Zavi tells us that mankind has violated the laws of nature by reproducing more than any other species. He tells us that mankind's population growth must be managed, because mankind must learn to inhabit the universe in harmony with nature. He tells us that the death of four billion people was merely expiation for our past sins against nature.

Is Gren mad? What does he possibly think the human race—an entire species—could gain by exterminating itself? There is nothing to gain! No! Gren is a despot trying to exterminate the very source of life that has supported and nurtured him. We, of the Federation, shall never comprehend the monstrosity of his actions.

And now Gren threatens to crash Luna II onto Earth

AWAKENING

unless we surrender to him. What basis does he have for his demands? Is he in possession of some sort of absolute truth? No! He possesses nothing more than his own demented dogma. Is the entire Federation completely enfeebled, corrupt, and degenerate? Again, the answer is no. Many good, capable citizens have fought bravely against the threat from Zeon, and we are still strong and alive! So, then, does Zeon actually possess an overwhelming military superiority over the Federation? Again, the answer is NO!

Fellow citizens! Listen to what I say! Gren's threats are a mere bluff. Unworthy as I am of my good fortune, I was captured rather than killed by Zeon forces and thus was afforded the opportunity to see the Zeon nation firsthand. I therefore can assure you that the people of Zeon are exhausted, and there is no way they can possibly strengthen their forces enough to carry out their threats. So I say to you, Gren Zavi, if you think you can send Luna II crashing to Earth, well then, go ahead and try!

When General Revil had said this on television, it was as if he were staring Gren Zavi straight in the eyes.

Zeon's strength was expended in the Battle of Ruum. There is no way they can create new soldiers overnight, and Gren Zavi knows it. I therefore appeal to all the citizens of the Earth Federation, to each and every one of you. Zeon is exhausted! Now is not the time for us to kneel before Zeon. It is time for us to rise! Now, more than ever, is our chance to defeat Zeon!

After hearing General Revil's speech, Rear Admiral Krishia was said to have been so enraged that she tried to smash the negotiating table. An explosive shift in public opinion occurred throughout the Earth Federation, with the result that the Antarctic negotiations concluded not in surrender but in a treaty that merely banned the following: the use of chemical and nuclear weapons and attacks on the transport ships that both sides used to ferry critical resources, particularly helium from Jupiter.

After his speech, not everything went well for General Revil. Rumors swirled of a possible demotion by the Earth Federation government, but he had already become a global hero, and there was little they could do.

An opportunity was thus lost. The inability of the Federation government to come up with any bold initiative combined with the uncompromising stance of Zeon, led to the continuation of the war, and it quickly slid into a protracted stalemate. It was almost as if so many people had already died in the conflict that out of resentment their souls had enveloped the world and tried to ensnare the remaining survivors.

Gren was said to have once had the following conversation with his father, the Archduke Degin Sod Zavi.

"We've killed off too many people, Father. We need a certain number of people in the solar system just to keep the infrastructure of civilization going."

"You know, son, Zeon Zum Daikun once prophesied that some day mankind will undergo a transformation. Should that come to pass, mankind may give birth to a new race of men who by themselves will rule the universe."

"Mankind will give birth to a new race?"

"Yes. What he called a New Type of human."

"Well, surely he must have been talking about us, on Zeon."

"Your arrogance is showing, son. That is not what Zeon

AWAKENING

Zum Daikun was thinking of when he founded the Zeon Republic.''

"But we're a superior race, Father. Why aren't we good enough to rule over mankind, solve its overpopulation problem, and then, having achieved a proper balance in accordance with the laws of nature, forever prosper?"

"Because we're not good enough. Men who lust for power are doomed to become relics of an obsolete age."

"Father, are you including me?"

"You've heard of Adolf Hitler, haven't you? Well, son, you're following directly in his footsteps."

"Father! How can you say that?"

"You're not what Zeon Daikun meant by a New Type."

From that moment on Gren began to have murderous thoughts about his father.

Back on Luna II, General Revil was saying, "At ease, troops." He then made himself comfortable on a sofa and lit a cigar. "Sorry this makes such a stink," he added, glancing at Warrant Officer Mirai.

"It doesn't bother me, sir," she reassured him.

Mirai decided she liked this general, who seemed as shy as a boy in front of her, and she knew she would have no problem whatsoever following his commands. It was clear that he possessed a quality as good as gold in an officer—the ability to inspire confidence. Come to think of it, when he had mentioned the cigar smoke, maybe she should have told him what she really thought. She had never smelled tobacco smoke before, but she already knew she did not like it.

Revil continued. "Even though you young men and women were only able to pick up three Mobile Suits from Side 7, I can't thank you enough. We've just begun massproducing the GM model Mobile Suit and currently only have thirty or so machines. That means your three Mobile Suits are even more important and for the time being will form the core of the Federation Mobile Suit Corps.

"The problem is that some top officials in our Federation government have been tentatively discussing an attack on Zeon's *Solomon* base. To get to the point, I know you're all a motley crew of inexperienced officer trainees, thrown together by accident, but I find it extremely interesting that you nonetheless managed to bring back a damaged warship such as the *Pegasus*, to successfully operate the Mobile Suits, and to win two battles with the enemy. Now, I fully realize that both the *Pegasus* and its Mobile Suits can outperform anything the Federation's had in its arsenal before. So maybe your success shouldn't surprise me. But it does."

The general looked around the room at everyone's face once more. Then, turning to Captain Watkins, he said, "They do look awfully young, don't they?"

"Yessir. Absolutely right," Watkins replied, glancing coolly at Amuro.

Revil continued. "I first heard the words New Type when I was a prisoner on Zeon. It refers to a new breed of human, part of a new space generation with enhanced mental powers. But not special powers—just what you might casually call intellectual awareness, or simple consciousness, I guess, but on a higher level. The basic idea seems to be that the traditional type of man, the Earthbound variety, will evolve into something different in a space environment. Unfortunately, if I may say so, the old Earthbound type of consciousness is still dominant in the political structure of our Federation, so this idea obviously hasn't gained much credence there. Even the Zeon government—or the Zavi family, as the case may be—still officially denies the validity of the New Type concept, but select circles in academia have already advanced theories to support it."

AWAKENING

The general, finally pausing, stared straight into Amuro's eyes for the first time. Returning his pensive gaze, Amuro again felt a chill. He sensed he was in the presence of a man with enormous insight.

"Having learned of the accomplishments of you youngsters," he said, still looking at Amuro, "I'm almost ready to believe in New Types."

Then he smiled and gazed at everyone assembled.

"Although the Zeon government has officially rejected the New Type theory, I have come to the following conclusion. I think they have a plan to deploy actual New Type humans in combat, or that they are already using them, and that their public negation of the theory is really a smoke screen."

This elicited immediate questions from the group: "You mean some sort of a New Type corps?" and "Is this a group of people with superpowers?"

"Of course they don't have superpowers," Revil replied. "We live in a real world. And real people don't undergo dramatic physical evolution overnight. But take Zeon's Lieutenant Commander Sha—the Red Comet—for example. Now, he could conceivably be a New Type. His performance in combat has been extraordinary. That's probably the level of ability we're talking about. He's not a superman in the traditional sense of the word. The best thing about the New Type theory is that it predicts that the entire human race will eventually shed its collective skin, so to speak, and experience an expanded consciousness. This seems even more fantastic than science fiction, don't you think?"

The general stubbed out his cigar on an ashtray balanced on his knee.

"On a long shot," he said, "I took the liberty of checking into your past records. I may be getting senile, but my idea was that if there are such things as New Types, we'd better take full advantage of them. Much to my regret, I have to tell you that by military standards none of you have particularly spectacular grades. On the contrary, they've been terrible.''

The general smiled when he said this, and Amuro and the others could not help but laugh. Amuro actually had not had *bad* grades in the past, but he paled in comparison to someone like General Revil, who had been at the head of his class all the way from kindergarten to Officer's Academy.

''Now, of course I realize,'' the general explained, ''that your performance may simply have been heightened by the crisis you were in, but nonetheless I find the high level at which you operated in all areas—from operating the *Pegasus* to piloting the Mobile Suits—to be astonishing. For rank amateurs with poor grades, frankly, I find it incredible.''

Brite interjected with an overly serious ''Yessir!'' making the group once again burst out into laughter.

''But I want to believe in the existence of New Types,'' the general added. ''And I want you yourselves to test the theory.''

Mirai was quick to answer. '' 'Test,' Sir? We only did our best given the situation. And we were lucky. Like you said, our performance was probably heightened by a sense of crisis. Who knows, maybe the planets were all in alignment or something astrological. We've no way of knowing if we're New Types or not, and frankly I don't see how we can test ourselves. You surely don't mean in combat, do you?''

''Warrant Officer Mirai Yashima, isn't it? Let me tell you, young lady, I think the way you handled yourself through those two battles was most impressive. But let me also make an announcement here and now. The *Pegasus* and its crew have been formed into the 13th Autonomous Corps, under the command of Lieutenant junior grade Brite now, and you'll all be participating in the Star One campaign.''

AWAKENING

"But sir, I'm only an ensign."

General Revil ignored Brite's protest and stood up. "I believe I've made myself clear. Everything is now up to you. We'll get together again sometime and have more discussions on the future of mankind."

As he started to leave the room, Brite commanded the others: "Attention! Salute!"

Afterward, Watkins began handing out written commissions to everyone present. "Hmph," he muttered. "I'd like to boost you all up a few more notches, but the Federation Forces are so rank inflated you'll have to be patient for now. We could only promote you enough to bring your rank a little more in line with your level of responsibility. It wouldn't look right otherwise."

Looking at his new papers, Amuro could not help but exclaim, "An ensign? Me, sir?"

"Heck, even an ensign isn't enough. They ought to make you a lieutenant commander. After all, you're going to be using a beam rifle with as much destructive power as an entire warship."

Everyone assembled had reached officer rank.

Then Watkins laughed and said, "I know it's going to be hard for four pilots to operate three Mobile Suits, but you'll just have to work things out among yourselves for now. It's not easy to locate potential New Types."

Amuro, for one, was not ready to believe for a minute that he had some weird new type of blood circulating in his veins. He was mostly worried about Fra Bow.

Saila Mas, perhaps because of her military-related training and the fact that she had volunteered for service on Side 7, was granted the rank and uniform of petty officer second class in the Federation Forces. She had always tried to avoid anything directly connected to the war, so the commission didn't make her happy.

After all, although her companions were unaware of it, Saila's father had been Zeon Zum Daikun, one of the first persons to advocate the independence of space colonies, the leader of the revolution on Side 3, and founder of the Zeon Republic. If he had not died, the Zavi family never would have been able to seize power and pervert the revolution. But be that as it may, the rebel Zeon Archduchy now existed, it bore her father's name, and it was supposed to be her enemy.

Saila's adoptive father, Zinba Ral, had always told her, "Your father was a New Type. He was a great man who showed us how we should live in space, and while still young he had millions of followers, some of whom spoke of him as though he were the second coming of Christ or Buddha. Degin Sod Zavi helped him form the Zeon Republic, but that was really part of a scheme on the part of Gren, Degin's son. Gren was responsible for everything that went wrong after that, including your father's assassination."

At that point Saila usually grew tired of the old story and cut off her foster parent, saying, "We're living on Earth, Father, and we're just ordinary citizens now."

To avoid the war and all its unpleasant associations with her family, Saila eventually emigrated to the new frontier of Side 7, where she hoped to live in peace. Her brother Caspar, on the other hand, became so completely obsessed with their foster father's story that he infiltrated Zeon, using the alias Sha, to "kill Gren Zavi and restore Zeon to its true glory." Although Saila had always been very close to her brother and he had always treated her with great kindness, she frankly felt he was too rash and too obsessed. She wished she had asked him before he had left Earth how in the world his military exploits were possibly going to avenge their father's death. She knew their father would have disapproved, and even now she dreamed of somehow meeting her brother again and changing his mind. It was highly unlikely, but at least joining the Earth Federation Forces would increase the odds of being able to do so. No Federation civilian, after all, would ever be able to travel to Zeon. This thought more than any other helped Saila overcome her inner resistance to wearing a military uniform.

"Well, what're you gonna do?" Amuro again asked Fra while glancing over at the three noisy young children playing with computer games in the corner of the mess hall.

"I'll work here on Luna II, Amuro," she said, her mind apparently made up. "There was some talk of sending me back to Side 7, but there's no one I know there anymore. Look at these poor kids. Luckily, the nursery agreed to look after them till their parents can be tracked down."

"But what if you have to start taking care of them."

"Because their parents are dead?" Fra finally uttered the words she had been afraid to speak. "Oh, I don't know. I'm tired, Amuro. I've never seen so many seriously wounded people before."

Amuro then realized how badly Fra had been shaken by events. It also explained why, in retrospect, when she, Amuro, and the children had eaten together earlier, Fra had not taken a single bite of the meat on her plate.

"So where are you going to live?"

"In Karol; Sector Number 32, South." She was referring to the Luna II refugee camp.

"I know they'll try to draft me into doing things like tightening bolts on an assembly line, Amuro, but I'm no good at it. I should probably try to get an ele-car mechanic's license or something so I can at least support myself. So much for my dream of becoming a fashion designer, huh?"

"Really, Fra, I think you ought to continue studying design. This war won't last forever, you know." Amuro meant what he said. He could easily imagine her as a fashion designer, but the thought of her becoming a grease monkey had never occurred to him.

"I hope so, but how many years do you think I'll have to stay here on Luna II?"

"This is a military base, and heck, it could be attacked any day, Fra. And if Gren Zavi ever makes it here and gets his way, he'll carry out his threat to crash the entire asteroid onto Earth, with you on it."

He said the last sentence half in jest, but Fra took it seriously and nodded.

Then a child's voice broke the ice. "Can you gimme some more coins?" It was Kika, the youngest. She ran over from the video games and clung to Fra's legs, hungry for any kind of affection while at the same time keeping up a guard against Amuro. Later Amuro heard she had said he looked "scary."

A crowd of forty or fifty crewmen poured into the mess hall, so Fra and Amuro stood up from their table to leave. They knew that there was nothing they could do about their future, that they were at the mercy of their own fates.

"Amuro . . ." Fra started to say something but paused and reached out to take his hand. An awkward silence ensued. She had never done that before. On Side 7, she had always acted like a sister to him, or even a mother, always telling him to eat properly, take a bath, wash his clothes, or wipe the sleep from his eyes.

"Can I count on you?" she said.

What a silly question, Amuro thought. Here he was, talking like this with her and depending on her friendship as much as she on his. But there was something vague and sweet about the way she had said it and the way she had

AWAKENING

reached out to hold his hand. He knew they were not meeting because they were in love or anything like that, or at least he thought so. But neither, then, were they just getting together for an idle chat. It was more like meeting someone really close, like a family member, even a sister.

"Heck, Fra, you know we're both in this together."

Fra smiled happily, showing her beautiful white teeth. Then she whispered, "I love you, Amuro."

And he knew they were more than just friends.

CHAPTER 5 ZEON

Archduke Degin Sod Zavi, the nominal ruler of Zeon, looked far older than his actual years. For nearly ten years real power had rested in his eldest son, Gren. After seizing power from the revolutionary Zeon Zum Daikun, Degin had successfully reigned for a while by appeasing the members of the Daikun faction. But then some of his own more hardline supporters accused him of being too idealistic and out of touch with the real world. They formed a separate faction in the Zeon Assembly that supported not Degin but his son Gren, and they succeeded in reducing Degin's role to that of a virtual puppet.

Three days before the death of his youngest son, Garma, Degin Zavi received a video letter. "Father," Garma said in it, "I'd hate to have my countrymen laugh at me if I someday become general or supreme commander and say it's just because I'm the son of the nation's leader. Be patient, Father, and I promise I'll distinguish myself in war and achieve the rank of general on my own merits." It was a message from a pure-hearted youth, and it warmed Degin's heart. Garma, it seemed, had inherited many of the

AWAKENING

virtues of his gentle mother, Narsia. How different he was from his brothers and sisters.

Out of concern for Garma's development, Degin had kept the Zeon media away from him until he entered the Officer's Academy. But when a news tape was finally released announcing his matriculation, Garma became a national idol overnight. His delicate, almost nervous features conveyed great nobility. The tone of his voice sometimes made him seem a little aloof, but he chose his words carefully and always addressed his countrymen with kindness. No matter what the situation, his public speeches began with the sentence "Thank you, friends, for giving me the opportunity to address you." And as almost everyone on Zeon seemed to know, he was fond of saying in private that although he was the baby of the Zavi family, he was not going to let anyone take him for granted.

Needless to say, Garma's public popularity gave his father immense, almost childlike pleasure. Degin had become a mere puppet on Zeon, but through Garma he secretly hoped to control his oldest son, Gren. It was the vain hope of an overly doting father, and it was dashed with Garma's death.

"Father, what are you doing?" It was Degin's daughter, Rear Admiral Krishia. "Please get up. The people are waiting for your appearance at the funeral ceremonies."

Degin muttered, "Why . . . of course . . ." and slowly stood, feeling as if an enormous weight had descended on his shoulders. He looked at Krishia, and she seemed to read his thoughts.

"If you don't perform your duties as the Archduke of Zeon today, Father," she said icily, "we'll lose control over our subjects."

It was hard for Degin to get up and walk out there, but

he had to if he did not want to hear any more snide reminders of his figurehead role from his own daughter.

The crowd began to chant "ZAVI! ZAVI!" and the roar of their two hundred thousand voices shook the air. Funeral cannon were fired, and then the chants were suddenly accompanied by the thunder of the crowd stamping their feet. The enormous vibrations shook the colony's artificial earth and for a nanosecond or two skewed the axis around which it revolved. Looking out over the crowd from a giant center stage, Degin noticed how young most of them seemed, and he began to grind his teeth in frustration. With this kind of support, and with Garma's help, he thought, he would surely have been able to depose Gren.

A fifty-meter-square portrait of Garma Zavi had been placed atop an altar in the middle of the stage, and it was surrounded by cascading flower arrangements on either side. Degin strode forth, sat down in the throne reserved for him, and gazed out again at the giant assembly before him. There were at least two hundred thousand people gathered, and twenty million more watching the televised speech. "Garma, my son," he whispered, thinking again that if only Garma were still alive, they might really have been able to counter Gren. It was a good thing Garma's mother, Narsia, had passed away before all this happened. If she had been alive, she would probably have gone insane.

As the nominal sovereign of Zeon, Degin sat at the center of the stage. To his right and below him were arrayed his remaining children, Gren, Dozzle, and Krishia, in that order. Below and to his left were top government officials and other Zavi family members.

Why did the citizens of Zeon support Gren Zavi and his evil ways? One reason was that he was always careful to appoint people unrelated to the Zavi family to positions of

AWAKENING

power in the government and military. Many were pure Zavi puppets, but some were also talented, brilliant men with New Type potential, such as the forty-two-year-old Darshia Baharo, the current prime minister of Zeon. Now delivering the opening address to the assembly, he was perfectly suited for his job and was beloved by the people of Zeon. He was also a testimony to the success of Supreme Commander Gren Zavi's deliberate strategy to preserve his own power.

On stage, Dozzle Zavi whispered bitterly to his elder sister, Krishia, standing to his right. "I hear you're planning to take Sha Aznable under your wing, sister. I don't like it. I cashiered him as an example to my men. It won't look good."

"Well, you kicked him out, didn't you?" Krishia defiantly hissed back. "Why should it concern you what I do with him? There's no problem with it legally. He wasn't able to protect Garma, and you've punished him enough."

"But . . . but how do you think Garma would feel?"

"That was then, and this is now. Lieutenant Commander Sha has extraordinary abilities. We can't afford to waste them."

While this interchange took place, their father, Archduke Degin Zavi, publicly expressed his profound sadness at the death of his beloved son and noted his gratitude to the Zeon citizenry, who so clearly shared his sentiments. Then representatives of each sector of society read seemingly endless speeches of mourning.

And the whispered spats among the Zavi siblings continued.

"Dozzle, you've made your point with Krishia," Gren said with an utterly expressionless face. "If you're really worried how Garma would have felt, keep your nose out of this business. Remember, Garma was also one of those naive people who actually believed Zeon Zum Daikun was mankind's savior."

"I know, I know. He was an idealist," Dozzle replied. "But frankly, he was the type of person even I would have felt honored to serve under. I'd even hoped he would rise to the rank of general or admiral. Understand how I feel, Gren? You're a politician. A plotter. But Garma wasn't like that. He could have become a real military leader."

"My, my, how blunt you are, brothers," Krishia whispered, laughing softly. "And how respectful of your brother's spirit."

Archduke Degin Zavi sat down on his throne and resumed staring vacantly out at the crowd before him. From a distance it gave him the look of a rather dignified father figure, but in the eyes of his son Gren, Degin was lower than human filth, a constant thorn in his side. Gren had heard a rumor that Prime Minister Darshia had been talking with his father, and if it was true, it meant his father could become a major obstacle to his plans. Things would go a lot better, he thought, if only the funeral ceremony were being held for his father, Degin Sod Zavi, instead of his brother, Garma.

Then the crowd of two hundred thousand began chanting, "Gren Zavi! Our supreme commander!" and stomping with their feet. It was Gren's turn to state his thanks for statements of mourning delivered by the people's representatives. He stood up straight and walked over to the podium on the stage, his tall, erect bearing giving him an air of nobility. And he spoke: *"Honorable citizens of Zeon! Listen!"*

Gren's words cut through the air, and the two hundred thousand in the audience plus the twenty million watching a live broadcast of the ceremonies waited hungrily for more.

AWAKENING

One out of every five families in the Zeon principality had lost a member in the war, and now their suffering was shared by the Zavi family. Now the Zavi family would be able to understand their loss. This they appreciated. The supreme commander would give them an uplifting speech about the responsibilities they all shared and a goal to pursue. He would give them a sense of direction and, at least for the time being, help them forget their pain and suffering.

> *. . . I know you have all lost friends and lovers, parents and children, in the war, and I know you mourn your loss. But let me ask you. Since the Battle of Ruum, is it not possible that we have all become too soft? Is it not possible that some of us have even begun to secretly believe there is nothing wrong with submitting to the Federation, given their size and overwhelming material superiority? It is time to reaffirm our convictions! We, the people of Zeon, are a chosen people. Why should we even think of giving in to Federation corruption? Never forget what Zeon Zum Daikun, the heroic founder of our nation, taught us!*

In reality, it bothered Gren to have to use Zeon Zum Daikun's name. Zeon Daikun had been a revolutionary and one of the first to advocate the right of the colonies to govern themselves. Now that he had been enshrined as a near deity by the people, his name was essential in public speeches like this.

> *The peoples of space have always looked upon Earth as the birthplace of all mankind, as a sacred place that needs careful protection. In order to save it, it was necessary for us to leave it. But some of the older generations refused to leave. They continue to try to control and rule*

us, the Space People, from Earth. They do not realize that the vastness and infinity of the universe works to expand our awareness and that it teaches us we no longer needed to be connected to the old Earthbound generations. What, after all, can we, the new space generations, do under the control of the old Earth generations? We need to remove the Earth generations, to protect the sacredness of Earth, and to lead mankind into eternal prosperity. We may dwell in a solar system that is only a remote speck in the galaxy, but we are nonetheless the torchbearers of civilization. As you know, this is the reason the Zeon nation was founded. Why, then, do some of you, merely because of your personal difficulties or the death of your relatives, think of submitting to the old Earth generation? Remember the spirit in which the Zeon nation was founded!

Side 3, the frontier most distant from Earth, is the Side your mothers and fathers elected to live on! It is here that the chosen race of mankind began! None of us can ever forget the powerful speech given by Zeon Zum Daikun, titled To the New People. *As he said, "Never forget! The people of Zeon are a chosen people! It is our destiny to forever protect all of mankind!"*

Lt. Comdr. Sha Aznable, unable to protect his superior, Garma Zavi, incurred the wrath of Vice Adm. Dozzle Zavi and was cashiered from the Mobile Assault Forces. But shortly thereafter he received a visit from an officer in Rear Admiral Krishia's Guards, who offered him the rank of commander.

"Rear Admiral Krishia," the officer had said, "is extremely interested in the fact you have had contact with the Flanagan Agency about New Types. She wants you to pro-

AWAKENING

ceed immediately to the Balda colony on Side 6 and initiate talks with them for her."

He then added that a new mobile cruiser, the *Zanzibar*, had been readied for Sha, and as he proudly noted, it was vastly superior to the standard *Musai*-class cruiser in both maneuverability and power. Its smooth outline—compared to the uneven, protrusion-covered surface of the *Musai*— also allowed for greatly improved armor.

"Is there a time factor involved?" Sha asked.

"Yes, sir. For the last six months or so Rear Admiral Krishia has been receiving some very specific information from the Flanagan Agency, and she has used it to help develop what we call the psychom, sir."

"The psychom?" Sha feigned ignorance, although he already knew about the weapon interface. He did not particularly like the young officer's obsequious manner.

"I can't discuss the matter here with you, sir," the officer replied. "You'd best ask Doctor Flanagan directly at the agency."

Sha thought to himself: *"Commander" is nice, but everyone is so protocol-obsessed around here, I wish they'd made me a captain instead.* He almost said it out loud but thought better of it. He had other reasons for accepting this assignment besides the promotion, and one of them he would not have admitted under the pain of death. By going to Side 6, he would get to see Lala Sun again.

"We also have some Mobile Armor we'd like you to deliver to the Flanagan Agency, sir. An engineer on the *Zanzibar* will brief you on it."

"Mobile Armor?" It was a term Sha had never heard.

"Yes, sir. It's different from a traditional Mobile Suit. It replaces suits that rely primarily on traditional means of delivering their firepower. It's composed of two components: the Elmeth and its support units, Bits."

"Hmmph." Sha nodded. How interesting, he thought, that although Vice Adm. Dozzle Zavi seemed to have absolutely no interest in the New Type theories, Krishia Zavi appeared to be thinking already about forming an operational combat corps of potential New Types.

After formally accepting his new commission and his new orders from this exceedingly polite, cautious officer, Sha boarded the *Zanzibar* and took off from Zeon's Zum City colony for Balda Bay on Side 6.

During the trip the ship's engineer, Lieutenant Muramasa, showed him the Elmeth. It was stowed in the *Zanzibar*'s hangar next to his beloved red Zak, which Krishia had apparently been able to retrieve from Dozzle. To his surprise, the Elmeth was utterly unlike any Mobile Suit he had ever seen. It had no arms or legs and bore a faint resemblance to an old-style aircraft. And it was equipped with only two mega-particle cannons. Muramasa nonetheless boasted, "If everything goes according to plan, this thing'll be one hell of a weapon."

"Even better than the Red Comet?" Sha asked sarcastically.

"Well, it depends on the pilot, of course. But I don't see why not."

As Lieutenant Muramasa filled Sha in on the specs of the new machine, he spoke persuasively and with conviction. More than the hardware itself, Sha found himself again awed by the New Type concept of humans on which the machine relied. The first pilot scheduled to use the Elmeth-Bit system, he thought, would have to be an extraordinary person.

Side 6, or Lia, as it was also known, was governed by the Rank administration and generally regarded as neutral territory. But the truth was far more complex. If the Zeon

Archduchy prevailed in the war, it would need a safe base from which to control the defeated Federation territory. Gren, Krishia, and the other Zavi leaders had therefore deliberately spared Side 6 from the destruction and co-opted the supposedly autonomous Rank administration. Side 6 was in reality a Zeon puppet.

"And how is Lala Sun?" Sha asked in the lobby of the Flanagan Agency.

"A wonderful girl. The best, in fact," Doctor Flanagan replied with a slight grin.

As on the first time he had met Doctor Flanagan, Sha felt a negative reaction. For a seventy-year-old engaged in the supposedly noble profession of science, the man was far too worldly. But, as Sha had to admit, it was probably that same quality that had enabled him to ingratiate himself with Krishia and achieve recognition for his organization.

"Well," he said, "that's good to hear." He had had a strange feeling about Lala Sun when he had first encountered her as a newly orphaned young woman in this strange place some time earlier. Something about her had made him think she might have some sort of New Type potential, and now that he sensed he had been right, he could already see new possibilities emerging. It made him feel good when his hunches played out. And now, with Krishia Zavi backing the Flanagan Agency, the wheel of fortune might slowly be turning in his favor.

"In looking at your combat record, Commander, it's even occurred to me that *you* might have New Type potential."

"I'm a down-to-earth type of man, Doctor, and frankly, I don't believe in supermen or New Types. I'm just bringing you the Elmeth-Bit system from Rear Admiral Krishia Zavi for testing. I want to meet the Elmeth pilot and run the test. We don't have much time."

"Commander, I must say I'm surprised by your words."

"That I don't believe in New Types?" Sha repeated the line for effect.

Sha felt Flanagan's doubting eyes trying to probe through his face mask and further resolved never to trust the man fully. He clearly had his own agenda. But that did not mean Sha had abandoned hopes for the research the scientist's team was doing. If New Types ever went beyond the theoretical stage and were proved in practice, he knew they could also be used as a real weapon to topple the Zavi family and even control the Earth Federation. If not, he never would have entrusted Lala Sun to a man like Flanagan.

New Type humans were still a vague idea, but if they possessed even limited special powers, it was only a matter of time before someone employed them in combat. With individually piloted Mobile Suits now the centerpiece of modern warfare strategy, there would be plenty of places to apply their talents. The Flanagan Agency, an intelligence organization, could be put to great use performing needed research. Sha would use the worldly Flanagan and in turn be used by him. He would just have to deal with the man carefully, from a position of strength.

Then Sha heard the sound of silk brushing against silk. He turned and saw Lala Sun.

"Well, if it isn't Sha Aznable!"

Lala's clear voice resonated pleasantly in his ears. She wore a pale yellow one-piece outfit with long billowing sleeves trailing in the air as she walked, and it made her tawny skin appear almost glistening black. There was something quite incongruous about the sight of her in the impersonal lobby of an agency charged with developing new fighters for the Zeon forces. Smack in the middle of her forehead, almost like the light-emitting third eye of a bodhisattva, was a beauty mark. Her real eyes were emerald-green and hinted at an ancestry more complex than that of most Asians. Her limbs moved with grace as she glided directly up to him. She lacked any natural fragrance and had an altogether ethereal quality to her.

Turning to Doctor Flanagan, a shocked Sha exclaimed in spite of himself, "This potential pilot you've been talking about for the Elmeth-Bit system . . . You meant Lala, didn't you?"

"Correct."

When Flanagan replied, his eyes probed the proper-looking Sha with a lecherous look, as if to ask, *"Well, don't you think she's developed into a fine woman in the six months since you last saw her?"*

"Now, about the performance of New Types, Professor . . ." Sha looked into Lala's eyes and wished he had not started to say it, but it was too late, and besides, he could not restrain the impulse to mock Flanagan a little. As he paused, Lala laughed as if she understood and seemed to urge him on. "Do you think it makes a difference," he continued, secretly thrilled, "if they're virgins or not?"

Caught off guard, Flanagan looked away in embarrassment. Perhaps, he thought with fear, Sha could read his thoughts. He had spent too much time studying people with paranormal abilities—from potential New Types to those purported to have real superpowers—not to be suspicious.

"That's . . . that's . . . a difficult question," he answered, flustered. "We really don't have enough test samples to yield solid data yet."

"Hmph. That's no good," Sha said. "Everyone's always making such grandiose claims about the Flanagan Agency, I wondered how thorough you really are."

"Please, Commander, spare us your sarcasm. New Types still haven't been clearly defined yet. It would be much easier if we were dealing with garden-variety paranormal abilities."

"Well, how about starting out by showing me some of the more simple tricks they can do."

"My dear Commander, I don't know what type of relationship you have to Her Excellency Krishia, but you should know that the Flanagan Agency is an organization under her direct control. Please cease this mockery of yours and get to the point."

"Mockery? Heaven forbid. I just wanted to help clear your mind of some depraved notions and have you show me what you've been able to actually accomplish with the New Type idea," Sha said with a grin.

It occurred to Flanagan then that Sha himself might be a true New Type. They generally had remarkably refined insight, which they often referred to as hunches. Until he knew exactly what sort of ability Sha had, he would have to engage him with extreme care.

"Well?" Sha said, as if further confirming Flanagan's suspicion. "How is she?"

"There's no doubt about it, Commander. You were absolutely on target in recommending Lala Sun. She's a second-generation space colonist, from the Ruum colony on Side 5, and although her family was killed later in flight, the very fact that they were spared *during* the Battle of Ruum may in large measure be due to Lala's own considerable abilities."

Sha could tell from the way Flanagan was talking that Lala had been forced to retell her own history more than once. The poor kid, he thought, feeling a twinge of guilt. He knew such painful memories were normally best left alone and that he himself was partly responsible for their being dredged up.

"You've done well, Lala," he said.

AWAKENING

"Thank you, Commander," she replied clearly, looking up at him.

Somehow their exchange left Doctor Flanagan with no doubts—he knew he was not witnessing any ordinary infatuation. The relationship between Sha and Lala was characterized more by a type of tension, the type that occurs when two psyches suddenly click together perfectly. It was a powerful bond.

In a laboratory, one of the agency's younger scientists gave Sha a formal presentation on the progress of their research. There was some machinery and, somewhat distanced from it, a ten-cubic-meter transparent glass enclosure with about twenty mechanical manipulators inside. Standing before the machinery, the researcher first noted how honored he felt in the presence of Zeon's famous commander and then began his explanation. His cheeks were flushed with excitement.

"First of all," he said, pointing, "this mechanism, which we call the psychom, is used to conduct brain waves. The extremely weak electrical signals emitted by a human brain are detected by this receiver, amplified, and then transmitted to the controls that operate the manipulators. We say transmitted, but in reality the brain waves themselves become an integral part of the electrical oscillation that drives the manipulators."

"Can't you just show us how it works?" Sha asked.

"Er . . . why, yessir!"

On Doctor Flanagan's order, the young researcher began to double-check the connections on the machine. As he traced each lead wire running into the amplifier, his cheeks reddened even more. The whole process took so long, they could easily have had a cup of coffee.

"Lala," Sha asked. "Tell me. Does this thing always take so long to set up?"

She laughed and replied in the affirmative.

Turning to Doctor Flanagan, Sha asked, "Does a fear coefficient or any type of negative coefficient adversely effect the device's operation?"

"It does. And we know this for certain. For example, when Lala used the system to handle dead animals, she would emit a negative reaction, which limited effectiveness to a degree. In fact, her negative reaction is even stronger than that of the average human."

"Hmm," Sha said. "That makes sense, I suppose." Then he suddenly asked Lala, "What kind of corpses did they have you handle?"

"Frogs, rats, rabbits, horses, and humans." She replied so matter-of-factly that Sha decided not to pursue the matter further.

When the young researcher resumed his presentation, he noted that the manipulators in the enclosure could move faster and with greater precision than a human hand.

"I'm now going to release one fly and one mosquito," he announced. "Lala, I'd like you to catch them as soon as you can."

He then inserted the insects into the enclosure from an opening in one side. They were so small that they were hard to see, but Sha could tell there was definitely something flying around inside. Lala donned a special cap containing the receiver circuitry and stared inside the glass enclosure. Seconds later, one of the manipulators in the case suddenly moved.

The researcher announced, "Both of the insects have been caught," then added in a somewhat disappointed tone, "but crushed."

AWAKENING

Sha had to ask. "You mean sometimes the hands don't crush them?"

"Yessir. The flies, at least."

The manipulators had responded almost instantly and precisely and demonstrated the psychom system's astounding ability to amplify brain waves. Lala had operated the manipulators without having to move her hands or feet.

Sha stepped closer to the enclosure. He turned around and looked at Lala, seated several meters away. Then he inspected the manipulators she had operated. Sure enough, between the fingers of one of them was a fly and a mosquito. "Well, I'll be . . ." he whispered to himself. Turning to Lala, he smiled. "This is incredible."

"In the beginning it used to wear me out. Now I can do it anytime."

"But isn't operating Mobile Armor a lot harder than this?"

It was Flanagan's turn to make an icy comment. "Her Excellency Krishia loaned the agency a simulator, Commander, sir. Using it, Lala has already become an expert pilot of the Mobile Armor, sir."

"Doctor Flanagan. Forgive the way I acted earlier. I was out of line. But do me a favor. I may be a commander in the Zeon forces, but you don't need to be so formal with me—I'm almost young enough to be your grandson. Can we agree?"

Flanagan uttered a strained laugh and said, "I didn't mean to sound too obsequious, Commander. I'll try not to be *overly* polite."

"Good. Let's get back to business, then, and attach this psychom device to the Elmeth-Bits system. We have to let Lala get used to it."

"Understood, Commander," Flanagan said. "We'll

speed things up." He extended his right hand, and for the first time the two men shook hands.

When the test with Lala and the psychom was over, Sha invited her to join him in the agency's dining room. She was now formally under his command as he carried a commission for her, signed by Rear Admiral Krishia, which made her an ensign. His real task was to introduce her into actual combat and turn her into a true soldier for Zeon. Right now she still looked too much like an innocent young girl.

There were only four or five of the agency's off-duty researchers relaxing in the room, all engrossed in a video broadcast of the speech Gren Zavi had given at Garma's funeral.

The old generations of the Earth Federation have no vision, and if we place our trust in them, mankind is doomed. They speak only of a vague notion that, somehow, their system of government by "absolute democracy" and a "perfect parliament" will result in peace and happiness for mankind! But their system leads only to more incompetence of every sort, and to continued overpopulation. And the result? Instead of an enlightened civilization, the Federation is producing a race of incompetents who will multiply out of control, upset the balance of nature, and defile our universe!

History shows that when the members of any given animal population—be it rats, locusts, or ants—increase too much and reach an abnormal level in the natural order of things, that species instinctively knows enough to commit mass suicide or abandon itself to the gardener of natural selection. This is the most virtuous, altruistic act any form of life can perform for the good of nature. Yet what

AWAKENING

of mankind? Simply because he has intelligence, he insults nature with his arrogance. And he becomes lazy. The Zeon nation, however, with your united support and your powers of perception, has struck a blow for nature. For the last eight months we have helped atone for the sins of mankind against nature. I know you all remember why!

"Well?" Sha asked Lala. "What would you like?" He handed her a menu, knowing she probably had it memorized from eating in the same place so often.

She merely glanced at it and said, "I'm not hungry. I'll just have some juice."

"Well, I hope you don't mind if I go ahead and eat, then."

"No, of course not. Please, be my guest."

Their table was in one of the best spots in the dining hall, bathed in natural sunlight beamed in from outside the colony. Since the atmosphere of Balda City was kept at the same temperature at the forty-fifth parallel on Earth, it felt like spring everywhere. Gren's speech continued.

Remember, honorable citizens of Zeon, that our beloved Garma has joined your friends and relatives and died for the cause! Why did he sacrifice himself?

Sha muttered to himself, "Because he was a naive kid."

"Did you say something?" Lala asked, unable to hear him clearly. She showed absolutely no interest in the broadcast and had been gazing outside the dining hall. There were so many things she wanted to ask him, but she did not know where to begin. She was beginning to get irritated with herself.

"No," Sha replied, with a gentle smile. Gren's speech was just reaching its climax.

> *Garma Zavi died to spur those of us who have tired of fighting to greater effort! Garma—the Garma you loved— died crying out to us not to let our warriors die in vain! He died shouting "Glory to Zeon!" Why? Because he knew that you, the wise people of Zeon, are the true people, the chosen race in this world! Yes, he died shouting "Glory to Zeon!" Open your eyes, fellow citizens! Now, more than ever, we must unite and strike at the enfeebled Federation!*

"Lala?"

"Yes?"

"I know the researchers at the agency must have inspected every pore in your body and analyzed every memory you have. I want to apologize."

"You don't need to, Commander," she said, placing her hand on top of his and shaking her head. "When my parents died, I was devastated. You gave me a reason to go on living. And I'm grateful for it. And besides, this assignment means I'll be with you. I'm happy."

"That makes me feel better, Lala."

"I was picked up by a Zeon warship after I lost my mother and father, and I did whatever I had to to survive until I arrived here at Side 6. I had no choice. And it was the same after I got here. I'm just grateful that I met you as soon as I did, before I became a physical and mental wreck. Now I'm going to be working with you. Just think of it. Suddenly, I've even been made an ensign!" Somehow Lala managed to laugh.

"Funny how fate works, isn't it?" Sha said, smiling with her. He could imagine what she had been through in the two months before he had met her, and he knew it must have been rough. She still had the look of a young girl, but her face was almost too beautiful. She was the type of woman who drove men crazy.

"I'm . . . I'm no saint, or even a gentleman, Lala. I'm just like other men. And I've no right to criticize the way you've lived. But I keep wondering what your life was like before this all happened."

She said nothing, merely stared at Sha's mask. He looked into her eyes and saw something terribly honest. He knew that there was more he had to say but also that he would have to take off the mask in order to continue. He was silent for a second and then looked around the dining hall. The broadcast of Gren's speech was over, and everyone else had left. He removed his mask and turned to Lala.

She squinted as if staring at something bright. "How did . . . how did it happen?" she asked, referring to the deep scar that ran diagonally across his forehead.

"In a fencing match with a man called Garma Zavi, when I was in Officer's Academy."

It was a lie. Sha had deliberately done it to himself before even entering the school. It had been part of his oath of revenge. In order to get close to the Zavi family in the future, he knew he would have to hide his real identity. An ugly scar would help distract people from noticing any trace of his father's features and even give him a pretext to wear a face mask. But the pain was something he would never forget.

"Frankly, Lala, I nearly managed to forget about you on a personal level over the last six months. But now, seeing you again, I like what I see. Tell me, what do you think of me?"

Lala stared at Sha. His eyes seemed so clear.

"This is about as romantic as I ever get," he said. He

suddenly felt very young. It was sad, but at the same time his rational mind was warning him to be careful.

"I . . . I'll do my best for you, Commander . . ."

Lala chose her words very carefully, but tears began to well up in her eyes. "Right now, I'm very, very happy."

CHAPTER 6: THE TEXAS ZONE

"Hail Zeon! Hail Zeon! Hail Zeon!"

The roar of two hundred thousand citizens capped the end of Garma Zavi's funeral in Zeon's Zum City. Amuro, watching the ceremony on a Federation news broadcast thousands of miles away, heard his video speakers vibrate and was taken aback when the cameras zoomed in on the giant photograph of Garma Zavi displayed on the altar. They showed the face of a decent, gentle man, utterly lacking in the qualities one would expect of an evil "enemy." It had never occurred to Amuro when he had tried so hard to knock out the Gow carrier that it had been commanded by Garma Zavi.

The Federation announcer continued:

And that was the face of the young Zeon officer Garma Zavi, who recently met his demise at the hands of the new Federation warship, the Pegasus. *If Zeon, in order to incite its citizens to further slaughter, must stoop to portraying the ignominious death of one of its ruling family members as a glorious event, then its days are clearly numbered. The cries of "Hail Zeon!" are the last flicker of light for the Zeon Archduchy before total darkness descends!*

"Hah!" Lieutenant Brite muttered to anyone in range. "I'll say. And did you get a load of Gren Zavi's speech? The man who hijacked Zeon and turned it into a Zavi dictatorship?" Then he turned to the crew of the *Pegasus* around him and spoke in a louder voice.

"We launch from Luna II in two hours, so there'll be no time for rest. There are twenty GMs, the new mass-produced type of MS, on other ships in the fleet, but they're pretty useless compared to the three Mobile Suits we have on our ship, unfortunately. That means that we're the main force going up against the enemy. Understood?"

The Federation's Star One campaign was finally being put into action. The *Pegasus*, as part of the 13th Autonomous Corps, was a key player in the strike force because of its three Mobile Suits. Before embarking, Amuro called Fra Bow on the vid-phone to say good-bye, but he was at a loss for the right words. All he could think of was "They say it's a big operation, Fra."

"I suppose this is a funny thing to say to someone going out to defend us with his life, but do be careful, Amuro."

"Don't worry, Fra . . . I'm not going to die."

"What'd you say?"

"I said I'm not going to die. I promise I'll return."

"Good. That's the right attitude, isn't it? I'll be waiting for you, Amuro."

"Thanks."

Just then Kai Shiden came by and thumped Amuro on the back. "Well, what're you waiting for, Ensign? You've got equipment checks to perform, don't you? Hey, get busy!" And then he zipped off on a lift-grip.

"I'll . . . I'll see you later, Fra." Amuro grabbed one

AWAKENING

of the lift-grips, but as he did so, out of the corner of his eye he saw the expression on her face on the video screen. He knew she wanted to talk more. The vid-phone was coin-operated, and he probably had another thirty seconds left. But there was too much work to be done to engage in small talk.

Because of the chronic labor shortage, none of the Federation warships carried the required number of mechamen, and as soon as the supply or maintenance personnel finished one task, they were off in a flash to another. To ensure that the three Mobile Suits were always operational, Hayato Kobayashi and Ryu Jose themselves often had to go haggle with the Supply Department for spares. And on the *Pegasus* even mundane chores such as cleaning up and putting away tools were left to the pilots. It was simple but important work; a Mobile Suit might not overheat if a screw were dropped into its exhaust system, but a single loose bolt could wreak havoc on the catapult mechanism that launched the suit. The pilots therefore had to carefully wipe everything in the area clean with rags.

It seemed as though the *Pegasus* would never be combat-ready. Not only was she understaffed, but on Luna II ten or twenty new mechamen and gunners had joined the regular crew, and they were still utterly disoriented. Once Brite accidentally left the switch on the captain's phone on ship wide, and the entire ship had the chance to overhear an interchange between him and one of the newcomers. "What the hell's taking so long?" Brite yelled, his voice booming throughout the ship.

"Jeez, how should I know?" the crewman answered. "I'm not here 'cause I wanna be. I don't even know where I've been assigned yet."

"State your name and rank before you gripe, mister!"

"Hey, not so loud, man. I'm Sleggar Row, lieutenant junior grade. I came here with the Gunnery Corps. I'm going to be in charge of the antiship cannon."

"I'm the captain of this ship, Sleggar. Don't forget, I make the decisions around here, and I want you to watch your language!"

"You? Lieutenant? You're the ship's captain? You gotta be kidding!"

To the disappointment of those eavesdropping, some dogooder then switched off the bridge phone so no more could be heard. As far as anyone knew, Brite probably slugged Sleggar for insolence.

Fifteen minutes before the ship's scheduled departure time some critically needed parts arrived from Matilda Ajan's unit in the Supply Corps. And then the 13th Autonomous finally sailed out of the Luna II port. The *Pegasus* was preceded by a *Magellan*-class warship, the *Hal*, and followed port and starboard by two *Salamis*-class cruisers, the *Cisco* and the *Saphron*. Six smaller Public attack ships were deployed in a defensive perimeter around the entire strike force.

Kai Shiden joked weakly to anyone in sight. "Hey, tell me I'm hallucinating. This has gotta be just a routine exercise, right? It can't be for real."

"The goal of the Star One campaign," Brite finally and confidently announced to the crew, "is the destruction of Zeon's most powerful moon base, *Granada*. Once this is accomplished, we can easily take the heartland of Zeon itself. Our forces—the Federation Forces—are several times larger than Zeon's, so if we knock out *Granada* and get past *Solomon*, they won't stand a chance. The fleet we're part of, the 13th Autonomous, will try to enter the *Texas* Zone and draw out Zeon's *Granada* fleet. Then the main Federation force under the command of General Revil will attack both *Granada* and *Solomon*. I expect each and every one of you to be fully aware of the importance of the role assigned us and to put the training you received to maximum effect."

Kai, irreverent as always, whispered to his friends, "Amazing, isn't it? Give the guy a promotion, and he suddenly starts to sound like a real skipper."

Amuro wondered out loud: "Do you really think we'll be able to pull it off?"

"It won't be easy," Ryu said. "We're the decoy in this strategy—the bait."

Amuro envied the calm way Ryu said it, as though he were already prepared for the worst. He was not so sure about himself; he had already accomplished more than he had ever hoped as an MS pilot, but he still had a reservoir of fear. He clung to the precious hope that he might survive all this somehow and let his confidence be boosted by a new anger he was starting to feel—directed not only at the Zavi family but at the whole trail of human sins and failings that had seemed to lead to their emergence.

Until the end of the twentieth century the history of mankind—the "progress of civilization"—had really been nothing but an endless series of wars. When the world had converted to the new Universal Century calendar, it therefore had done so not only to commemorate its advance into space but also to help usher in what it hoped would be a new era of peace. And for over seventy years it seemed to work; man did almost forget war. But then fighting erupted again. For all their fancy statements about being a new, chosen people of space, Amuro knew that the Zavis were trying to dominate their fellow men with violence and that they were really no different from their rapacious, power-hungry ancestors throughout the ages.

Gren Zavi, the de facto ruler of Zeon, always claimed that a new type of human with an expanded consciousness—the New Types of Zeon, presumably—should "manage" the rest of mankind. But it seemed to Amuro that if Gren's notion of New Types was the true one, they were a barbaric crowd and he would rather have nothing to do with them. As he told his friends, "General Revil's gotta be mistaken, don't you think? If New Types are a new kind of human and they're anything like the Zavi family, then they'll treat the rest of us like the lowest form of life imaginable." Everyone seemed to agree.

When Lieutenant Brite finally finished briefing the crew, Hayato wryly commented, "Damned if I'm gonna let Zeon blow me up in the *Texas* Zone. I'm gonna go all the way to *Granada*, and nothin's gonna stop me!" Without missing so much as a beat, Kai chimed in in agreement.

Once the *Pegasus* was clear of Luna II's jurisdiction, Amuro and his fellow pilots began intensive practice in takeoff and landing with the three Mobile Suits. They missed the jeers of Lieutenant Ralv, who had first trained them. Now the four of them were no longer cadets but MS regular pilots. Their shared experiences had bonded them together like brothers, but in actual combat that would not be enough. Rehearsing in formation around Ryu Jose, who was technically the senior pilot by virtue of being the oldest, somehow things did not quite come together. The true state of everyone's feelings was hinted at by Ryu, who said he was more interested in becoming a Gun Cannon specialist and not really that eager to be the point man. And by Hayato, who said he wanted to pilot the Gundam but was told by Kai it was Amuro's role, as Amuro was already twice combat tested in the machine.

AWAKENING

The fleet itself nonetheless went ahead with a relentless training program, and Amuro found himself having to perform mock space duels with two GM suits from the flagship *Hal*. To his shock, he realized for the first time that the GM actually outclassed the Gundam in firepower at close range. Like the Gun Cannon, the GM had a single panel of glass where its eyes would have been, which gave the sighting monitor a clearer image. The Gundam designers for some reason had felt it necessary to make their machine look much more human and had installed two cameras, linked to the system's sight-scope, to approximate a human face. The result, it seemed to Amuro, was that the scope tended to cloud over more easily and was often a tad out of sync. He believed that the simpler a mechanism was designed, the better. But the Gundam had far more power in its vernier jets and could outperform the GM in almost every other aspect.

Supported by Kai and Ryu in the Gun Cannons, the Gundam and two GMs practiced making mock attacks on the *Cisco*. They practiced attacking simultaneously, first in a lateral, then in a vertical formation. They practiced timing their attacks and staggering their approach. It was Amuro's first formal training in tactics, and it seemed to him that they practiced everything possible, repeating moves over and over again until he just wished it would all end. His throat was starting to feel parched, and the undergarment he wore beneath his Normal Suit was soaked with sweat.

Then the order finally came to return to the flagship *Hal*. It was time for a critique of the mock combat sessions and further study of formation tactics. The Earth Federation Forces had only a rudimentary, almost primitive, combat manual for use with the Mobile Suits; it had been written by officers with no actual combat experience who could only imagine how Zeon's Zaks actually operated. Rumor had it that the manual had really been patched together from a surreptitiously obtained Zak manual and from information on old-style fighters. An enormous number of errors needed to be corrected as a result. The Federation MS pilots were clearly in an awkward position. They were inexperienced and vastly outnumbered by Zaks. They would have to rely instead on a great deal of creativity.

Lt. Comdr. Rudolph Ramski, who led the sessions in the ship's mess, announced, "We don't have a lot of time, men, so I'm going to talk while you chow down." He was popular, an engineer involved with Mobile Suits since they were first developed. "Mock battles are good training for novices," he said, "but you all tend to rely too much on the performance of your Mobile Suits. Don't expect them to always compensate for you."

His little audience groaned.

"I say this," he continued, "because I want you to stay alive. Keep in mind that what I say is true of almost all weapons systems while they're being developed. Think of yourselves as test pilots. 'Course you've probably never heard of test pilots going into combat, have you? The big shots in the Federation don't fully realize what they're asking you suckers to do, so you don't even get a special test pilot bonus. Of course you're all free to step down from the Mobile Suit Corps if you so decide, but your pay will also be taken down a few notches."

Ramski's forthright manner made Amuro and the others like him even more, but they knew that there was a big difference between his theoretical approach and the reality of combat.

"One point the communications operators on all our ships have stressed in their group meetings is that all you pilots are a little slow in transmitting your call signs. It's hard for

AWAKENING

them to track you in battle with radar. Laser signals work better. And it's especially important to get those calls out promptly when the warships go into action against each other—unless you want to be hit from behind by friendly fire!"

The pilots were aware of the flaws in this logic, of course. Both the communications operators and the navigators on the *Pegasus* were inexperienced. Would they really be able to read the call signs properly even if they were issued? When the area was heavily saturated with Minovski particles, radio broadcasts were effective only up to twenty miles, and the petty officer in charge of wireless communications was Saila Mas. She was a rank amateur, and there was an awful lot of communications jargon and terminology she did not yet understand.

"Saila's got a lot to learn, but I love the sound of her voice," Kai whispered to Amuro. "It gives me goose bumps."

"Saila?" When Amuro had first glimpsed her on his display monitor, it was true she had looked beautiful, but she had a habit of jutting out her lower jaw that made her seem a little too nervous for his tastes, and he hated the formal, prissy sound of her voice. *"If I say anything incorrectly,"* she always said, *"please inform me. I'll soon learn the right way."*

Amuro hissed a reply to Kai's comment. "She tries too hard to be like us."

"Of course, stupid," Kai said. "That's what makes her so cute!"

The lieutenant commander interrupted them. "Ensign Amuro—you're the Gundam pilot, right?" When Amuro answered in the affirmative, he continued. "The Vulcan cannons built into the Gundam's head are auxiliary weapons for close-in fighting. You rely on them too much. And you're not using your throttle properly. You should be able to control your vertical roll better."

After critiques of each MS pilot's performance, lectures followed: first on the various types of Zeon warships and the specific formations they flew in, then on Zak combat flight patterns. To be truly useful, the lieutenant commander's theoretical approach had to be augmented by comments from the MS combat veterans. But since the pilots tended to articulate their experiences in a limited, fragmented fashion, the lieutenant commander tried to help them mold their impressions into a larger conceptual framework that described Zak tactics.

"I wish I could show you how Sha operated," Amuro said apologetically as the rest of the pilots listened intently, "but I can't. When I was engaged with him, I wasn't even aware the Gundam had special combat sequence video recorders. But I can tell you that Sha Aznable is unlike any other MS pilot. I know this sounds incredible, but he almost seems to see the beams coming at him and then somehow finds a way to initiate evasive maneuvers—in advance. I can frame him in the cross hairs of my beam rifle scope when he's moving laterally, but the instant I pull the trigger, he's gone."

Then someone asked the question: "Think he's one of these New Types we keep hearing about?"

"I don't know. I was too busy trying to stay alive to think about that. If I hadn't put the Gundam through evasive maneuvers at top speed, though, Sha's rifle blasts would have pulverized me. Both the Gundam and the GM seem to have enough armor to withstand about two hits, but not by a marksman aiming directly at the same place twice."

During the nearly six hours that the lectures and critiques took, the Gundam and Gun Cannon Mobile Suits were transported from the *Hal* to the *Pegasus*. Amuro and the other pilots followed later in a space launch.

People on Earth referred to the moon's invisible half as its "dark side," or "back side," but from the perspective of the Zeon Archduchy it was the front side. They had a major moon base, *Granada*, located at the southern tip of the Soviet mountains, from which their warships regularly landed and took off, and to counter increasing Federation intrusions into the area a Zeon fleet under Rear Admiral Krishia's command had begun to reinforce its presence there. It included Captain Ma Kube's squadron, with its single heavy cruiser and three light cruisers, which was assigned to defend the *Texas* Zone.

The *Texas* Zone was an area in space around the Lagrange point where the Battle of Ruum, the last major conflict between Zeon and the Federation, had taken place. It got its name from the sole surviving Side 5 colony in the area—*Texas*—which had once been used exclusively for sightseeing and large-scale cattle ranching. An old-style colony only three kilometers in diameter and thirty-two in length, *Texas* had been built to simulate the mountains and plains of the western regions of the North American continent and was even equipped with cowboys, herds of cows, and covered wagons; people had come from throughout the space colonies to *Texas* to enjoy camping, horseback riding, and the experience of rafting down a replica of the Rio Grande. Although the colony had been attacked several times during the Battle of Ruum, it had not been completely destroyed, but the motors that drove the mirrors used to radiate sunlight into the colony had been wrecked, leaving them stuck perpetually in a sunset mode. The colony still had air, but the humidity had fallen so low that eight months after the Battle of Ruum, *Texas* had become a near desert. The livestock had all been seized by Zeon forces, and the former residents had escaped to Federation territory or surrendered to Zeon. The colony was now totally deserted.

The space around the colony was filled with remnants of other Side 5 colonies destroyed in the war, creating a shoal region even more dangerous than that around Luna II, and when a heavy concentration of Minovski particles was used, the combination made the region almost impenetrable. Both Zeon and Federation forces feared entering the *Texas* Zone because enemy ships were too hard to spot and ambushes were too easy.

Captain Ma Kube, to whom the defense of the *Texas* Zone had been entrusted, enjoyed the full confidence of Rear Admiral Krishia because of his political position rather than his military skills. Should Zeon triumph over the Federation, he was destined to become her right-hand man; for now, however, he had to bide his time. But there was one thing that bothered him about his superior's actions.

"Sha Aznable," he muttered while admiring one of his prized white china vases from the northern Sung dynasty. "I don't like the idea of that kid working with the Flanagan Agency on Side 6 to form a New Type combat unit. How can someone who couldn't even protect Captain Garma possibly be qualified to lead New Types? Seems like he's up to something behind our backs. And Doctor Flanagan can't be trusted. Look who he's hooked up with. Her Excellency is far too impulsive for her own good. How can she place her faith in a lowlife like Flanagan when the existence of New Types hasn't even been fully proved?"

Until Krishia had declared her intention of rehabilitating Sha, Ma Kube had planned to cut off all payments to the Flanagan Agency. Why waste any more money on research that produced no results? Why not spend it instead to improve the Zak design or further develop the new Rik Dom Suit? Surely the Zeon auditor general would not like the idea of wasting precious research money on some unproven Mobile Armor—the Elmeth or Bits or whatever the thing was called.

Moreover, Ma Kube had learned that before Sha had left Granada, Krishia had given him command of a new advanced mobile cruiser, the *Zanzibar*. Coming on top of that, a formal decision to use the Elmeth-type weapons was like a stab in the back. He remembered with bitterness the words Krishia had laughingly tossed out at him: *"You worry too much, Ma Kube."*

But there was something else Ma Kube was also worrying about. He knew that a man like Sha, who obviously had talent running out of his ears, could be dangerous and would eventually become his enemy. There was something too calculating about the man's overly proper behavior and the way he cozied up to authority. First he leeched on to Vice Admiral Dozzle, and then to Her Excellency Krishia.

Why, he thought, *the man acts like he's Krishia's favorite pet.* He liked this idea and subtly began popularizing it with the help of his men. It caught on among the troops, who soon began joking among themselves that Sha was "Krishia's pet, 'cause he's got a nice ass."

Meanwhile, Sha, on the *Zanzibar*, had left from Side 6's Balda Bay and was proceeding to the *Texas* Zone; he planned to test the new Elmeth-Bits Mobile Armor, now equipped with the psychom interface, inside the deserted *Texas* colony. It would have been possible to conduct the tests in open space, but Sha did not want to take any chances. Lala Sun would be operating the system, and he wanted to avoid exposing her too fast to what was essentially a vast battlefield. New Type–operated weaponry, he sensed, had to be handled carefully. New Types, after all, possessed nothing like the superpowers of comic book heroes and merely had a finely honed sense of intuition. As for the psychom, it was part of a system that amplified the New Type operator's intuition and both projected and fed off an expanded consciousness. It was itself an astonishing device, especially since its signals, unlike normal electromagnetic waves, could overcome any Minovski particle interference. But the system was not without its problems. It was still unclear what kind of person was really capable of projecting clearly defined brain waves—"willpower waves," for lack of a better term—that could be amplified. Sha and Doctor Flanagan's discovery of Lala Sun had been a fluke. To isolate and quantify the characteristics required for a New Type Mobile Armor pilot would require testing of far more potential candidates.

On the bridge of the *Zanzibar*, Sha turned and looked at Lala Sun, who was seated deferentially in a chair in the corner. He smiled and whispered to himself, "I wonder if I'd be able to pilot the Elmeth-Bits system?" She was seated too far away to have been able to hear him, but to his astonishment she replied.

"You, Commander? Why, of course . . . and much better than I, I'm sure."

Sha's eyes widened. He had not even fully verbalized his statement. "You . . . understood me?" he asked.

"You tend to be very logical, so it's fairly easy to deduce what you're thinking."

Lala giggled softly as she said this, almost reflexively. It was one habit of hers he did not care for. He suddenly announced, "I'll see you later, Lala," turned away, and began walking in the direction of the captain's quarters.

She let her eyes follow him out the door and was suddenly

AWAKENING

seized with melancholy. She was not sure why. She imagined herself in the embrace of his arms and broad shoulders and reminded herself that he was everything she had ever hoped for. But she knew there was something else. The coldness he sometimes exhibited stemmed from the fact that his goals in life were very different from hers. Whatever they might be, they were clearly a vital component of his being, and they would make it impossible for him to ever lead a normal life. When Lala used her New Type intuition to try to probe the core of his consciousness, she could feel him try to shut her out, and she then knew he was almost a full New Type himself. But in the unformed thoughts she contacted, in the depths of a mind trying to conceptualize its surrounding reality, she sensed dark, brooding hatred. It was this hatred, she knew, that manifested itself in his detached manner, and explained why, when she was talking alone with him, his mind always seemed to be elsewhere.

To the Commander, I'm a means to an end.

It was something she had realized only recently, and it was one of her greatest fears. It was not that he had no love for her. She knew he did. Love was a solid reality in the swirling interface of their shared consciousness. But it was at this point that Lala's femininity exerted itself in a grand compromise; if she loved him and she could help him, what could possibly be wrong with being a tool for him?

On the *Pegasus* officers and enlisted men normally ate in separate mess halls. Since Amuro and his colleagues had just been promoted, he could have eaten with the officers, but he still felt more comfortable with the enlisted men. He got his meal tray from the mess hall self-service window and proceeded out of habit to a table in the right-hand corner of the room, only to find it occupied. Ensign Mirai Yashima, having finished eating, stood up to leave when he approached, but her companion, a Wave petty officer, did not.

"Nice to see you, Ensign," Mirai said with a smile as she walked by him. He stuttered a pleasantry in response, thinking how pretty her eyes were. Her full figure was apparent beneath the sharp lines of her uniform.

Mirai tended to act like an older sister to the younger men, and it was no wonder she was one of the most popular of the ship's Waves. Amuro recalled Kai having once said, *"Wife material. That's what she is. Two years older than me . . . but, yep, I like that idea."* And of course Hayato had agreed wholeheartedly. But Mirai was also as smart as a whip and had another side to her. She had an uncanny ability to discover shoddy work, and more than one young crewman had had his ears boxed by her. It was this dual personality, perhaps, that made her so attractive. Ryu had once boasted, *"Hell, I never screw up, so she never slaps me,"* whereupon someone else chimed in, *"Hey, when she does, it feels good!"*

Amuro was about to seat himself somewhere else when he realized he had seen the other Wave at Mirai's table before. Then he remembered her name and blushed to the tips of his ears. Saila Mas, having finished her meal, was savoring a cup of coffee and reading what looked like a manual. Amuro and the other young pilots knew her only from the three-inch image they saw on their MS cockpit monitors. It was hard to connect that to the real thing.

Everyone knew Saila Mas was technically ill suited to be the ship's communications specialist. Most of the crew members were not about to follow an order telling them to move from Sector A to Sector D if it was simply parroted by someone relaying it from above. They wanted to know

AWAKENING

why they were supposed to do something, and even if no one could tell them, they still wanted to hear something, anything. It did not matter if it was true or not. If told something as simple as "Keep up the good work," even a stubborn idiot would run happily to perform his task, his head full of sweet thoughts for the pretty face that gave the order. This fact of male psychology was the main reason Waves were often used to transmit orders throughout the ship.

But for whatever reason, Saila could not bring herself to act that way, with the result that crewmen often ignored her messages, and chaos resulted. She became known, therefore, as "the Bungler."

Standing in front of Saila with his meal tray in hand, Amuro knew that as an ensign he now technically outranked her. But he also knew she was older than he. With one factor offsetting the other, he figured they ought to be on equal ranking. Gathering up his courage, he ventured, "May I join you?"

"Oh . . . uh, of course, Ensign . . . er . . ."

Amuro knew she was having trouble remembering his name—an automatic demerit for a communications specialist. She glanced at his tray and looked up as if to say, *"What are you doing here?"* Looking down at her, he instantly cursed himself for having addressed her. His heart started pounding again, and he felt his attempt to act like a sophisticated ensign collapse in ashes. He accidentally put his tray down on the table too hard, and to his embarrassment it clattered.

"Er . . . excuse me . . ." he said, thinking for a second perhaps he had better move to another table, then realizing it was too late to turn back. He knew he should say something else before he started his meal . . .

"I used to see you at the Zeravi library on Side 7," he ventured, hoping this was a good approach.

"You were there, too, Ensign?" Saila said, with a thin smile.

"Uh . . . yeah . . . I . . . I lived on Side 7 for two years before I joined up."

"Really?" Her overly formal smile suddenly brightened.

The Federation military was a collection of so many types of people that when a crewman ran into anyone from the same Side, it was like meeting an old acquaintance. If it was someone from the same colony, it was like meeting a bosom buddy. Amuro felt ecstatic. Here was Saila, smiling, really smiling, not on a display monitor but right before his eyes.

"When you were in the library," he said haltingly, "uh, I . . . actually I didn't go there very often, but once, ten days before I signed up, I thought I'd say hello to you, and actually I started going every day, but . . . uh . . . I . . . uh."

"You should have said something. But please, go ahead before your food gets cold."

"Uh . . . thanks." He picked up a forkload of noodles and began shoveling them into his mouth, but his mind was not on the taste.

"When I used to see you in the library, Saila, I only knew of you as the, er—'scuse me—the Blonde. It was a nickname I gave you."

"Well, gee, I'm awfully glad to know you're from Side 7, Ensign. I'm the only one of us Side 7 folks on the *Pegasus* bridge. I didn't join the military through normal channels, and there's an awful lot I don't know yet, so if it wasn't for Mirai's help, I don't know what I'd do. I can't tell you how happy I am to know there's somebody else from my Side, especially when it's an ace pilot like you!"

AWAKENING 151

Amuro was in seventh heaven, but Saila was shocked at herself for the way she had spoken to him. In her communications with the MS pilot over the video monitors, she had always sensed something in common with him, and now, meeting him in the flesh, it was almost as though she could not stop herself. The guy stammering in front of her was younger than she was, and cute, and hardly resembled the ensign she had been seeing on the communications monitors.

Something about the way he transcended his age also reminded her of the talk going around the bridge about New Types and made her wonder if he might really be one. It was a quality Amuro shared with her brother, Sha, aka Caspar. Her foster father, Zinba Ral, had often told her that her real dad, Zeon Zum Daikun, had been a New Type. *"It's an expanded consciousness resulting from mankind's leap into outer space,"* he would say. *"A New Type of human. Your father was a great man, Artesia. And you are his offspring. Someday you must realize your own New Type potential, destroy the Zavi family, and help lead mankind back to a world of peace!"* In the end, Zinba Ral always came back to the same point: the need to overthrow the Zavi family on Zeon.

Sitting and talking with Amuro, Saila began to sense that the New Type potential mentioned by her foster father indeed might appear in other people as well. It was a farfetched notion, but when she thought of the millions who had died in vain in the war, she hoped it was true.

"Ensign . . ." she began as Amuro suddenly looked up. "Have you ever heard the words New Type?" Something about the fact that he was younger made it easier for her to talk freely.

"Well, I've heard General Revil use the term," Amuro

answered, "but, hey, I don't believe in Superman or anything with superpowers."

"Still, you've heard the Zavi family thinks they're New Types, haven't you?"

"Are you kidding? If they're what New Types are all about, then what's the point of staying alive? I heard Gren Zavi's speech the other day, and the man's a maniac. His idea of paradise is to enslave the peoples of the Earth Federation, and frankly, I don't like it."

When Saila heard blunt talk like that from Amuro, it made her feel even happier. "I agree," she said, "but have you ever read about the legend of Zeon Zum Daikun?"

"I only know what I read in my school textbooks. He's the man who claimed that in order to feel truly at home in the solar system, mankind would have to start thinking differently. And didn't he also say man shouldn't cling to his home planet? I understand all that, but it hardly seems to apply to the Zavi family. Don't you think they're kind of living anachronisms from a feudal past, to say the least?"

Saila had to restrain a smile of satisfaction. The shy, stammering youth of a few minutes ago was turning rather eloquent.

"When men get into positions of power, they always seem to forget about people, even the people who helped put them there. Heck, look at the Earth Federation government. 'Absolute democracy' sounds great, but the parliament can't do a thing without a two-thirds majority, so the politicians spend all their time scheming, and nobody thinks about the people anymore. No wonder the Zavi family calls them spineless. The Federation government's ruled by bureaucrats and incapable of change. As far as I'm concerned, I don't care if it collapses."

"So why are you fighting in this war, Ensign?"

"Mainly because I don't want to die. War is about killing

AWAKENING

each other. But to get back to your New Types, I'm willing to believe in the idea if it means a type of person capable of putting the Federation organization back in the hands of the people. I mean, sometimes people have an almost intuitive understanding of each other. If that kind of awareness could link not only individuals but all of mankind, well, then maybe we really could all live in harmony. If that's what New Types are all about, I'm all for them. Heck, I'd even like to be one."

"That's exactly the kind of person Zeon Zum Daikun was talking about when he used the term New Type, people with that type of consciousness."

"Really?" Amuro looked at Saila and saw what looked like sadness or loneliness. "You seem to know an awful lot about this guy Zeon."

"Why . . . no . . . I really don't." For a second Saila panicked, and she knew Amuro had noticed.

"New Types . . . hmm," he said. "Well, it's an interesting idea, but I don't see how people can change so easily."

"Yes . . . yes, you're quite right, and even if real New Types did appear among us, well, it wouldn't be easy. Giving birth to something totally new is usually painful."

Suddenly Amuro had a powerful, subjective understanding of what she was trying to say. "Saila, you're really convinced New Types are going to appear soon, aren't you?"

Almost reflexively, she responded to his sudden question with a smile. He stared at her. For a second the two of them interacted on a new emotive level, but then she shifted the focus. It made her too nervous.

"I just think it would be nice," she said.

In reality, she yearned to meet a real New Type if they did exist. She was not exactly sure why, but being separated from her brother and having no close friends to speak of, she found herself more fascinated by people than ever before. If only she could be sure that, as she earnestly hoped, true New Types possessed some intangible essence of humanity, she might be able to use that knowledge to change the mind of her brother, Caspar, or Sha. Zinba Ral had always said that her father, Zeon Zum Daikun, was a New Type and that he had referred to a sort of future renaissance among humans that would help propel them into a true space-based existence. If he was right, perhaps in some odd way the huge conflagration taking place in space between the Federation and Zeon was a prelude to it. Perhaps it would provide a catalyst, allowing mankind to collectively shed its old-type skin.

Saila looked deep into Amuro's eyes and tried as hard as she could to project a thought: *If you're really a New Type, Amuro, give me a sign. Show me if there's any hope for us!* She knew he would not understand something so desperate. And she was right. Her earnest look registered on him, but he interpreted it in an entirely different way. Amuro Rey was still a virgin.

The Zeon squadron led by Captain Ma Kube in the heavy cruiser *Chibe* was on patrol, making a wide sweep around the *Texas* Zone.

"There's the *Zanzibar*, sir!" one of the men on watch yelled.

Ma Kube automatically sprang out of his captain's seat. He knew the *Zanzibar* had left Side 6, but no one had informed him of its movements after that. Sure enough, there, looking as though it would practically slice off the starboard wing of his bridge, he could see the enormous shape of the *Zanzibar* silently drifting by, blinking out a signal.

"What're they saying?" he demanded of Lieutenant Ur-

AWAKENING

agan on the bridge. Ma Kube could not read old-fashioned Morse code.

Uragan's hoarse, subdued voiced slowly responded, *"TO-THE-MA-KUBE-SQUADRON. GOOD-LUCK-IN-BATTLE!* sir."

"Hmph. I'll bet."

Keeping his eye on the brightly lit bridge of the *Zanzibar* as it drifted by, he ordered Uragan to reply. "Tell them, 'We await the triumphant return of the Red Comet and the Elmeth. Go in glory! Ma Kube' "

"Did you say Elmeth, sir?"

"That's right. And don't forget the 'Go in glory' part, either."

Ma Kube's message was flashed from the *Chibe* over to the *Zanzibar*, where it was deciphered by Lieutenant Maligan and conveyed to Sha, who frowned and remarked, "The man's like a rose with too many thorns." He knew that if he ever had the opportunity, he should do something about Ma Kube, and he groused aloud that as far as he was concerned, "the man would be far better off chasing skirts." He had no way of knowing, of course, that at the same time his rival was calling him "Krishia's pet."

Ma Kube's ships and the *Zanzibar* then silently went their different ways in the darkness—the *Zanzibar* to dock at the *Texas* colony, the Ma Kube squadron to eventually encounter the Federation's 13th Autonomous Corps under Captain Watkins's command. The rendezvous between the two fleets came much earlier than anyone expected.

"Enemy ship above the Number 3 combat line!" called out Chief Petty Officer Mark Kran from the operator's boom chair suspended on the *Pegasus*'s bridge.

"But we're in the *Texas* Zone!" Lieutenant Brite yelled. "Are you positive?"

"The computer data base readout identifies it as the *Chibe*, a Zeon heavy cruiser, sir! It's too close a match in weight and size to be an asteroid."

From the ship's helm it was Ensign Mirai's turn to comment. "We've got a message from the *Hal* requesting us to assume Number 2 combat formation!" she yelled.

Brite reached for the captain's phone and switched it shipwide. *"All crew! Assume Number 2 combat formation!"* He repeated the announcement twice. Ensign Gilal, Petty Officer Saila, and the other communications crew would make sure that everyone moved to the proper sectors and took up the right stations.

Saila announced: *"Decks One and Two, open launch hatches! Mobile Suits stand by for takeoff!"*

Before she could get all the words out, a response came from Ensign Amuro. "All systems go on Gundam!" he yelled. "Beam rifle ready! Catapult set!" He was ready thirty seconds faster than Ryu and Kai in their Gun Cannons.

Mark, the operator, shouted from his perch. "The enemy will reach the Number 2 combat line in one minute! One heavy cruiser, two regular! Estimated number of Zaks . . . eleven!"

After Saila relayed the information to each pilot, what sounded like a wail came from Kai in his Mobile Suit. "Jeez! We're outnumbered more than two to one!"

"Saila!" Brite called angrily. "Tell Kai to cut the personal chitchat!"

"Yessir," she replied.

Mark started counting aloud as if to confirm the number of enemy Mobile Suits. "Four . . . Five . . . Six . . . Ten! Eleven!"

Brite looked up at the display on the ceiling of the *Peg-*

AWAKENING 157

asus's bridge, where computer graphics showed a simulated model of enemy ship locations. "Launch Mobile Suits!" he ordered.

Just before the radio link to each Mobile Suit was severed, Saila's final communication reached the pilots. "Mark's estimate was correct," she said. "There are eleven Zaks."

On the Federation side, the six Public attack ships were not designed for aerial combat like fighters, but they were still more maneuverable than cruisers or other warships. Six of them deployed themselves in a wedge formation facing the direction of the Zak approach and were followed by the Mobile Suits: the Gun Cannons, the Gundam, and the two GMs from the *Hal*.

As soon as the lead Public fired two large Lim missiles at the oncoming formation of eleven Zaks, it peeled away from the main force. The timed missiles then went on to explode in the general area where it was assumed the Zaks would be. It was a crude method, one that would have surely puzzled a military man from the old days, when radar-linked, computer-controlled weapons were taken for granted.

Two bursts of light appeared to swallow the Zak formation, but it was only an illusion. Before the light had completely dissipated, several darkened shapes—Zaks—came into view. The five remaining Publics in the Federation formation, rather than waste their Lim missiles, launched a barrage of smaller ones, and some seemed to hit. Two enormous balls of white light mushroomed in space with a shape unique to an exploding nuclear fusion engine. They overwhelmed the visual spectrum; in the Mobile Suits, even with the orthoscopic monitor's automatic exposure control on full, the light was blinding.

"Here they come!" Amuro cried seconds later, spotting

something bright soar toward him from the upper right corner of his field of vision. It was a single Zak, and if the earlier explosion had not diverted him, he never would have noticed it bearing down on him. Then he saw something flash in the area of its torso. Simultaneously, he pulled on the Gundam's control levers, jammed his feet on the pedals, and dodged a blast from the Zak's hyperbazooka with only about ten centimeters to spare.

Damn! he thought, trying to aim with his beam rifle. The enemy Zak was not as fast as the Red Comet, but almost. Their relative speeds made them cross paths before the Zak had a chance to fire another blast. Amuro tried to spin his Gundam around in time but gave up. From then on the battle would be a free-for-all. The same Zak would either spot another target or become a target itself. Amuro checked the upper left display in his cockpit, then switched to the orthoscopic monitor and spotted another Suit. It was a Gun Cannon.

Amuro pushed the swivel-mounted gun scope away from his face, realizing that his trajectory was taking him away from the enemy. In relation to the plane of the ecliptic, he was too far north, or above them. For a moment he wondered if he might have opened the Gundam's throttle too much, perhaps out of fear or even a subconscious desire to avoid the enemy. He began a broad curving maneuver to his right, hunting for enemy Suits. The light of the Earth passed over his orthoscopic monitor, and for a second he thought it was an attacking Zak and felt a shiver run down his spine. *It's going to take me years to really get used to this,* he thought, and in the same second he spotted a real Zak.

Incredibly, it was only five kilometers to his right, descending parallel to him and seemingly oblivious to his presence. In hot pursuit of some other prey, it was already sighting down the barrel of its bazooka rifle. Amuro swung his beam rifle around ninety degrees and pulled the trigger.

For a fraction of a second the entire Gundam shook as heavy metal particles bundled by a laser beam were blasted out the gun barrel. Even with a shock absorber system built into the beam rifle and into the Gundam's shoulder, it was impossible to avoid some sort of kick. But by the time Amuro felt it, the enemy Zak had already been blown several kilometers away, with the initial explosion colored by the residual light from the beam. Then came the main blast as the Zak reactor went. Averting his eyes, Amuro spun the Gundam around 180 degrees, and as he did so he suddenly spotted several other Mobile Suits in the area, illuminated in the light of the blast. There were a lot fewer Zaks than he had expected. For a moment he wondered if the other Federation pilots had been able to take out the Zaks, but he knew that was too much to wish for; all of them, including the GM pilots, were essentially still novices.

Then, just as Amuro had always feared, several Zaks began closing in on the four Federation warships under Captain Watkins's command. The ships began evasive maneuvers and unleashed a barrage of antiair fire in all directions, but Amuro knew the Zaks were cannily taking advantage of the fleet's feeble defensive perimeter. He cursed them for trying to make fools out of him and his friends, and then, spotting a flash from a Zak bazooka far off to his right, he put the Gundam into a high-speed swoop toward the Zaks around the ships, careful at the same time to avoid friendly gun and missile fire.

We all have to die sometime . . . but God help me, 'cuz here I go.

Amuro did not vocalize the words, nor was it likely that he remembered them later. His action was an intuitive response to the fact that the Zaks were perfectly positioned for him to attack. Zak squad leaders were normally identified by a decorative antennalike rod protruding from their machines, and sure enough, Amuro immediately spotted one. The enemy assumed a defensive posture as Amuro closed in and raised its bazooka as if to fire, but Amuro fired his beam rifle first and scored a direct hit. A ball of light mushroomed from the exploding Zak and nearly enveloped Amuro's Gundam, which flashed by without a second to spare.

"Two down," he exulted.

MS pilots wore helmets wired not only for radio transmissions but also for localized sounds, and as the Gundam shook violently from the Zak's explosion, Amuro heard a crackling sound, as though something were burning inside the cockpit. He let his body roll with the MS and checked around him. He was not expecting to find any major damage; if a critical condition warranted abandoning the MS, a computer readout on the upper right instrument panel would notify him, and then the escape mechanism in the Gundam's Core Fighter system would be activated—assuming, of course, that the system had survived an attack.

The two or three seconds Amuro used to check the inside of his cockpit nearly cost him his life.

"Jeez!" he suddenly yelled in terror. From the bottom of his monitor he saw a third Zak soar up toward him and almost overwhelm the screen.

Thanks to automatic avoidance circuitry in the Gundam, which mercifully worked properly, the Zak's heat hawk/battle-ax slashed through empty space rather than hacking off one of the Gundam's legs. The Zak's first attack thwarted, it next fired a laser burner built into its left hand. Using the Gundam's shield, Amuro managed to deflect what would otherwise have been a direct hit, but the blast nonetheless struck his Suit with an inaudible *whomp!* and a burst of light. And then the Zak sliced through space again with its heat ax.

Amuro felt something like a spark deep inside his brain, and a rainbow of light shot through his consciousness. He knew that unless he acted, the Gundam's head section would be split open like a watermelon. The instant the light in his brain turned to blackness, he found himself staring into an abyss in his own consciousness and confronting a force that transcended all time and tugged on him like a magnet. It was colorless, transparent, and utterly black. And then he felt it. He felt a leap in his awareness.

Amuro's right arm moved so fast that it threatened to overwhelm the Gundam's safety mechanisms; the Suit's arm, moving in response, groaned. Wielding the magazine of the beam rifle, Amuro intercepted the swing of the Zak's heat ax and stopped it with only a millimeter to spare. He could see the blade of the heat ax glowing bright red, almost screaming. Sparks from the severed laser oscillator in the Gundam's beam rifle sprayed light between it and the Zak. And then suddenly, as if confused, the Zak's mono-eye flickered and seemed to go out.

Something in Amuro yelled, *I did it!* It did not come from his conscious mind. It came from whatever had caused the leap in his awareness. He felt as though he had been guided by some external force and led out of a crisis. It was almost as though the scream had come not from within him at all but from a larger, independent consciousness.

Amuro made the Gundam discard its now-useless beam rifle and used the freed right arm to reach back over the Suit's shoulder and grab the hilt of one of the beam sabers. When the Zak's mono-eye flashed again, he slashed downward through its head, driving the glowing pink saber blade all the way through to its chest. The Zak, nearly severed in two, collapsed forward at the waist, molten metal fragments spraying from its innards like magma spewing from a volcano. Amuro turned off the saber's laser oscillation beam and put the Gundam in reverse to get away from the explosion he knew would occur. And then he was enveloped in the light of another nuclear fusion blast.

"Three down," he whispered to himself.

Then Amuro turned the Gundam toward the remaining Zaks attacking the Federation ships. Luckily, almost all the Zaks would have already exhausted their supply of bazooka rockets, because without his beam rifle he would have no choice but to use the beam saber in close-quarter combat.

At exactly the instant when the Zaks changed course to avoid a barrage from the Federation ships, he plunged the Gundam into their midst. The fourth Zak he severed in two before it had time to draw its heat ax. The fifth tried to parry with its heat ax, but the Gundam's beam saber melted it in an instant and sliced diagonally down through its shoulder to its waist.

"Five down."

That was the end of the fight. Ryu's Gun Cannon had bagged one Zak. A GM had finished off another. The remaining four retreated. Federation losses included two Public attack ships destroyed and four ships slightly damaged. Or so it seemed.

When Amuro returned to the *Pegasus*, Saila's face appeared on the miniature monitor in his cockpit. The few words she uttered were so official and shocking that he forgot to release his seat belt and sat temporarily speechless. Of the *Pegasus*'s MS team, only Amuro's Gundam and Kai's Gun Cannon had returned. "You must be kidding," he groaned.

"No. It's true," she said. "I just received confirmation from the bridge."

The hatch on the *Pegasus*'s catapult deck was still open, as if waiting for Ryu Jose to return in his Gun Cannon any minute. Death in battle, it seemed to Amuro, was too sudden. It had happened to Sean Crane and now to Ryu. One instant they were there, and the next they were gone. And they would never come back. That was it.

When Amuro climbed out of the Gundam and made his way to the briefing room, sure enough, there was the chair Ryu had been sitting in before they had all taken off. The original five pilot cadets now had been reduced to three.

Kai Shiden entered the room, looked at Amuro, and merely shrugged his shoulders. Hayato Kobayashi, who had stayed behind on the ship during the battle, turned to Kai and exploded with grief.

"Why? Why couldn't you protect him?" he yelled.

"Who the hell do you think I am?" Kai retorted. "Some kind of invincible veteran MS space ace?"

Hayato said nothing, and when Amuro turned and stared at him, he started to leave the room with an expression of utter despair.

Kai yelled at his back, "Next battle, you're *on*, partner! You were brought along on this ship as a backup for Amuro! He knocked out five Zaks! And you're telling us we should have saved Ryu?"

"Okay, enough!" Hayato broke under Kai's blast. His anger spent, he turned around, slumped into a chair, and exclaimed "Dammit!" in frustration. Instead of Hayato, it was Kai who left the room.

Amuro walked over to one of the reclining chairs in the room, eased himself into it, and strapped on the seat belt. If they were going to be on round-the-clock standby for combat, he thought to himself, they should at least have two more alternate pilots. His pulse was still racing from the adrenaline of combat, but he knew he was exhausted. He would not have time for a good sleep, but he would at least try to take a short nap. He popped a tranquilizer and called out to Hayato, "Wake me up if anything happens."

Because of the battle between the 13th Autonomous and Captain Ma Kube's fleet, Zeon might decide to send out reinforcements, but by then General Revil and the main Federation force should have started closing in on Zeon's *Solomon* fortress in the area around Side 1. Any Zeon reinforcements coming to the *Texas* Zone would have to leave from either Zeon's *Granada* moon base or *Solomon*, and General Revil's fleet might be able to respond accordingly. It was too early to tell if the final showdown would take place around *Granada* or *Solomon*, but either way, the accomplishment of the 13th Autonomous—especially the *Pegasus* and the *Hal*—had opened the door to a major battle.

Immediately after receiving his letter of commendation for downing five Zaks from Captain Watkins, Amuro had to go out again. An enemy fleet had been detected coming out of *Granada*, so if at all possible, in advance of its arrival at the *Texas* Zone, the 13th was to destroy Captain Ma Kube's squadron and then wait for a major fleet offensive to shape up. Unknown to Watkins and the other Federation commanders, however, Commander Sha Aznable and the *Zanzibar* were already on the *Texas* colony.

CHAPTER 7
LALA SUN

"Judging by the damage the Federation pilots inflicted on us," Captain Ma Kube said, sifting through reports from his men, "we're dealing with a fairly powerful opponent."

"Yessir," Lieutenant Uragan replied. "We have reason to believe there were over ten enemy Mobile Suits, but it is possible that the count was slightly inflated if, for example, two of our pilots reported downing the same machine. Still, I agree, we shouldn't have lost seven Suits. An enemy MS can't possibly be more powerful than a Zak."

"Hold your tongue for a second, Lieutenant," Ma Kube said. Uragan always talked too much, which irritated him. He wished he had brought along his little white marble Tang dynasty statue of the goddess of mercy. Its gentle expression could soothe the spirit of any who gazed upon it, and he often used it to help collect his thoughts. Right now he was also disgusted by his own carelessness. Who would have dreamed he would run into a Federation fleet on what was supposed to be a routine patrol mission?

"How many Mobile Suits do you think the Federation Horse can carry?" he asked, referring to the *Pegasus*.

"Well . . . er . . . according to the information from Lieutenant Commander Sha, sir—"

"He's a full commander now, Uragan," Ma Kube said, interrupting.

"Yessir! General Staff Headquarters, based on information from the commander, has determined it can hold between six and eight Suits."

"Well, that's the number we're looking at, then. Even if their Mobile Suits perform twice as well as ours, they still don't have any veteran pilots. It seems to me, then, that we're looking at no more than eight. Don't you agree, Uragan?"

"Why, yes . . . yessir!"

"I don't know what Commander Sha and the *Zanzibar* are up to at the *Texas* colony, but send an emissary requesting they go into action to support us. The Federation Forces will make the next move."

Sure enough, Ma Kube was right.

Twenty minutes after Amuro received his commendation from Captain Watkins, Saila broke the news to him over the video link that he had been ordered on a scouting mission. "You all right, Amuro?" she said softly. "Brite tried his best to get Watkins to rescind his order, but we apparently lost track of the Zeon fleet that launched the Zaks earlier, and—"

"Brite? Brite did that for me?"

As far as Amuro was concerned, Brite was usually preoccupied with yelling orders from the bridge, and it was hard to imagine him looking out for any of his pilots. As it turned out, however, at first Hayato had been scheduled to launch in Amuro's stead, but Brite had refused. And his refusal had angered Watkins.

AWAKENING

"Why can't Hayato go? Amuro asked. "What's wrong with sending him out?"

Saila answered lightly. "I think the skipper trusts you, Amuro." And then, "We can see asteroids from the bridge. Be careful."

Since their conversation in the mess hall, Saila had begun to let down her guard with Amuro. He, for that matter, had been unable to forget the strangely beautiful blue color of her eyes. There was something in her eyes that hinted of a great personal burden. There was something different about the woman he had always thought of as the Blonde, and he knew it was more than his imagination.

Later, while doing a preflight check on the Gundam, he wondered to himself if *she* might even be a New Type.

After checking the signal shells, the beam rifle, the bazooka, and its spare rockets, he called out: "Gundam, ready for takeoff!"

Saila wished him luck over the video link, and then he felt the *g* force of the launch. It felt better than he remembered.

"Hey, Hayato!" Kai called out to his friend, watching the Gundam launch on the monitor in the *Pegasus*'s briefing room. "Be thankful it's Amuro. It lessens the odds we'll buy the farm."

"But I'm a full ensign, just like him!" Hayato exclaimed. "How come I'm still just an alternate Gundam pilot?"

"Tough luck. We're not New Types. We're Gun Cannon specialists now, Hayato."

"What are you getting at?"

"Well, don't you think Amuro's a little different than we are?"

"Nope. I still don't have the foggiest idea what people mean by New Types."

"Well, since we're just average Joes, they're basically telling us to take a backseat. Nothin' wrong with that, as far as I can see. Heck, I don't want to meet the same fate Ryu did."

Hayato, his eyes glued to the video monitor, said nothing. On the launch deck the mechamen were scurrying about, doing last-minute maintenance on the Gun Cannon. This time there was nothing for the pilots to do but wait. Noticing after a while that Kai had fallen silent, he turned and looked at his friend and found him sound asleep in his reclining chair.

Pilots were specially chosen officers, and Hayato had no reason to think he was incompetent, but when he thought of his peer, Amuro, carrying out difficult and dangerous assignments, he could not help feeling a trace of self-disgust. If, as General Revil had suggested, New Types symbolized a transformation of all mankind, then they clearly were not mere comic-book-style supermen. And if, as implied, a human "consciousness raising" was going to herald a new stage in man's evolution, well, that would be almost too good to be true. In the past, man's progress had always seemed dependent on his periodically destroying the very civilization he had built; if that could be changed, who would need something as terrible as war?

But it seemed to Hayato that there was something about all this that smacked of nonsense. If the Zeon government was really planning to form a special New Type Corps, its members could hardly represent a total transformation of humanity. Surely they would simply be a group of murderous supermen, even superbutchers. Weren't New Types just some kind of freak-mutants? Hayato had never heard of any people with special powers—at least not with powers of the type currently being whispered about—who had made so much as a dent in history. New Types, Hayato concluded,

AWAKENING

were really just deviant personalities. There was no other way he could comfortably compare himself to Amuro. His pride would not allow it.

Wending his way around asteroids up to two kilometers in diameter, Amuro traced his way in the Gundam over the Federation squadron's planned course. Captain Watkins was not so foolish as to leave the advance scouting to the Gundam alone; the four surviving Public attack ships were deployed in a supporting role, above, below, and to either side of him.

As the formation navigated past another asteroid, Amuro encountered a giant piece of wall panel over a kilometer long, a remnant of one of the Side 5 colonies destroyed in the Battle of Ruum. Sensing something odd, he tilted the Gundam forward and started to maneuver around the wall. Far off in the distance to the left, he could see *Texas*. The moon, as usual, appeared so enormous that it nearly overwhelmed his optic nerves. If the enemy was lying in wait on the other side of the wall, he realized they would be in the perfect position to ambush the Federation fleet when it came by.

Just as he was puzzling over what he sensed, a corner of the wall seemed to ignite, and a group of particle beams stabbed through the space toward his Suit. He responded reflexively, and the incredible speed of his movements was transmitted to the Gundam, which creaked and groaned as if tortured. The core of the enemy beams missed, but a few diffused particles on their periphery pierced the Gundam's armor; the bazooka fastened to the machine's back was blown to smithereens.

"What the heck happened?"

Just when his guard was down, he had been hit by a particle beam attack! He had evaded it. And that was that. He knew an enemy MS could easily have been waiting to ambush him from behind the wall, but the beams aimed at him were far too powerful.

Putting his MS though a wide evasive maneuver, he slipped around to the other side of the wall and found himself staring at a small squadron of Zeon ships—looking up at their bottoms, from his perspective. Scattered smaller fire—both particle beams and missiles—streaked toward him, missing but nonetheless unnerving him. No wonder he had sensed something odd. One heavy cruiser and two *Musai*-class ships had been lying in wait for him, and the first blasts that had zapped out at him through the darkness had come from their main cannons. The thought made his flesh crawl. It was a miracle that he had not been pulverized.

Without hesitating, Amuro moved into action. The *Musai*-class ship immediately in front of him blocked his view of the heavy cruiser *Chibe*, making a direct hit on it with his beam rifle impossible. He therefore trained his rifle sights at the *Musai*-class ship and pulled the trigger. Three beam blasts pierced the engine on one side of the vessel, but just before the entire craft blew, the *Chibe* and the other *Musai*-class ship accelerated forward, and two Zaks that had been hiding behind them came toward him, firing rockets from their bazookas. One smashed into the Gundam's right arm.

"Damn!"

The Zaks had seized the perfect moment to attack. Amuro was still drunk with his own success at bagging the *Musai* cruiser. He cursed his foolishness.

Luckily, although his Suit's right arm had received a direct hit, the joint had been spared, and the arm still functioned. But the power lines connecting the main engine to the beam rifle mechanism had been damaged, leaving it unusable, and there was no time to switch the rifle to the

AWAKENING

Gundam's left hand, which was holding the shield. Amuro therefore tried to ward off attacking blasts with the shield while he bolted the rifle onto a restraining fixture on the Gundam's hip. Then he unsheathed the beam saber hilt from his backpack. Positioning himself between the two oncoming Zaks, he thanked the stars the Gundam's beam saber and rifle had independent power lines; if not, he would have been a goner.

With a *zap!* the saber hilt projected a blade of beam particles over ten meters in length, which sliced into the left shoulder of one of the oncoming Zaks. Amuro knew he had connected with the enemy MS, but he did not have time to check if he had delivered a mortal blow; they were both streaking toward the giant cylinder of the *Texas* colony, and unless he was careful, he himself would crash into its walls. Turning and accelerating the Gundam way into the tach redline, he swooped right in front of the Zaks. Carefully avoiding the colony's giant extended mirrors, he glanced at his rearview monitor and for the first time saw concrete proof of his kill in the form of a fading burst of light from an explosion. But what about the other Zak? He would have to be extra careful; it had had the insignia of a squad leader on it.

He badly needed to check the damage to the Gundam's right arm. As he soared alongside the colony, he spotted its docking bay and decided to enter and take cover. It was on the "sunny side" of the huge cylinder (having been abandoned by the Colony Administration, it now had a rotation one-fifth slower than normal, and its axis was permanently skewed), but at least he would be temporarily out of sight of the Zaks.

The Gundam Mobile Suit, as Amuro found once he parked in the bay and took a close look, could withstand a lot. The armor in its damaged right arm was constructed of a triple-layered, compound honeycomb material and had a four- or five-centimeter dent in it and what looked like a hole. The arm would still work, but using it to hold the beam rifle was out of the question. What he really needed at this point was a bazooka. Beam rifles were formidable weapons, but they taxed the concentration of already overburdened pilots because they required great marksmanship; unlike bazookas and other old-style weapons, which created a more diffuse explosion and required a less precise aim, with a beam rifle anything less than a direct hit was meaningless. And as Amuro's earlier skirmish had proved, MS pilots had to operate on a hair-trigger basis, with no room for mistakes. During the two or three seconds of exultation over hitting a *Musai* his overconfidence had almost led to disaster; he had let down his guard and almost let a Zak blindside him.

Now parked inside the *Texas* colony docking bay, he had no idea where the enemy, especially the surviving Zak, was. Nor did he know who its pilot was. He knew he was not dealing with the Red Comet, but judging by the earlier action, he felt certain its pilot was a veteran of more than one battle.

On the Zeon cruiser *Chibe*, Captain Ma Kube was livid. "What?" he said. "No response from Commander Sha?"

A Federation squadron of four ships had already arrived on the scene, and his ship, as well as the cruiser *Kwamel*, had come under fire. True, like him, the Federation Forces did not have much firepower. But the mobile cruiser *Zanzibar* Sha was on, now supposedly docked on *Texas*, was far more powerful and agile than any *Musai*-class ship and should have been able to arrive on the scene in a few minutes. If it would only come to his aid, he thought, he could hit the Federation ships broadside and destroy them all.

AWAKENING   173

Now here he was, in the midst of a battle, with particle beams from cannons on both sides crisscrossing through space, unable to deliver fatal blows but pulverizing several small asteroids in the process. Luckily for Ma Kube, his men were brave. Two of his Zaks even courageously managed to approach the Federation fleet flagship, *Hal*. If only that white enemy MS had not appeared on the scene so fast and spoiled his surprise earlier, Ma Kube was convinced his carefully planned ambush would have wiped out the Federation's entire 13th Autonomous Corps.

Perhaps he had given away his position by being too hasty to attack the Gundam, but he was not the type to dwell on the pros and cons of past decisions. His was a simple philosophy: If a crisis arose, it had to be solved. He was also pragmatic enough to put his personal grudges aside for the moment and really did wish Sha were around to help him now. After all, he had lost the *Tolmeth*, a *Musai*-class cruiser, and eight Zaks. He had an account to settle.

Ma Kube's *Chibe* concentrated a barrage of fire on the Federation Magellan-class flagship, *Hal*. Dodging blasts of friendly fire, the two Zeon Zaks also contributed their own firepower. Under normal circumstances that would have been an absurd strategy, but Ma Kube knew he had no other choice if he wished to get the upper hand.

"Lieutenants Rolm and Zerol are piloting our Zaks, are they not?"

"Yes, sir." Lieutenant Uragan wondered why his captain would ask such a question at a time like this.

"Well, I certainly feel proud of those men today," Ma Kube exclaimed in his subordinate's face just as a shout went up from the other officers and men on the bridge. The main engine on the *Hal* had turned into a ball of light.

"That's the way!" Ma Kube exulted, standing at attention on the bridge and urging on his forces while the mushrooming orb of light threatened to envelop them. "Now go for the Horse! Turn your guns on the Horse!"

But Zeon guns were not the only ones capable of hitting their targets. Several blasts from Federation beam cannon also scored direct hits on the *Chibe*. Then eight missiles struck home. Then two more. The main foredeck cannons were knocked out of action, and to use the aft cannon to maximum effect Ma Kube had no choice but to swing his ship around, exposing his right flank to the enemy.

Lieutenant Uragan yelled out a report. "Lieutenant Rolm's Zak has reached the cruiser on our port side, sir!"

"Excellent!" Ma Kube exulted. "Steady your aim!"

Beams streaked forth from the *Chibe*'s three linked aft cannon as the Federation cruiser *Saphron*, on the right wing of the formation, suddenly pulled in front of the *Pegasus*. It looked unscathed. An intense barrage of mega-particle blasts followed.

Over on the *Pegasus*, Brite was livid. "What? Hayato's taken off on his own? The kid's crazy to go out there in the midst of a battle between fleets. Order him back at once!"

Saila knew the best way to get her skipper to calm down was to let him rant and rave. With the loss of the flagship *Hal*, the *Pegasus* was more exposed than ever, and Brite was understandably distraught. She acknowledged his command and radioed Hayato's Gun Cannon, knowing full well her message could not reach him.

"Pegasus *to Gun Cannon! Ensign Hayato, return to ship immediately! Return to ship!*"

It was madness for Hayato to have taken off in the middle of the cross fire between enemy warships, but once he was outside the immediate area, the incredible latticework of light he saw looked like beautiful shining threads. It was hard to imagine being hit by them. It made him realize why, in the vastness of space, it really was difficult to achieve a direct hit on anything.

Homing in on the beams of light coming from the enemy, Hayato could see that the Zeon cruiser *Chibe* was half-destroyed but still pursuing the attack. He marveled how calm he felt as he trained his sights on its aft deck cannon. Indulging in a little self-satisfaction, he concluded that he had finally become a seasoned combat veteran. He pulled the trigger, and the two cannon built into the shoulders of his Suit belched forth flames.

"Three . . . two . . . one . . ." He did a countdown by himself while putting the Gun Cannon into a broad curve to the left and training his sights on the other *Musai*-class cruiser on the other side of the *Chibe*. And just then the aft deck cannon on the *Chibe* exploded.

"Bull's-eye!" Hayato yelled.

Ma Kube's ship gave its final gasp, and then a ball of light equal to that made by the *Hal* earlier highlighted both the asteroids and the surviving warships in the area. In the midst of all this, the *Kwamel*, the last *Musai*-class cruiser in the Zeon squad, heeled about sharply, desperately trying to escape.

"Can't let them get away," Hayato swore to himself in the narrow confines of his Gun Cannon cockpit as he swooped after the *Kwamel*. The *Pegasus* fired a signal flare indicating that all forces should regroup, but Hayato was too preoccupied to notice.

Over by the *Texas* colony, the Zeon Zak squad leader following Amuro closed in for the kill outside the docking bay. Since the colony port was nearly four hundred meters in diameter, he fired two rockets from his bazooka as cover before entering and then, without waiting for the explosion to clear, plunged inside.

Amuro quickly retreated behind an old transport ship scuttled in the center of the colony's port. He could physically sense the intruder's presence—he was learning to sense things from inside a cockpit—and he was seized by a crazy idea. He would try to grab the bazooka from the Zak.

And then he saw the girl.

It was such an odd sight that for a moment he wondered if he was seeing things. She was standing in a corner of what used to be the colony's control core, behind the multilayered glass of its observation window. And from his perspective, she was upside down. Despite the distance, her emerald-green eyes were strikingly beautiful, almost transparent and glowing, and he sensed something indescribably powerful, even vast in them. Remembering what he had sensed in Saila once before, he felt a vague sense of déjà vu. What could it be? he wondered. Even more important, was the girl real?

The control core of the abandoned colony was unmanned, and the lights should have been extinguished long ago. The girl was standing in darkness, yet around her there was a faint glow. The notion of a ghost crossed Amuro's mind but was soon canceled by a powerful realization that this girl did in fact exist, that she was *there*. He did not know exactly where his realization came from and wondered if it was a projection of her own conscious thought, an awareness that she was deliberately creating in him.

Without verbalizing, something in Amuro's mind nearly screamed, <Who are you?>

And again: <Who are you?>

The question was pleading, almost desperate, almost a physical yell.

AWAKENING

"What do you want from me?"

Could she hear him? She appeared to smile, and when a transparent light seemed to pierce the center of her forehead, he hoped it was all an illusion. But then he understood it was real. She had parted her jet-black hair in the middle of her head and gathered it in buns on either side. Her skin was a glistening tan, and the contrast made her emerald-green eyes seem almost transparent. Her dress also surprised him. It was nothing more than folds of cloth hung over her neck and draped around her body, an awfully mature outfit for someone so young. But then another realization welled up inside him. She was the same age as he was! It was a physical sensation and undeniable. It was incredible.

Then he felt a growing awareness of a new sensation—a darker force, like a shadow—run through his cerebral lobes. He sensed Z-A-K.

The enemy had brazenly managed to sneak up behind him and was now so close that he could have finished the Gundam off with a bazooka blast. But he did not. Instead, the Zak swung its glowing heat ax toward the Gundam's hips in an attempt to connect with and destroy the Gundam's power train. But Amuro forced his Suit to move so fast that the metal screamed and dodged the blow in the nick of time. Like a knife slicing through butter, instead of Gundam armor, the Zak's heat ax sliced through the wall of the abandoned transport.

Seizing the moment, Amuro raised the beam rifle in the Gundam's functioning left hand and slammed its stock into the Zak's left shoulder, sending it smashing into the side of the transport. The ship's framework shook, and as the Zak rebounded from it, Amuro jammed his rifle muzzle into its cockpit area. He knew there was a human pilot inside, and when he pulled the rifle trigger, it felt colder than normal.

The beam from his gun pierced the Zak, sliced through the wrecked transport, and even reached the control core on the other side of the port.

Heaving a sigh of relief at his narrow escape, Amuro shoved the fallen Zak out toward the colony port exit. It scraped and bounced on the deck once, spun crazily, and then drifted out and off toward the sun. Somehow, Amuro did not want the girl to see what he had done. The fight with the Zak had taken only a few seconds in all, and he had not even glanced at the monitor that earlier had shown the girl, but he was afraid she might have become frightened and disappeared. For him that would have been a disaster. He had no idea who she was, but she had seemed easily capable of understanding his intentions. To lose contact with her would be terrifying. She had made him realize something profound—that he was not alone, that she was a kindred spirit he must meet.

It was an intuitive realization, the recognition of one New Type by another, yet even Amuro himself was not fully aware of what was happening. While pushing the Zak corpse out the docking bay, fearing she was no longer there, he suddenly sensed her presence. He mentally "saw" her. He knew she was still there. He knew her name was Lala Sun. And he knew she was real.

Unable to stand the idea of looking at her over a video monitor, Amuro yanked the lever for the Gundam's main hatch. The orthoscopic monitor lowered, and the double-layered hatch door opened up and outward. He unbuckled his seat belt, stood up, and looked straight at her. If he had not still been in the vacuum of space in the colony's docking bay, he would even have removed his Normal Suit helmet. And if he could have, he would have smashed the glass panels of the control core window that still separated them. There was too much between them. He could sense her

AWAKENING

physical presence, but visually she was still too unclear, too unstable. With her still standing upside down from his perspective, he stared straight into her eyes and asked: "Lala, what are you doing here?"

He knew there was no voice channel available. But she responded anyway, as if she had physically heard. Her hands floated up to her cheeks, and her nearly transparent emerald-green eyes seemed to cloud over in sadness.

He knew her spirit was wavering. He knew she was afraid but could not tell why. He cursed the limitations of trying to understand her mind. But then he clearly sensed a thought from her directed at him, assaulting his brain like a wave. It was a perception so powerful that it threw his mind off balance for a second and allowed her to connect directly with his consciousness.

<You're too late!>

<What do you mean?>

<I've already fallen in love with Sha!>

Amuro felt like a hole was being bored in his brain, splitting his nervous system in two. What did she mean? Who was the Sha she spoke of? Who was too late? "Love"? All he could think of was "Who are you?"

<Why?>

Suddenly, as the girl gradually began to express herself, several thoughts struck the confused Amuro simultaneously. And behind them he could still sense sadness and anxiety.

<Why are you so late? It took you too long to get here!>

The thoughts were clear and filled Amuro's awareness.

<I had no idea you existed!>

"What are you talking about? What has all this got to do with me?" Amuro tried to answer but then stopped. She had mentioned Sha! Could she possibly mean the same Sha he knew as the Red Comet? Sha Aznable?

This time Amuro's words were not received by Lala Sun.

Their form of communication was unlike telepathy, which never needed spoken words. Nor was it triggering some sort of leap in consciousness. As impressions were traded back and forth, an awareness that transcended conscious thought was built up. What seemed like an exchange of fragmentary ideas created the context for understanding another person. It was not a simple means of communication. It was more like a weaving together of two minds.

And it allowed Amuro to feel the sadness behind Lala Sun's words.

<You are too late. I just realized now that you are the one I was waiting for. But you're too late . . .>

<My name's Amuro Rey. I'm from the Federation. I don't understand why you'd be waiting for me here, in *Texas*, of all places. Do you mean you were waiting for some sort of kindred spirit?>

<Yes, and it was a new person . . . It was you, not the commander. This is too cruel.>

Amuro's next thought was like a dagger to Lala's heart.

<I don't think a true New Type . . . would make a mistake like that.>

<How can you say such a cruel thing? Why didn't you contact me?>

With that, Amuro had a profound realization of his own basic weakness. And he lamented it deeply.

<Because. Because I don't think I'm really a New Type.>

<We . . . we are both imperfect, Amuro.>

<Maybe. But listen, Lala Sun. What can we do about it? We're supposed to be enemies!>

<I don't know. I just know I'm supposed to be the pilot of this Mobile Armor. I'm the first pilot in our New Type combat unit, but I can't believe this is my only mission in life. Meeting you has convinced me. But that said, I'm—>

<I get it.>

AWAKENING

Amuro had a powerful, sudden insight. New Types might be real, after all. And it just might be possible, as he and Saila Mas had once discussed, that people *could* learn to communicate on a new level. It was an incredible idea, but perhaps hundreds, thousands, even millions of different levels of awareness *could* overlap, and perhaps mankind *could* one day finally leave its prejudices behind and achieve a universal wisdom.

Amuro had to believe in the idea. He had no other way of comprehending the thoughts flowing back and forth between him and Lala Sun. But he answered based on an objective reality.

<I hope you're right!>

Lala sensed his meaning and the implications of what failure would mean and fell deeper into despair.

Amuro, for his part, realized that he just might have a spark of New Type insight within him, pointing the way toward his own destiny.

<Amuro! It's too cruel. Amuro! You've got to stop me!>
<What?>

He did not understand. He saw her emerald-green eyes, her tawny skin that seemed to melt into the surrounding darkness, her long, supple limbs, and her beautiful head of hair. She appeared to waver and then tried to smash through the glass barrier that separated them. He was taken aback by her abrupt change in behavior and was completely at a loss how to respond.

Then a door opened behind Lala, and through the light it let in, Amuro made out the shadow of a quickly moving man. A sound like static violently intruded on his and Lala's thought communication. There was a perceptual spark and then a fragmentary interruption by a third thought form overlaid on his and Lala's. It was not words. It was a ruptured type of noise, and it assumed an aura of hate.

The man was wearing a red military uniform with a platinum-colored helmet and face mask, and he appeared to be an officer of the Zeon forces. A cape fluttered from his back. It was Commander Sha Aznable, aka Caspar Lem Daikun, of the Zeon forces.

So this is the Red Comet! Amuro thought to himself.

When Sha spoke, the words were real. "Lala!" he curtly ordered. "Get out of here! Now!"

"B-but Commander," she started to say, as if afraid.

The interruption resulted in confusion in all three's awareness, but the confusion was soon transformed to an instinct common to all mammals—a fighting instinct.

Through the glass window of the control core window, Sha saw the object of Lala's attention—a young Federation pilot dangling out of the cockpit hatch of a Gundam MS. Lala, glancing at Sha, was unable to hide her panic. She saw in him a lovable quality to which she was powerfully attracted, but she also saw emerging in him one of man's most despicable traits. She knew that the combination, in this situation, would be disaster for her.

Amuro, for his part, mournfully watched the couple in the control core. Too young and inexperienced to understand all the ways of men and women, he watched Lala tremble and thought: *So that's what she meant about being too late*.

As Amuro watched, the red-uniformed Zeon officer floated across the room and out the door with Lala in his arms. The door slammed shut, and the control core command center was again deserted.

Amuro craved more contact with the mysterious Lala Sun but he had just seen what he thought was incontrovertible evidence of her physical love for his archenemy. A thought

AWAKENING

suddenly ran through his brain in a way he did not fully understand. It was more than a sixth sense; it was subtle proof that he was developing an expanded awareness and power of insight. It said, <Time to scram!> He was in real danger.

Quickly shutting the Gundam hatch, he checked his beam rifle. It was low on energy, so he maneuvered the MS to pick up the bazooka left behind by the Zak he had earlier dispatched. It still had three rockets left in it. Then he moved over toward the colony port exit, where the Gundam instruments detected the *Pegasus* and its two accompanying cruisers nearby in space. Even the Gun Cannons were close enough to be identified. Amuro should have felt overjoyed, but he could not suppress a basic animal instinct welling up inside him. "Lala Sun . . ." he whispered. He wanted to see her close up. He wanted to touch her. He wanted her. His perception of danger was already beginning to fade, and he had no way of knowing what kind of enemy was really lying in wait inside *Texas*.

When encountering a member of the opposite sex with whom one had a powerful, intuitive understanding, physical desire could sometimes be masked. But when the actual thought waves of both individuals were almost perfectly intertwined, the encounter could also be a powerful aphrodisiac. Amuro was far too young to understand what was happening to him or to restrain himself. Instead of launching into space toward the *Pegasus*, he spun the Gundam around and walked toward the series of hatches at the other end of the colony port. Opening them one by one, he stepped through the last door that led inside *Texas*.

It was virtually impossible to see the inner surface of the colony from the final hatch. Giant external mirrors normally reflected sunlight inside the colony, but their automatic control mechanism was broken, and for the last few months they had been stuck on something equivalent to dawn or dusk. Atmospheric conditions inside the colony had deteriorated into violent windstorms, with sand-colored tornadoes often occurring around the colony's central axis.

Keeping his eyes on the Gundam's main monitor, Amuro watched a small whirlwind form next to him and twist through the air. Wondering where Lala might be in the 360-degree panorama in front of him, he tried to rely on his intuition. He closed his eyes and focused his mind, to no avail. It was frustrating. Only a few minutes earlier he had been so close to her that he could almost have physically called out to her. He asked himself: What to do?

The next instant he barely dodged an incoming bazooka rocket. But a fraction of a second before it burst next to him with a leaden *whomp!* he put the Gundam into a jump maneuver toward the direction of its origin, somewhere above to his right. He soared to an elevation of nearly five hundred meters off the colony floor, right through the middle of a brown twister cloud. There were fierce winds blowing throughout the colony, but luckily a true greenhouse effect had not occurred; without the cooling effect of the external walls, the place would have been an inferno.

As Amuro made a rapid descent into a corner of the *Texas* colony, for the first time he saw the grand scale of the place. Although he had spent the first few years of his life on Earth, his father, a construction engineer, had taken him into outer space almost as early as he could remember, and he had returned to Earth only three times after that, always to visit his mother. He was familiar only with the gentle mountains and temperate climate of her home and had never experienced anything like the wild environment of *Texas*.

The people who had designed *Texas* had done their best to represent nature in all its glory and had paid special attention to visual effects. Rivers and streams wound through

AWAKENING

steep canyons that appeared to have been carved by centuries of erosion; forests of evergreens spread on the foothills. The environment was totally artificial, but the scenery was more than enough to evoke images of the ancient reality on which it had been modeled. Although the plains were now desert, once tourists had delighted in the sight of hundreds of cattle herded by cowboys, imagined campfire smoke in the distance to be signals from Indians, crossed the colony's glass sections on giant bridges made to look like natural rock formations, and experienced a simulation of the wild and woolly days of the Wild West on Earth's North American continent.

The Gundam MS dropped out of a dust cloud on the verge of forming a vortex and sailed into a roaring wind. With his attention diverted by the scenery unfolding before him, Amuro nearly made a fatal mistake. But as before in the colony port area, a cool lightlike sensation seemed to bore into his forehead. As his awareness expanded to 360 degrees, he sensed a specific direction, and just in the nick of time he dodged another incoming enemy round.

"Where are you?" Amuro muttered, scanning the area around him. He knew it might be overconfidence, but he somehow felt he was better positioned to deal with the enemy—even if it was Sha Aznable, the Red Comet—than the enemy was to deal with him.

"Where are you?" he growled again, frustrated by the fact that his new awareness could not help him pinpoint a distant target. Perhaps, he thought, it was because of the turbid atmospheric conditions. But unknown to Amuro, Sha Aznable was already retreating with Lala Sun to the port on the opposite end of the colony cylinder, where the *Zanzibar* was anchored.

* * *

Earlier, inside the colony, Doctor Flanagan and his team of assistants had performed the first successful feasibility tests of the Elmeth-Bits Mobile Armor system with Lala. The Bits, equipped with beam cannon and explosive charges, were operated remotely and were made to attack when her willpower was channeled and amplified through the psychom interface. From the cockpit of the Elmeth, without using its beam cannon, she had simultaneously mobilized and fired the cannon on eight out of ten Bits and had effectively destroyed the test targets. It was after completing this test that she had wandered on her own to the control core of the colony's other port and encountered Amuro. When Sha had taken her away from the control core, he had put her under the care of the Flanagan team in the mobile trailer used to launch the Elmeth-Bits system and immediately moved to attack the infiltrator MS—Amuro and the Gundam.

Sha's mood had plunged to near despair.

The pilot's a New Type. He may not be as advanced as Lala, but there's no other way to explain the way he parries my attacks.

His worst fear on first encountering the white enemy MS— that there were New Types among the Federation pilots— had been borne out. He knew mankind might be in the midst of a transition, even a new type of evolution, but it was wartime. If there were to be a genesis of New Types, the real question was, when would the fetus begin quickening, and what kind of labor pains would result? He himself might have New Type potential. He was at least capable of one form of insight that the older, conservative Earthbound generations were not: he was able to recognize a true New Type when he saw one. And this time he had to believe his opponent was one. After all, a terrified young Federation recruit had nicknamed him the Red Comet. If he was not up against a New Type, his pride would crumble from the shame of his failure to defeat his opponent.

Damn! he thought. Making his way in his MS through the colony's evergreen belt, he checked all his monitors for any sign of the enemy. After parrying Sha's second barrage, the white MS had looked as if it would make a steep descent and come in for a hard landing on the colony floor. But the pilot might have anticipated his movement.

Sha began to doubt himself. Had he ordered too high a concentration of Minovski particles scattered in the area for Lala's test earlier? The scan lines on his MS radar display had turned to static.

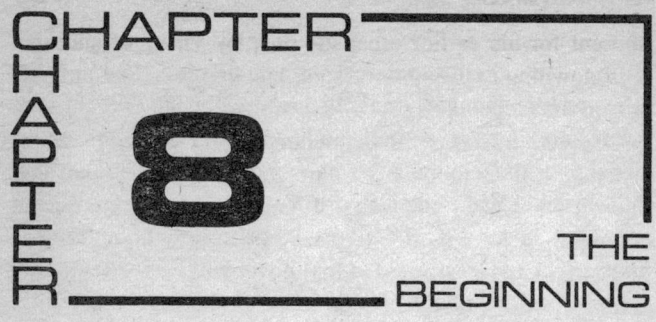

CHAPTER 8

THE BEGINNING

After ordering the two cruisers, *Cisco* and *Saphron*, to stand by outside, Lieutenant (jg) Brite moved the *Pegasus* inside the *Texas* colony port. The four layers of giant air lock doors in the port were all operational, and the second and third were already open. When the fourth and final hatch opened, the *Pegasus* passed through into the murky twilight of the colony's inner environment and was immediately enveloped in a cloud of swirling sand.

"Saila!" Brite yelled. "Detect any signal from Amuro's Gundam yet?"

"No, not a thing," she replied haltingly. "There's . . . there's an extremely high Minovski level in here, sir."

She looked pale. Turning around, she slowly stood up and asked, "Could someone spell me?"

As far as Brite could tell, she was not faking it. She looked bad. "Bammus!" he ordered a petty officer on the bridge. "I want you to relieve Saila. And I want Ensign Kai Shiden to take over from Hayato in the Gun Cannon and to launch a search for the Gundam immediately. Get Hayato up here on the bridge with me." Hayato had escaped punishment for his earlier escapade only by virtue of successfully downing two Zeon cruisers, but Brite was not anxious to turn him loose again.

"Do you think we're safe anchored here, skipper?" Mirai queried, still manning the helm. "It might be dangerous. There's no way to tell what's going on at the port on the other end of the colony cylinder."

"Hmm . . . maybe you're right." Brite found himself agreeing with her once again.

"Lift off!" Mirai cried.

"Mirai?" Brite was so stunned by the way she had unilaterally initiated the order that he forgot to countermand her and just stared. She was right, though. If any enemy forces were at the colony's other port, they would be directly opposite the *Pegasus* in the cylinder; firing straight down the colony cylinder would be like shooting fish in a barrel.

"Hmm . . . I wonder if we should . . ." he wondered out loud.

"It's worth it, skipper," Mirai replied instantly. Brite did not have to complete the sentence. She knew exactly what he was thinking.

He turned and barked: "Prepare a barrage of Model Six missiles in the fore section! Fire when ready!"

The *Pegasus* moved out of the core of the port area and began descending to the colony's outer walls, firing groups of twelve missiles at three-second intervals. With a diameter of two hundred meters, the port on the opposite end of the cylinder was hard not to hit, and sure enough, the atmosphere inside the colony soon reverberated with the sound of explosions and torn metal.

Mirai and Brite were right: A Zeon ship, the *Zanzibar*, had been moored directly opposite them. But they had no way of knowing that two layers of hatches had saved it from final destruction or that firing one more volley of missiles would have done the job.

On the bridge of the *Zanzibar*, Captain Burman immediately ordered his four Zaks to go into action inside the colony and resolved to follow them with his ships. If the enemy forces were merely remnants of the Federation fleet encountered by his fellow officer Captain Ma Kube earlier, he was convinced he could destroy them with his Zaks. Ma Kube, as far as he was concerned, was a rank amateur when it came to fleet battles.

His own ship, the *Zanzibar*, was no ordinary warship but a state-of-the-art Mobile Cruiser equipped with four regular Zaks piloted by combat veterans. If he had to, he could rely on Sha's Red Comet, and if worse came to worst, there was even the new Elmeth-Bits system. Its true capability was untested, but he was sure that at the very least it could outperform a mass-produced GM Mobile Suit.

Inside the *Pegasus*, Saila began running down a corridor, seized by an overpowering growing feeling that if she moved fast, she might somehow be able to contact her brother, Caspar. She knew it was now or never.

Normally she never suffered from headaches, but she had a fierce one now. Pressing her palm against her head, she tried to restrain the growing pain, and just when it seemed to hurt so much that she felt nauseous, the *Pegasus* rocked. She stumbled, cried out, and fell. Picking herself up and resuming running, she wondered if the ship had touched down on the colony floor or been hit by enemy fire. She ducked into an air lock and started to don a Normal Suit. The door from there led into a hangar where she knew there was a dune buggy. *I just hope the ship's actually landed*, she thought between stabs of pain as she struggled to put on the suit. She had experienced only two trial ground landings before. Cursing her poor coordination and bad memory, she used her now-gloved hands to pull her sweat-soaked locks away from her face.

With the *Pegasus* still hovering forward around five meters off the ground, Saila punched the accelerator on the dune buggy and flew out of the *Pegasus* hatch, hit the ground, and bounced, kicking up a cloud of sand. If she had not been wearing a Normal Suit, she would have been rendered unconscious by the shock. Luckily, the colony had enough atmosphere left to breathe, but she still had to keep her helmet visor down to keep the dust out of her eyes. Somehow she knew which direction to go.

Sha, meanwhile, sensed danger approaching and felt a shiver run up his spine. If the white Federation MS was about to emerge from the evergreen forest to his right, he was not sure he could stop it. He was a realist, and he knew his limits. He never hesitated to confront an enemy when he had to, but he never let his ego get in the way when prudence called for a retreat; he knew he could figure out a way to come back and destroy him later. But the opponent he now faced was different. It would not let him get away. It had become too powerful.

Then, to his astonishment, he heard the missiles explode in the port where the *Zanzibar* was moored. He refused to believe that an enemy warship had infiltrated the colony, but there were too many blasts to have come from a Mobile Suit. *Besides,* he thought, *the pilot of the white MS wouldn't waste its ammo like that. He's too smart.* In his mind the white MS was like a lion obsessively stalking a lone rabbit. It would train its sights on Sha first, even if it knew the *Zanzibar* was in the colony. Yes, that was the way a true opponent would surely act, especially if he were a New

Type. Sha had great faith in his ability to outthink his opponents.

Lala Sun was riding with Doctor Flanagan in the cab of the mobile trailer carrying the Elmeth-Bit system when the Federation missiles exploded. Turning to him, she suddenly pleaded, "Doctor, stop! We don't have a minute to lose! Let me take off in the Elmeth and attack the enemy!"

"What are you talking about? You know it hasn't been perfected yet!"

"It doesn't matter. The enemy in here is too powerful! We can't afford to lose a single Mobile Armor machine, and if we don't do something, we might even lose the *Zanzibar*!"

Her last words made Flanagan tremble. If the *Zanzibar* was destroyed, they might be stranded on *Texas*, and that was unthinkable. "Well . . ." he said, hesitating, "I . . . I did adjust the psychom in the test earlier. I guess we've no choice, have we? But you've got to wear your Normal Suit." Flanagan was, after all, a scientist, and he could rationalize anything.

Ignoring him, Lala jumped down from the cab of the trailer and, without bothering to don her Normal Suit, climbed in the Elmeth cockpit. The Elmeth had two megaparticle cannons and finlike protrusions on both sides and the top and bottom that acted as antennae, projecting her amplified consciousness from the psychom interface. From the front it looked like a trifurcated projectile, but because the fuselage contained a disproportionately large and powerful engine, from the side it had a silhouette rather like that of the Kobatan, an exotic Amazonian parrot. Using the psychom interface, Lala could operate the engine by will, and she could also remotely control up to ten armed Bits— miniature flying orbs, that flew behind the Elmeth.

AWAKENING

The four Zeon pilots dispatched from the *Zanzibar* performed low-altitude jumps in their Zaks, moving toward the colony port where the Federation Forces were believed to have infiltrated.

Amuro, crouching low in the forest with his Gundam, let them go by. Sha, he deduced, would expect him to attack them. Then a vague sensation flared in a corner of his brain. It seemed to indicate a direction, and he gambled on it. A few heartbeats after the Zaks had passed by, he ignited the Gundam's backpack jets and jumped. As he rose into the air, his field of vision automatically expanded, and on the other side of a river he spotted a different Zak turning away from him. There was a cloud of sand between them, but he could tell the Zak was red. His hunch had been right. Fearing he was too late, he fired. The beam from the Gundam's rifle streaked straight toward the red Zak, particles from it scorching the earth below and then whooshing into a ball of flame.

"What?" Amuro gasped. The Zak's right leg was gone, severed below the knee, but incredibly, it still managed to soar like a red comet into the air just in the nick of time. Amuro shuddered. Even as his own powers of perception seemed to be increasing, Sha seemed to be increasing his ability to avoid his attacks. Maybe General Revil was right, Amuro thought. Maybe Sha really was a New Type.

Unfortunately for Amuro, he did not see Sha put a spin on his Zak in midair; he had barely had time to maneuver his shield into position after seeing the bazooka blast, and—*wham!*—it was blown to smithereens.

"Whoa!" he yelled as the Gundam fuselage shook violently and the immense force of several *g*'s bore down on him. Somehow managing to keep his eyes wide open, he fired a blast from the Vulcan cannon in the Gundam's head as a feint and increased the power in the backpack jets. He knew he had to get above the Zak. To attack, to even threaten an enemy required gaining some tactical advantage. No matter how weightless an environment, it was still important to get above the upper limit of the enemy's field of vision.

The Gundam had a lot more power than any Zak, perhaps, but to Amuro's distress, it had nowhere near the amount he needed. Losing faith in his machine, he thought, *I'm a goner.*

Unknown to Amuro, Sha was feeling exactly the same way.

"Damn!" he cursed as he made his Zak utilize the force of the blast to soar into the air. "My MS's no match in power for the white Suit . . ." He was climbing four times faster than normal, but it still was not enough. The enemy MS rose toward him fast enough to pass him and launched another attack. Within seconds the shield on the Zak's left shoulder had been blown away, and if Sha had not had his safety harness on and if there had not been an air bag in his cockpit, the shock would have snapped his spine in two. Then a whirlwind enveloped the battling suits, and both pilots took evasive action.

"Only two rounds left?" Sha checked his magazine indicator and gnashed his teeth in frustration. If only his Zak had a beam rifle.

Not far away, Saila gripped the wheel of her dune buggy even tighter and cursed her brother. If his goal was to avenge their father's death, what good would it possibly do him to die in this worthless, out-of-the-way *Texas* colony? She kicked herself for not having spoken more frankly to him when they had met accidentally on Side 7, for not having tried to steer him away from his crazy obsession. Neither she nor Caspar knew for certain what their father really would have thought, but given his idealistic view of the world, she was absolutely certain revenge would not be part of it. "Caspar," she lamented, "can't you join the real world?"

In the distance she saw flashes of light. Slamming the buggy accelerator to the floor, she steered toward them.

When the four Zeon Zaks finally closed in on the *Pegasus* at the other end of the colony, Ensign Kai turned his Gun Cannon around and abandoned his search for Amuro and the Gundam. He did not know if Amuro was still alive, but he knew what he had to do—defend his mother ship.

Fighting inside a cylinder only three kilometers in diameter was no ordinary feat, and neither the Zak pilots nor Kai could maneuver their machines with anywhere near the skill of Sha or Amuro. They were used to the vastness of space, but now sand and dust obscured their field of vision, and gravity forced them to adopt what amounted to old Earth-style hand-to-hand combat techniques. The Zak pilots, maneuvering on the ground, could not just slip in to attack the *Pegasus*'s underbelly. Nor, for that matter, could the *Pegasus* easily repel the Zaks. Missiles and shells fired by both parties missed their mark and wreaked havoc on the colony's artificial ground cover.

When the Federation Forces stationed outside the colony learned of the assault on the *Pegasus*, they immediately sent in reinforcements, but the colony environment exacted a toll on them, too. Of three Public attack ships, two promptly became disoriented in the dust clouds and smashed into the colony's earthen floor. Similarly, when a GM Suit followed the ships into the colony, it crashed into a Zak, and both machines vanished in a swirl of dust.

* * *

In the midst of all this, Kai spotted a flare from a Zak bazooka and immediately put his Gun Cannon into a two-hundred-meter jump, swinging behind the enemy just as he was about to pump another round into the *Pegasus*. Kai knew it was a gamble—under normal conditions a Zak would have easily anticipated his move—but he went ahead anyway. Poor visibility affected them both equally, and he might as well put it to work for his own advantage.

His tactic worked. Two shells from the Gun Cannon scored a direct hit on the Zak, instantly pulverizing its upper torso. Miraculously, the engine did not blow; since the *Pegasus* was maneuvering only five hundred meters above, a nuclear fusion blast might have wounded her mortally. Flush with success, Kai moved on to his next quarry.

Burman, the skipper of the *Zanzibar*, was far less lucky. Twenty kilometers ahead he saw flashes of defensive fire put up by the *Pegasus*, and when the clouds of sand parted, he suddenly spotted the ship itself. He unleashed a barrage of mega-particle beams from all four front cannon and scored direct hits on the *Pegasus*'s port and starboard foredecks, causing the ship to shudder violently. But then Burman made a fatal mistake. Instead of firing more blasts to polish off the enemy, he waited for another break in visibility and thus gave Brite the opportunity he needed. Brite ordered all his surviving guns fired in the direction of the flashes. In a showdown between a brash youth and a cautious veteran, youth won out. Two particle beams, along with three volleys from the main cannon and three missiles, streaked forth from the *Pegasus* and smashed directly into the *Zanzibar*.

Both ships were heavily damaged, and—needless to say in a colony three kilometers in diameter—there was no room for either to take evasive action or make an easy escape.

AWAKENING

Although holes had been blown in the colony walls, none were yet large enough for an entire warship to slip through.

In the Elmeth, the instant Lala Sun saw the *Zanzibar* burst into flames, she knew her commander was in mortal danger. She had no way of knowing for sure, but she surmised that the Gundam had jumped into a trap Sha had laid and had proved more difficult to handle than anticipated.

In her mind an awareness of two people appeared and became entangled; the thoughts of one—Amuro—turned directly into a white light and began to destroy the other—Sha. Shuddering, she recalled her shock and sadness on meeting the young Amuro earlier. She knew he might be a New Type, too, and she was seized by a sudden desire to abandon the Elmeth. *Why couldn't I have met him earlier?* she lamented, but it was too late. Her consciousness was already linked to the psychom interface, and while her confusion might prevent her from properly controlling the remotely operated Bits, she was the pilot of the Elmeth and, as such, already an integral part of a highly sophisticated weapons system.

The surviving Federation Public attack ship spotted the Elmeth through the sand clouds, approached, and unleashed four missiles. Horrified, Lala automatically began evasive action in her Elmeth and concentrated her thoughts on the missiles. The danger level she sensed automatically triggered subconscious self-preservation instincts and further stimulated her latent powers of perception. Waves emitted from her brain were sensed by the psychom interface and amplified. When this neural information was transmitted to the remote bits carried on the Elmeth, they went into action.

Brain waves are essentially electrical signals, and Doctor Flanagan had developed a computer-based system that converted them into pulse signals for amplification. But from his research on people with paranormal abilities, he knew that human consciousness was composed of far more than electricity and that it also included other waveforms such as the psycho wave. With new biocomputer technology, he therefore had succeeded in creating a device called a psycho-communicator, or psychom, which could interface with a brainwave amplification apparatus. As it turned out, the total system failed to function properly with human operators of average paranormal abilities and worked only with those who possessed unique, expanded powers of insight or intuition.

Early experiments had proved problematic for Doctor Flanagan and his assistants. They demonstrated the existence of mysterious different "types" of humans and the wide range of abilities they possessed. But it proved infinitely more difficult than first anticipated to categorize those abilities. Clearly, the psychom interface worked best with subjects who had enhanced powers of intuition—with the so-called New Types—but that only led to the question of how to define, or for that matter how to even find, New Types. There was no guarantee of finding them in any great number among the truly gifted members of society—the geniuses in the arts and sciences. Nor were average persons with superior intuition always New Types. They could even exist among extremely ordinary, traditional people with a rigid sense of self and relatively little heightened awareness.

Lala Sun was herself a case in point, as the Flanagan team realized from the moment she had joined the project as a subject. She had no higher education to speak of. Nor was her IQ particularly outstanding. But her ability to activate the psychom interface was so unusual that they could scarcely believe their own data.

What, they then began to wonder, was a true New Type?

AWAKENING

Unable to come up with a single concrete definition, they were forced to conclude merely that New Type subjects were characterized mainly by a power of insight greater than anything ever before recorded in research on human consciousness. New Types were different from ordinary geniuses or the highly gifted and different from people with already identified extrasensory powers, such as telepathy, prescience, psychic photography, teleportation, and even channeling. New Types were also capable of simultaneously addressing multiple problems and of projecting their thoughts externally.

Doctor Flanagan's greatest scientific achievement came when he realized that the New Type concept symbolized not just a unique individual ability but a positive transformation that all mankind could potentially achieve. It was an idea with universal appeal, but in Zeon it especially caught the attention of Krishia Zavi, who realized at once that the psychom interface also could be utilized for military ends, and immediately banned any further public mention of the New Type concept. Human nature being what it was, however, people tiring of the war nonetheless began to whisper in wishful terms about a New Type transformation of all mankind. In reality, of course, nothing had changed at all yet.

Yet now, on *Texas*, a young woman—a true New Type— was going into action. Controlling four Bit modules from the cockpit on her Elmeth Mobile Armor, she destroyed each individual incoming missile as well as the Public attack ship that had launched them. It was more than just a demonstration of New Type potential. It was a terrifying testimony to the abilities of the developers of the Elmeth-Bit military machine—the scientists of the Flanagan Agency and the weapons experts under Krishia's command. Lala had simply sighted the incoming missiles and their mother ship and willed an attack on them from her Elmeth. The mega-particle cannons in each Bit—a six-meter-diameter machine composed primarily of a small nuclear fusion engine—had automatically trained their sights on the targets and destroyed them all.

Perhaps because thought waves flowed in reverse from the Elmeth's psychom interface, the action also served to heighten Lala's awareness. Through the psychom she became aware of the presence of Amuro and Sha in the area and of something terrifying. Something screaming, symbolizing man's basic fighting instinct, rushed toward her like a dark wall of water. There were no audible words or describable sounds, but she knew what it represented. It was the screams and yells of two men locked in mortal combat, the war cries of two independent conscious beings merging in screams, anger, and fear.

Lala was no stranger to the horrors of war, yet she was terrified. In the past, when two Federation warships had raked the colony she lived on, she had trembled in fear of her own death, only to experience true horror and despair on learning that her parents, from whom she had become separated, had been killed. But those were memories, something experienced on the periphery of battle. She had imagined before what it would be like for two people to deliberately try to kill each other in combat, but the reality of what she now faced was far more frightening. A torrent of conscious thoughts rushed toward her, thoughts trying mightily to dispel fear of death, trying at all costs to avoid being killed. They seemed like a maelstrom, a dark, foreboding image like that of ancient Japanese hell scrolls, of two demons locked in mortal combat, devouring each other's flesh.

She glanced out her cockpit window and beheld a Federation Gundam MS and a Zeon Zak with weapons flashing.

AWAKENING

The Gundam's beam saber slashed, and the Zak's heat ax seared the air. The Zak was clearly outclassed.

Lala screamed, "Commander!" But then she sensed yet another thought emerging from the two men's blurred consciousness. It was sharp and clear, like a bright, beautiful light, something that could only involve skill or art. How ironic, she thought, that killing could be perfected only by something so beautiful. From the terror of two men trying to slice each other in two came a force that penetrated right through her. With a sense of sadness tinged with despair, she realized that it was in fact the very same mental quality required to vanquish an enemy in combat.

It occurred to Sha that he had made an unforgivable error, trying to be a New Type when he was not one. He cursed his carelessness but had no time to dwell on it; the Gundam never gave him a chance.

Victory in combat could be assured only by taking advantage of every possible opportunity. History at the very least taught that the best warriors never left victory up to their own fighting spirit or to mere chance. When one was outclassed by an opponent, an appropriate strategy was all the more essential. Only in comic books were battles determined by brute strength alone.

I should never have let this business about the Red Comet go to my head, Sha thought. The Gundam's beam saber had him completely on the defensive, but he was not ready to concede victory yet. "You may be a New Type," he screamed in the direction of the Gundam pilot, "but you don't have a psychom interface . . ."

The Gundam, he realized, was without doubt a mechanical marvel, but therein also lay its biggest weakness. There was no evidence that the Federation had developed an MS with anything like a psychom interface. While parrying yet another blow of the Gundam's beam saber, Sha swung his heat ax at the enemy's extended right arm.

Amuro swore. The Gundam's drive system was already at the breaking point, but it worked well enough to avoid the Zak's thrust one more time. Leaning his machine forward and to the side, Amuro brought the MS's right leg up in a kick to the Zak's right wrist and sent the heat ax flying into the sand. And then he heard what sounded like a moan or gasp. It did not come from Sha. It was a sensation that surged through his brain, from his frontal lobes to the rear, creating an almost audible <S-t-o-p> and forcing him to rivet his attention to it.

A thud brought Amuro back to a more immediate reality. Much to his horror, the Zak had crashed into the Gundam, and the laser burners in its left fingers were already burning deep into its backpack. Cursing, he countered by smashing the Zak's mono-eye with the Gundam's left hand and then using the right, which was holding the beam saber, to try to slash down through the base of the Zak's neck in a diagonal trajectory.

As the Gundam's saber beam zapped and flickered, sparks showered on Sha's head inside the Zak cockpit from severed coils and circuitry. "What the—" he yelled. While marveling at the performance of the enemy weapon, he quickly activated his auxiliary camera eye and with the laser burners in the Zak's left fingers took aim at the Gundam's "eyes" and fired. With a *whoosh!* the blast made a hole between the Gundam's eyes and nose. Next Sha took aim at his opponent's neck. If he could, he wanted to fire a direct laser blast into the MS torso. But then the Gundam's right hand pulled out the beam saber and tried to thrust it through the Zak's left side.

AWAKENING

Sha yelled in surprise. His Zak's left arm was no longer usable. And then he heard something that should not have been physically possible; he heard Lala scream "Commander!"

Lala was frantic at the plight of her superior, and her thoughts had turned in wrath on the Gundam, thereby activating and sending the eight remote-control Bits on the attack. But Amuro, in the Gundam, had already sensed the presence of another enemy. Disengaging from the Zak, he ignited the Gundam's verniers and jumped high into the dust clouds, completely avoiding the beam blasts directed at him from the Bits.

Lala shook with terror. The Elmeth-Bit combination was supposed to have been invincible, yet the Gundam had easily outmaneuvered her.

Meanwhile, the *Pegasus* and the *Zanzibar* were about to cross paths in the middle of the colony cylinder. Although few direct hits had been scored, barrages of fire had heavily damaged both warships, and the intense explosions had created enormous cracks here and there in the colony walls. On the *Pegasus*, Lieutenant (jg) Brite and Ensign Mirai had decided that for their final gamble they would try to cut the enemy off inside the colony. Outside the cylinder, the *Pegasus*'s consort ships, the *Saphron* and the *Cisco*, trained their beam cannons through one of the largest holes in the colony wall and waited.

Because both the *Pegasus* and the *Zanzibar* were in such close proximity, Brite knew his opponent would try to knock his ship out with a single blow or try to increase speed and avoid him. To preempt either action, he immediately tried to destroy the *Zanzibar* bridge. The more rounded *Zanzibar* was better armored than the complex *Pegasus*, but it nonetheless had its weak spots.

First, to avoid crashing into the enemy ship, Mirai steered the *Pegasus* so low that it nearly creased the colony floor, and then she brought the *Pegasus*'s foredeck main cannon level with the *Zanzibar*'s bridge. When the cannon was fired, the blast smashed straight through the ship. Crippled, the ship crashed into the colony's central "mountain" and then rebounded, floating back in the opposite direction.

Firing retrorockets, Mirai braked the *Pegasus* and narrowly steered her through the five-hundred-meter space between the drifting *Zanzibar* and the colony floor. Then she swung the prow of her ship toward the *Zanzibar*'s aft megaparticle cannon. Ensign Hayato, waiting on the bridge for this very instant, directed a blast that smashed the Zeon ship's remaining cannon, leaving it a drifting metal hulk with only a few remaining operational missile launch tubes and ship guns.

Brite flashed a V sign at Mirai and called out, "Good work!" But just then the *Zanzibar* fired her main engines, and the force of the exhaust struck the *Pegasus*'s starboard prow, driving her skidding into the colony floor. The *Zanzibar* sliced through a cloud of dust on the parched plain, crashed again into the central mountain, and came to a halt. The entire colony shuddered as if an earthquake had struck.

As Petty Officer Second Class Saila Mas raced across the *Texas* plain in search of her brother, she saw a flash from the firing of the *Zanzibar*'s main engines, but she could not feel the tremor that followed; her dune buggy was bouncing too wildly.

And then she finally located her brother's red Zak. It had made an emergency landing and appeared heavily damaged, but the hatch opened, and out slid a red-suited young pilot in a platinum-colored helmet with the visor up, revealing an unforgettable face mask. Hitting the ground, he knelt and

AWAKENING

hunched over and appeared to be coughing, but on second glance Saila realized he was readying an oxygen tank. She checked the pressure gauge on her own Normal Suit and saw to her horror that it had dropped dramatically. Too many holes had been blasted in the colony walls.

Jumping out of her dune buggy and switching on the voice channel in her Normal Suit, she cried out, "Caspar! It's me, Artesia!"

The red-suited pilot looked up in surprise and reached for his sidearm, but then as recognition sunk in he yelled, "Artesia! What in the world are you . . ." There was no point in completing the sentence.

"Caspar!" Saila cried. "Listen, what good is it going to do you to fight on Zeon's side? Why can't you just forget about avenging Father?"

"Artesia . . . you've got it all wrong. Times have changed, and it isn't just revenge anymore. But this is no time to argue. We've got to get out of here!"

"Can't you rejoin the Federation?"

"Rejoin the Federation? Are you crazy? I'm Sha Aznable now, a commander in the Zeon forces! And I'm in love with a woman in the force. Her name's Lala Sun."

"Well, can't you at least leave the Zeon military?"

"There's no guarantee either of us'll get out of here alive, Artesia, but the answer's no."

"Why?"

"Because we've finally proved New Types exist, and there's so much to be done . . ."

"Proved New Types exist?"

"That's right. You know how people always said Father was a prophet of the first New Types? Well, you're his daughter, so you ought to be able to sense it—there are two New Types here in this colony now . . ."

"Are you talking about Amuro, Caspar?"

Even as she spoke, Saila wondered if some New Type potential might not be stirring in herself. Otherwise, she did not see how she could possibly have made it safely this far.

"The Gundam pilot? Probably so . . ." Then, fastening the air tank to his belt and putting on his oxygen mask, he asked in a muffled voice, "Artesia, are you coming with me or not?"

"To . . . to Zeon?" Her voice revealed her scorn.

"If not, sister, be a good girl and quit the Federation Forces. And don't ever show your face in front of me in uniform again! The military's not for you."

"Caspar . . ."

It was too late. He had already jumped in her dune buggy. As he roared off into a billowing cloud of dust, he yelled, "You've got to go back, Artesia! I'm sure a Federation ship'll pick you up."

"Caspar, wait!" she yelled. Ever since she was old enough to remember, it seemed she had yelled the same thing after her brother. And he had always left her behind.

Standing alone beside her brother's abandoned red Zak, Saila felt a tingling sensation inside her head. It was not a result of meeting him again. It was not pain. But it was nonetheless a physical sensation, and it pervaded her entire brain. She looked up at the sky. The voice channel inside her Normal Suit activated, and amid the static she heard the order *"All hands abandon ship!"* It was the *Pegasus*. The ship had finally been dealt a mortal blow.

Meanwhile, Lala Sun had entered maximum combat mode. The remotely controlled Bit units, oblivious to any and all obstacles, began to randomly attack the Gundam. One self-destructed on the MS's left leg and partly pulverized it.

Even strapped in his seat, Amuro's body was being tossed

around. His collarbone felt as if it would snap, and he groaned in pain, but he remained aware enough to sense the remaining seven Bits streaming toward him from Lala's Elmeth.

He saw no physical trail but rather the stream of consciousness that connected the Bits and Lala. It was like a trace of light reflected through his own brain. He knew they were coming, and he knew this time he had to wait. One more high-speed, high-*g* dodge would destroy the Gundam's already overloaded power train. He would have to gauge the angle of attack from the trace of lights he sensed and try to blow the Bits out of the air. *Here goes nothing,* he thought, knowing it was a gamble.

A narrow beam of light flashed out of the Gundam's rifle and miraculously knocked one Bit out of the air. Normally, concentrating so hard on one target would have left Amuro blind to another's movement, but when the other Bits attacked this time, it did not happen. Just as his awareness of the first trace seemed to peak, he sensed others headed toward the Gundam's other leg and its back. Infused with new self-confidence because of his growing powers of perception, he exulted. *"I can do it!"*

His attention quickly turned to the mother ship controlling the Bits. He had no way of knowing about the psychom system, but he knew that it was theoretically impossible to use radio-controlled weaponry in an area where there was such a high level of Minovski particles and that somehow the attacks were originating from the mother ship. It could present him with an opportunity.

The Gundam creaked badly but still managed to evade the other six attacking Bits. Amuro destroyed one, and while his MS swayed from the aftershock, the Elmeth mother ship fired a blast from its mega-particle cannon. And this time a clear thought pierced Amuro's brain like an exclamation mark; it was born of a hatred so intense that it revealed to him the beam's angle of impact before he could even see it. He easily evaded the attack.

Why? he thought. It was a double-edged query. Why, he thought angrily, was he being attacked like this? And why, thinking of himself, was he able to anticipate the angle of attack in advance? He spun the Gundam toward the direction where he sensed the Elmeth was and plunged through a cloud of sand.

As the rounded, flame-shaped Elmeth grew larger and larger on the Gundam's orthoscopic monitor, Amuro saw beyond its physical armor and wiring. He saw an image of grief.

And simultaneously, from the Elmeth, Lala Sun sensed the same thing in Amuro; she saw the grief that lay behind hatred.

An identical stream of thought linked two physical, flesh and blood forms.

<La-la! What are you doing here?> Amuro thought.

<Why did you attack?> Lala started to add the word "Sha" to her demand but never completed the thought. She loved Sha. It was a young woman's private, almost secret infatuation, the type tinged with melancholic yearning. Amuro's answer would be too obvious; they were at war.

But now a stream of Lala's thought was linked with that of Amuro's and was growing, expanding rapidly. When both streams fused completely into one, it seemed they would explode and soar forever. To her at least, the experience felt as if it held the potential for the universal transformation, even resurrection, that mankind seemed to be yearning for.

Then Amuro remembered the reality of their situation.

<Stop, Lala! It's not you I'm fighting. Stop!>

AWAKENING

<Amuro, I made a mistake. My feelings for Sha made me do it. And now it's too late! I can't stop this process!>

<You what? What do you mean you can't stop?> A scream from Amuro soared into the ether. <That's crazy! I'm here! Lala, I'll help you. I'll do anything!>

<Amuro! I love you!>

In the midst of despair, Amuro saw an image of Lala Sun; her emerald-green eyes widened, and the bodhisattva-like beauty mark in the middle of her brow flared into light.

<Amuro, I see you, too!>

There were no words spoken. Amuro simply knew. His thoughts were hers. Hers were his. They had fused together; a straight line of pure thought flared and soared straight into the heavens. It was perfect; two separate individuals experienced a perfect empathetic communion.

Amuro and Lala's fused consciousness ignited, expanded, and journeyed far into space. Before returning to lodge in human form, it presided over a world where chaos and confusion continued to reign and where a drama continued to unfold.

Saila Mas managed to use her Normal Suit vernier jets and escape through a hole in the colony, eventually alighting safely on the Saphron, *waiting outside.*

Ensign Mirai, her hand held by Lieutenant (jg) Brite, ran full speed toward the Texas *colony's port, as did Ensign Hayato, leading a group of the surviving crew members from the* Pegasus. *Ensign Kai, piloting the Gun Cannon, destroyed yet another Zak and then blasted into space.*

Sha Aznable resumed command of the Zeon fleet, with images of his smiling sister Artesia still in his mind.

Other images and sensations fused into one, of Mirai, Brite, and Fra Bow buffeted by wind; of the spirits of Lala's dead father and mother soaring through the heavens, of her mother smiling . . . Of tears in Lala's emerald-green eyes . . . Of the sound of crying . . . Of the sound of a life force from a woman's womb, crying its lungs out. Whose voice could it be? Mirai? Saila? Fra Bow? Matilda Ajan? Who was it? Lala? No, the Lala of the fused consciousness could only scream in grief. But somewhere there was an embryonic life, surrounded in warmth, with heart beating . . . A new life. Thump thump thump. *A strong, steady pulse. A vital pulse. The sound of life itself—so beautiful, so all-enriching.*

Lala and Amuro's fused consciousness flowed out in a wave of light over a panorama of Earth. Metamorphosing through the colors of the spectrum and finally becoming gold, the light passed by the Zeon fleet that left from the Granada moon base. Passed by the fierce fight that ensued between it and the defensive wing of General Revil's main fleet. Passed by before it was clear if Revil would get by Solomon and attack Granada directly.

The light, in a torrent, somehow testified to the fact that the Pegasus would survive. The sound of the heartbeat. The symbol of life, of survival.

Amuro and Lala's fused consciousness sensed beyond. The dark force of the Zavi ruling family . . . flowing into and disappearing in an instant of light . . . The light, without which no one would know how long mankind's future would last; no one would know . . .

The physical Lala tried to abandon herself to the flow of light . . . The fused part of her consciousness knew that once the two of them were no longer joined, they would no longer be able to see the flow of light. Would other New Types emerge in Lala's place? Were not she and Amuro gazing into the infinity of future precisely because history promised the appearance of New Types?

AWAKENING

All thoughts transpired in an instant. All thoughts transpired in an eternity.

The Gundam, under full power, smashed into the Elmeth.

Amuro's conscious mind awoke with a shock, and he tried at the last moment to deflect the trajectory of the Gundam's beam saber. But it was too late. The beam saber connected directly with the weakest section of the Elmeth—its cockpit. In an instant it incinerated Lala's young flesh and spirit and penetrated all the way to the engine. The Bits began flying madly and randomly in the colony air and smashed into its floor. Lala disappeared into a torrent of light and dissolved into the flow of eternal time.

Amuro had killed the person he needed more than anyone else in the whole universe. He screamed a cry of despair: *"What have I done?"*

In wretched disbelief, he put the Gundam in reverse, and the instant he did so, he saw the fuselage of the Elmeth suddenly mushroom in size. A second later his Gundam was blown by the fusion blast into the colony wall; the wall warped and ruptured, and then the Gundam was tossed into outer space. In a ball of light, the Gundam's cockpit escape mechanism went into action. The Mobile Suit's upper and lower torso separated, and the cockpit module transformed into the Core Fighter.

"Lala! Lala!" Amuro screamed, half-delirious. "Lala! Was it all a dream?"

As his Core Fighter was tossed from the area by the blast, he mercifully slipped into mumbling unconsciousness. But the fused awareness he had shared with Lala was not a dream. They had seen a future, and the future was one of promise. It was real, and it was burned into Amuro's mind. He knew that although only he and Lala had seen it, it did not belong only to them. It was vast. It was universal. And now he could rest. Sleep would be a but a brief respite before he emerged from the depths of despair to fulfill his final destiny.

Mankind still was not aware that New Types had awakened. But a new future had already begun.

It was 0080 U.C. And the war was still not over.

This is the conclusion of *Awakening*, the first volume of the GUNDAM series. Watch for the second volume—*Escalation*—coming from Del Rey Books in November 1990!

ABOUT THE AUTHOR

Yoshiyuki Tomino is the creator of GUNDAM, beginning with the first animated television series in 1979 in Japan. Later, he authored numerous novels, using the characters he developed, as well as other film and television projects in the GUNDAM universe. He lives in Tokyo, Japan.

ABOUT THE TRANSLATOR

Frederik L. Schodt is a writer, translator, and interpreter based in San Francisco. A long-time fan of Japanese fantasy, he also likes robots—both imaginary and real. Among the books he has authored are *Manga! Manga! The World of Japanese Comics*, and *Inside the Robot Kingdom: Japan, Mechatronics, and the Coming Robotopia* (Kodansha International, 1983 and 1988, respectively).